Gemini Rising

MarZe Scott

Debbie,
More than your hugs, your belief in
me is greatly appreciated! So glad you're
in my life. *MarZe Scott*

KeLacar Enterprises
Ypsilanti, Michigan

Gemini Rising by MarZe Scott
Publishing under KeLacar Enterprises
Copyright 2018

ISBN Paperback— 978-7323282-0-4
ISBN eBook— 978-1-7323282-1-1

Cover designed by: J.L. Woodson www.jlwoodson.com
Interior design by: Lissa Woodson www.naleighnakai.com
Cover Image: Woodson Creative Studio
www.woodsoncreativestudio.com

Printed in the United States of America

Dedication

This book is dedicated to my Ma, Freeda Mae Carter, who taught me only boring people get bored. The lessons about life and creativity you taught me will forever be with me. I love and miss you.

Acknowledgements

First and foremost I thank God—The Creator of all things thought it well to place the gift of storytelling within the fibers of my soul. I'm eternally grateful for this talent and will use it as long as there is a story to be told.

Thank you to my father, Carl Carter. Your encouraging words always came on time.

Thank you to my sister, Tamika Carter, who helps me to tease out all the ideas I have. God knew I needed someone to keep up with all of my overthinking.

Thank you to my brother, Cecil Carter, who is the consummate entrepreneur who always encourages me and prays for me to use my creativity to reach fame.

Thank you to Angela "Kim" Steed, whose heart grew exponentially dealing with me. If I ever had a question about my ability to write a good story, she encouraged me to believe that I don't write good stories, I write great stories. Early morning conversations and late night venting helped manage my sanity during this process.

Thank you to my five heartbeats, affectionately called The Royals, who told me not to mention their names. Their patience was bountiful, and without complaint as long as dinner was done.

Thank you to Aimee J. McVay, my Day One beta reader, whose eyes lit up when she read the raw, unedited version of this story. She cried the first tears for Aisha and was my first cheerleader.

Thank you to J. L. Woodson, graphic designer extraordinaire. I'm in love with my cover. Woodson Creative Studio does great work.

Thank you to my awesome team of beta readers and editors, J. L. Campbell, Christine Pauls, Felicia Thomas, and Mo Sytsma. Your time, service, energy, and feedback are greatly appreciated.

Thank you to Naleighna Kai's Tribe Called Success. Hands down the best literary support group I've ever had the honor of being a member.

A very special thank you to my developmental editor and friend, the phenomenal Lissa Woodson, who showed me how to make this story better than good. Words can't express the love and gratitude that I have for all that you've shown me.

To anyone who wasn't mentioned, you are loved and your support by word or deed makes my heart smile.

Chapter 1

Gemini

Pleasant memories blurred into a world of darkness the moment my mother gave me to Gillespie "Angel" Davis. The man did not live up to the beauty of his name. Several girls who walked the streets of Cincinnati every night to bring him that cold hard cash, could attest to that fact—and others.

Now twelve years later, the mirror in a darkened apartment bedroom shows the reflection of a woman I once knew. Angel calls her "Gemini." Her father named her Aisha Yasmin Mosley. The beauty of that name does not jibe with the woman in the silver glass. Hazel eyes glare back at me, chastising me for not knowing who owns the curly auburn hair, the swan-like neck, and honey-beige skin.

Orbs that bear resemblance to my Persian mother's bedroom eyes have seen far too much. The same eyes that examine the high cheekbones and full lips that were inherited from a Sudanese father now taunt the reflection in the foyer mirror in the first floor apartment Angel leased to be the humble beginnings of his budding enterprise.

The shadow person mimics every movement; every facial expression commands me to pay attention, reminding me she's not totally lost. Most days, I wish to forget how I got here; in this place where something as simple as remembering to buy tahini to make my favorite meal of chicken shawarma and rice becomes more unfamiliar as time passes.

When Angel's clients look into my eyes what do they really see? They say I'm beautiful. If I'm so beautiful, why continue to break me?

Then there is Zephyr Gray. He only knows the woman he sees at the office.

He has no idea about my past or what happens when I leave the building, Zephyr has proven time after time that there's a vested interest in seeing me succeed. He is the exact opposite of Angel. How would Zephyr feel if he knew the truth?

Once, a long time ago, visits to Belle Isle on an early Sunday morning walk along the Detroit River with my family was common place; a time before my innocence was a commodity traded for a nightmare.

Flying away has crossed my mind more times than I care to admit, but how does a bird fly with clipped wings?

* * *

I just want to go home ...

Only weeks before my tenth birthday, a dark blue sedan slowly approached the front yard where I played with Nina, a friend who had brought her dolls over to hold our make-believe class. The car pulled up and parked in front of my house. I paused and glanced up in time to see a boy not much older than me slide out of the driver's seat.

The stranger walked past us without speaking. Seconds later, his brown knuckles rapped against the front door. My mother answered wearing black leggings and one of my father's t-shirts that practically swallowed her petite frame. Brief eye contact and a smile between the two were exchanged before the teenager entered the house close in step behind my mother. A feeling of discomfort worked knots in my stomach as questions churned in my mind.

Nina and I focused on our plastic students as we were teaching them how to spell the words our teacher gave us to study in our summer homework packets.

"Aisha, come here," my mother yelled, cutting through the giggles that came as a result of not being able to remember how to spell "possibility."

"Yes, Ma'am. Coming," I answered, dropping the dolls into Nina's lap. My feet moved as though they were on fire. Keeping my mother waiting too long would result in pain that meant I couldn't walk for hours.

Panting from the short run from the front yard into the living room, I managed a breathy, "Yes, Ma'am?"

"I have a friend I want you to meet," she said in a cool tone that I recognized as irritation.

My father and brother died in a car accident a few months before on Memorial Day after making a bakery run for cupcakes that I wanted. Ever since that day, she stayed annoyed with me for everything—from the way I washed the dishes to how I wore my socks.

A shudder went through my body the second my mother introduced me to Ryan. He didn't have a menacing appearance. On the contrary, Ryan was a teenage boy—tall with cinnamon skin; dressed in faded black jeans with holes in the legs and sparkly threads. His grey hoodie with block letters across the chest was warmer than needed for an average day in July. The diamond stud glinted in his left ear in the same manner as his teeth when he gave me what was supposed to be a comforting smile. His sneakers were bright white as though he spent every waking hour keeping them clean. Nothing I could name made this boy threatening in any way.

"I have to run an errand," she said, though she didn't grab her favorite red leather purse or move toward the front entrance. "I need you to go with Ryan. His father and your father were friends, alright?"

"But Mama—" She shot a green-eyed glare at me that told me to shut up and fast.

"You'll be fine."

"Yes, Ma'am." Something wasn't right, even for my mother's usually sour moods. She was distant—no, she was ... absent. She remained on the huge, plush, white sectional sofa in the living room, staring through the picture window of our suburban, two-story home as she made a hollow effort to console me. Ryan stood near the entrance holding a large golden envelope.

"Her card and certificate are in the envelope," she said, making no attempt to leave or match up with the words spoken earlier. My gaze shifted between my mother, Ryan, and the envelope he held as moisture pooled in the palm of my hands.

"Mama, I'm scared." The small, fearful voice of a nine-year-old girl echoed in the cozy room. Sadly, it was my voice.

"I said you'll be fine, Aisha," she snapped, pulling her dark waist-length hair toward the front of her body. Thin, graceful fingers combed through her thick mane, something she only did when she was bored.

"Thank you for watching Aisha," she said to Ryan. *"I'll be contacting you soon."*

Ryan nodded, but said nothing. He smiled at me for a moment as though assuring me that everything would be all right. Then he extended his hand in my direction. I didn't make a move to place my smaller one in his. Instead, I turned a lingering look on the woman on the sofa. *"When will you be back, Mama?"*

"I'll call for you," she said dryly, hands twisting the auburn locs but for some reason unable to make the long braid that normally graced her head. *"Be a good girl and listen to Ryan, alright?"*

No, it wasn't alright. She had never sent me any place else for someone to babysit me while she ran errands. I followed Ryan, purely being obedient to my mother, to the dark blue sedan that had arrived and interrupted the happiest moment of my day. The July sun perched high in the afternoon sky, hurt my eyes, and nearly blinded me as I walked out of the house.

"Hey, Aisha. Where're ya going?" Nina asked, concern etched in her ivory face as she stared at Ryan.

I simply shrugged. Even if the huge lump in my throat would allow me to speak, I didn't have an answer. So, I followed Ryan, my gaze taking in the cracks along the familiar concrete path leading to the curb.

Ryan opened the rear passenger door and I slid across the warm, plush upholstery to the door behind the front passenger seat. Ryan's smile was warm and kind as he closed the door. My eyes left his and shifted toward the house, willing the uneasy feelings to go away. Peering through the window, I needed to see if my mother was standing at the door.

The front door closed without her stepping into the doorway. I was never much of a crybaby; something my father said made me his "Big Girl." But in that instant, hot tears welled in my eyes. My heart pounded in my ears as I struggled to hold in the urge to wail. I took a deep breath, my body trembling as though in the beginning stages of convulsions.

Inhale. Inhale.

Finally, a slow, pitiful hiss let loose behind teeth pressed together so tightly that my jaws stung.

Who is Ryan? Why can't I go to the store with my mama? Where is Ryan taking me?

All of these questions and more swirled in my mind, so much that my head pounded in the same frantic rhythm as my heartbeat.

The dolls splayed across the front lawn were swiftly forgotten. Nina's face, as sad looking as her favorite character Eeyore, was soon swept to the background, replaced by,

I just wanted my mama. As cold as she was.

I just wanted my mama. As mean as she could be.

I just wanted my mama.

The faster that blue car peeled down the streets of Dearborn, Michigan a harsh reality set in. This might be the last time I'd lay eyes on her again.

And it was.

Gemini

The knock at the door breaks the silence filling the room and the hold the mirror has had on me for nearly ten minutes.

"Who's there?" It's a rare occasion when anyone comes by to visit and Angel has a key.

"Baby, baby, baby, baby," croons a jazzy alto voice on the other side of the door. I peered through the peephole to find the only other person in my world outside of Zephyr and Angel. Caren sways her full hips to the music only she can hear.

Caren worked in the payroll department at McFadden and Tate, an accounting firm, but now fancies herself a singing artist. She loves to give unsuspecting audiences a free concert. Her musical repertoire is insane— the woman belts out Ella, Billie, Tom Jones, and Frank Sinatra like she trained with those legends. Today she's favoring some 2000's R&B.

"Baby, baby, baby, baby," I squeak trying to join the chorus of Ashanti's classic love ballad as Caren bounds over the threshold to the apartment.

"Girl, you know I love you, right?" Caren laughs. "I'm gonna need you to stick to facts and figures."

"I thought I sounded pretty good."

"Nah, Sweetie," she said shaking her head. "I wouldn't lie to you. Keep your day job."

Caren's voice is rich and deep, like her ebony complexion. She aspires to be a legend like her idol Tina Turner and if she didn't favor the casting couch approach, she might be. No reputable music agent would ever be caught dead in the dives she performs in. Local pubs to back alley hole-in-the-wall hangouts are more like karaoke nights in a bar, but it doesn't stop her from singing there. Besides, she gets "favors" from the club owners that secure her headline spots wherever she sings. Really when I think of it, she uses her body to get what she wants but she doesn't have to worry about getting killed if any of her suitors don't work out, which is a constant concern for me.

"What brings you here so early?" I ask, pulling my hair into a ponytail. "I've gotta get to work."

Her smile doesn't quite meet her eyes.

"I need a couple of dollars," she says as she burps and twists her face. "Dominic shorted me a hundred bucks, said that the till came up short."

"All of that and you still had money for drinks, huh?" I say with a chuckle.

Smelling like she's starting the day with her best friends Jack Daniels and his brother Johnny Walker Red, this is par for the course. Days when she's toasted not rested, or hung over, something went wrong the night before. Usually a club manager who she confused for a love interest slept with her and sent her off without giving her a job, a reference, or an orgasm.

Caren brushes past me over to the stainless steel fridge as the phone rings from the bedroom. I make a mad dash as she ransacks the shelves in search of snacks that can be miraculously transformed into three-course meals.

Pulling the cell from a purse and sitting on my freshly made bed, I find Angel's name displayed on the screen. Calls from him are never a good thing. Appointments for clients, or for his own personal engagement, the calls are never welcomed. I draw in a deep breath and put the phone to my ear as if it alone had the ability to harm me.

"Hey, Gemini," says the smooth bass voice on the other end without waiting for me to speak. Angel's voice would be sexy if it belonged to someone else. *Anyone* else. "How's everything with my baby girl?"

A sharp pain rips through me whenever he calls me "his baby girl." Once innocence is snatched in the horrific manner in which mine had been, growing into anything more than his baby girl has been almost impossible.

"Is there something you need, Angel?" I ask, unable to keep the impatience from sliding into my voice.

His throaty laughter makes me bristle. "Slow down, Baby Girl," he says in that slow, easy tone as if he has all the time in the world and my time is not important.

"I have company right now and I'm getting ready for work." Though plans of my escape stay at the front of my mind, old habit compels me to explain my every move whenever he calls.

"Company, hmmm?" He says sounding surprised.

I don't know why I didn't lie— guests of any sort aren't welcome if he hasn't arranged it.

"I'm leaving for work."

"Work," he laughs giving pause. "The worst thing I did was give you a 'time out' while I figured out what to do with you. So are you eating better now that you're a *working girl?*" he roars.

"What do you eat in this place," Caren yells from the kitchen. "I mean really, Aisha? A half-eaten beef kabob, a bag of lettuce, and rice milk?"

I clear my throat, but don't say anything to Angel or Caren.

"When's a good time to come by," he snarls. "You know, to collect the *payment* on that E Class."

The Mercedes E Class was supposed to be a twenty-first birthday gift, but somehow payment is always expected. The truth is the car is a good look to clients, but for what it has and will cost me for it to be parked in the lot, I'd rather he repossess it.

I take a well-deserved dramatic pause before answering, "Tonight, I guess. I'll be home around nine."

"Good," he says sounding amused before he delivers what could only be considered bad news, "I have an assignment for you. You'll need to take off the second week in June from *work*. Set that up today. I'll be at your place at 8:45."

A shudder of distaste quickly snakes up my spine as I disconnect. My hatred for Angel is absolute. Nothing about this man has ever been endearing. Not his voice, obsidian eyes that are as dark as his skin, his haughty posture, or attitude. Even though I'm taller than average at five-feet-nine inches, he towers over me by nearly a foot.

Gemini. The name he gave me the first day I arrived with Ryan at his home in Cincinnati. Hearing that word is nearly as offensive as when he calls me Baby Girl. For some reason, escaping the spider web of the life he's created for me seems hopeless. My mother. Ryan. Angel. All part of a net that has me bound for what feels like eternity; a web that creates an ocean of distance between Zephyr Gray and me— the same distance between normal life and a sordid existence.

Making my way into the kitchen, I try to sweep aside any stress since Caren can read me like a book. I don't need her worrying about me or pestering me about a secret life I never wish to share.

Caren has her head so far into the refrigerator she's about to kiss the condiments.

"Please, help yourself to the buffet," I tease, a mild sarcasm; a little irritated that she's ransacking the fridge.

"Girl, no wonder you stay so thin," she says looking over her shoulder and grimacing before giving me a onceover. "I guess I'll feast on whatever this ice maker puts out." Caren opens the cabinet and snatches a glass. "Yes, water on the rocks. We're just so fancy, aren't we?"

A laugh wants to break free at her silly antics, but the threat of Angel's presence and the mysterious assignment he has in store, makes feeling anything but impossible.

Gemini

Slinking in half an hour late like a mouse trying not to be detected by the family cat, works out well— the usual unofficial kiss-ass security missed my entrance.

The seventh story of McFadden and Tate's red brick and glass building houses the accounting department of the investment firm, where Zephyr Gray is the youngest account executive and only male person of color on the board. At thirty-three years old he has managed to bring the company more money than any other executive. With his assistance, the journey up the corporate ladder has been quick. He, along with Adelaide Forrester, an account manager, took me under their wings after working with me on a few projects. Zephyr took no time going to human resources to hire me permanently after I caught a discrepancy in one account that would've cost the company a million dollar account.

Every breath of the stuffy building air fills me with a sense of pride—it's the air of freedom.

For a while Angel was my only client and he only visited at night. I hoped that he no longer needed me to be a part of the enterprise. He brought other girls on board so I thought getting a legitimate job was a good idea. That was a lapse in judgment; soon after starting at McFadden &Tate the spider web pulled me back in with a new purpose and higher paying clients.

"Did you hear that McFadden is retiring," Sasha, the building gossip who doubles as the department receptionist asks.

"Oh yeah," Paul says leaning his portly body over the desk in Sasha's direction, sweat threatening to drip from his shiny brown bald head. "What do you know about it?"

"That he's retiring," Sasha crumples her nose as I zip by their exchange.

"I hear his last day is at the end of the month," freckled-faced Mark pipes up. The trio is so caught up in their conversation they don't give me a first or second glance as I tip past the front desk, slide by the supervisor's office, and make a pit stop at the water fountain. The door to my office is slightly ajar. *Unusual.* My shoulders tighten as I place a manicured hand on the natural wood and give it a little push.

From the threshold, I scan the desk, walls, and floor and find that everything is in place. Taking a seat in the leather chair makes me gasp because I accidentally kick a golden bag that's been placed underneath. A moment passes and thoughts of Angel flicker in my mind. No, he could not have invaded this space. My sanctuary.

Slowly, almost gingerly, I pull the sparkly, golden gift bag from its place. My heart races when I plunge my hand inside and lift out the ivory tissue paper that hides something heavy and expertly presented. Two boxes—one large cube-shaped, and wrapped in my favorite shade of mint green. The other, smaller and flat, has been wrapped in black-on-black embossed paper with a red satin ribbon fashioned into a loopy bow.

The small card attached reads:

Thinking of you
0721
Zephyr Gray

Zephyr Gray. The name brings the second smile of the day.

My cell rings but I ignore it. This moment is too precious to share with anyone.

Zephyr Gray. Somehow, it doesn't seem right to say the first name without the last; somehow lessens its power. The man is quite a beautiful specimen. His intelligence is awe-inspiring. He's been at McFadden & Tate for about three years, started in auditing and landed in account acquisitions.

Zephyr is tall and strong as though he's spent some time in the military. Eyes— dark as the midnight sky—his complexion the smooth, dark caramel of pecan pie, a strong jawline like my father's, and by that turn—like mine. Signature locs cascade down his back in little ropes pulled into a ponytail. He's the only man at the office whose hair is longer than mine.

Reginald McFadden, the CEO of the company, once told Zephyr to cut his hair close to fit the company's image. Filled with a confidence that is rare in men who work in this office, Zephyr explained, ever so cleverly, one major thing:

"I have no problem with compliance as long as it is *the clientele* who is offended," he stated, his dark-brown gaze locked on the older man. "Further, if *a client* should ever want this issue addressed, I will require written statements from each account holder to ensure that my appearance is the reason for their dissatisfaction with the company."

Well, damn. A woman's heart could fall right out of her bosom when a man is that fearless. Everyone in the place knew about this exchange word for word, and when I was hired even supervisors from other departments made sure I understood the level of respect that was to be given to him.

Zephyr can afford to be demanding and maybe a little arrogant. He draws in the multimillion-dollar contracts and he's damn good at what he does. He's increased McFadden's bottom line at least fifteen percent since gracing the doors of the firm that's been in business since 1989 and barely made it past the lean recession year. So far, no one has submitted any *formal* complaint about Zephyr's appearance, but why make a big deal about that if the man is making sure a company's bottom line is covered?

My finger strokes the edge of the small package, while I read the note again.

Thinking of me, huh? I wonder what he's thinking exactly?

The satin ribbon slips gracefully between my finger and thumb as the cell rings again. Savoring the thought of the possibilities inside this box keeps me spellbound while the call is ignored.

Curiosity and an opportunity to talk to Zephyr makes me close my door and pick up the office phone. His mellow tenor answers and straightaway my world is a little brighter.

"Good morning, Mr. Gray."

"And a glorious morning it is, Ms. Mosley." His warm and easy declaration paints the picture of a smile that's as wide as the east is from the west.

"I hope all is well with you." I close my eyes and press the phone to my face, imagining his cheek next to mine.

"All is magnificent … and has only gotten better now that I hear your voice." My middle finger glides over the edge of the folded paper.

"I have a bag of beautifully wrapped boxes in my office with a card that says it's from you."

"Absolutely. I'm sure you'll enjoy them."

One eyebrow flies up as I swivel in the chair. "And how are you so sure, Mr. Gray?"

"I've been told that I give great gifts. Yours is no exception."

If the packaging is any indication, he's been told the truth.

"Um— conceited much?" I ask with a chuckle.

"Indeed," he declares as laughter roars from the other end.

"Do you mind stopping by my office when you have a moment, so we can discuss … these gifts?"

"I don't mind at all. I have a few calls to make, then I'll be down to see you."

A small sliver of happiness shimmies its way into my heart. The few breaths that follow are filled with a delight that hasn't been felt since my father and brother died. Happiness. I've almost forgotten what that feels like.

The cell rings again and for a moment its intrusion into this wonderful moment brings resentment. I want to disregard the call a third time, but someone is being pretty damn persistent.

Angel.

Chapter 4

Zephyr

Aisha was a pleasant surprise from the first time I laid eyes on her and only became more so as time went on.

Tax season and annual audits come back to back every year. Extra people were needed on three accounts, two of which were seven figure clients that I personally brought to the company. The Monday that the temporary help walked through the doors of McFadden & Tate set my life on a course that I hadn't foreseen.

A small, but diverse band of young and eager individuals filed into the meeting room that was too big for the group. One woman, unlike the cohort she accompanied, entered the room observing the surroundings. Glances bounced from the dingy, white walls that were decorated with a few random pieces of art, to the ceiling tiles that needed replacing, to the rainbow speckled gray industrial carpeting, to the burgundy arm chairs that sat in three rows of six in front of a large white screen.

While the others, dressed in dark-colored slacks and ties or two-piece skirt suits, rushed my partner and the assistants for the project, the woman lingered away from the crowd wearing a knee-length black skirt that fit her curvaceous figure. The close-fitted royal blue cardigan was a perfect contrast to her auburn hair. Four-inch black patent leather heels that adorned her feet enhanced the contour of her legs and though she looked very strong in her posture, her presence made my knees weak. I'd been so challenged to kill my fever and the nature that was rapidly rising. I was grateful for the moment one enthusiastic man broke my trance.

"Good morning, Sir," said a young African-American man, who reminded me of some of my friends back home in Detroit, tried to shake my hand off my arm. "I'm Derek Winfree. "I'm excited to be working with the company."

"I appreciate your enthusiasm, Mr. Winfree." I chuckled. "I'm Zephyr Gray, one of the account executives on this project."

The young man laughed as he gave me a once over.

"I knew you were someone important, standing over here wearing a suit. The others thought you were another temp like us. I guess your locs have them confused."

"I guess so—" I laughed while still trying to keep my eyes on the lone new hire. "Well, Mr. Winfree, I'm sure you'll be a great asset to the company while you're here."

"Good morning, Miss…" I said, extending my hand while keeping a safe distance.

"Mosley. Aisha Mosley." A perfectly French-manicured hand gave me a firm handshake that made my heartbeat skip a beat.

"You give quite a handshake, Ms. Mosley."

"Thank you, Mr.—"

"Gray. Zephyr Gray, the lead account executive on this project."

Exquisite lips turned up into a warm smile that didn't quite reach her somber green eyes. "Do you have any questions?"

"Not yet, Sir." Her sultry voice sent chills down my spine. I wanted to ask more questions just so I could listen a little more and stare a little longer, but my vocabulary got caught in my throat.

* * *

I've been toeing close to the line of professionalism while being mindful not to cross it. Not only is she gorgeous, but also dedicated to great work and kind, always speaking to anyone who crosses her path and making herself available to help when her work is completed.

Even though it's not currently on the books, having a romantic relationship of any sort with co-workers is frowned upon. I find myself constantly wondering if breaking protocol will be worth the possible fallout.

After overhearing a lively conversation she and Caren in payroll had about some of her interests, I went out that same evening and picked up a few gifts for her. Besides, most days I'm not sure that her feelings are mutual. If we're not working on a project, she doesn't pay me any attention.

A working relationship with Aisha isn't enough. I've never believed in superstition, luck, or love at first sight.

Aisha has changed all of that for me.

Chapter 5

Gemini

Angel. Seeing that name on the screen drains all enthusiasm and leaves hope pooled on the carpet. Tapping the answer key on my screen, I hold my breath not knowing what he could possibly want.

"Are you ignoring my calls, Baby Girl?" Angel asks in a dark whisper as if he's gritting his teeth to hold in an intense level of anger.

"No, Sir."

"You didn't answer my call."

"I'm at work, Sir," I whisper as my shoulders tighten.

"There's a change of plans, Baby Girl," he says and my heart pounds a river of blood into places that are growing colder by the minute. "Meet me on the corner of Smyth and the Boulevard in a half hour."

"But I just got to work," I plead, trying to keep the panic at bay. "This doesn't even give me enough time to fake an illness."

"Who told you to get that job anyway?" he roared. "My business always comes first. Do what you gotta do, Baby Girl. I'll see you in thirty minutes."

Angel disconnects the call and the chills that run through my body are unrelenting. My heart races as I think about why the previous plans have changed. It took every minute of the morning to brace myself to see Angel tonight. His visits are nothing I look forward to, but to have one right now?

A sharp pain slices through my head starting at the nape of my neck before turning into a dull, pulsating ache. Suddenly, the reason for leaving work manifests itself without any dishonesty on my part. I cradle my head in my hands as hot tears well up in my eyes—it's a good thing no energy was wasted putting on eye makeup.

Zephyr knocks on the door and swings in before he's invited.

"Good morning, Miss …" His upbeat demeanor turns to worry as he closes the door behind him. "Are you alright?"

"I have a headache. It came out of nowhere."

He stares at me with his dark-brown orbs as though one look from him would be the cure to my pain.

"You should definitely go home and take care of that. I'll let your supervisor know."

The gesture is appreciated, but not necessary.

"Thanks, but I'll tell Mr. Webber."

"Are you sure?" Sincere concern is something I've never experienced from a man, which only makes him more attractive.

"Yes, I'm sure. Thanks again—and thanks for the gifts."

His eyes sparkle as a pair of luscious lips lift into a boyish grin. "I hope you like them."

"I'll let you know."

A glance at the gifts is met with an instant decision to put off opening them. I slide the bag further under my desk and grab my purse trying not to think too much about what's going to happen at this impromptu appointment.

Zephyr throws me a sympathetic gaze over his shoulder as I follow him out the door. The gifts, and the man who gave them, aren't forgotten. Something tells me I'll need something to bring me joy after whatever Angel has in store.

* * *

The walk to the Boulevard takes twenty minutes on an easy stroll, but I made it in twelve minutes today. Traffic zipped by while I wished for a bottle of water after my near sprint to the meeting place.

"Let's go," Angel demands from the front passenger seat as the tricked-out black Escalade pulls up to the curb. The door opens and a middle-aged, dark haired man I've never seen before is already seated in the back. Daytime assignments, like a father who wants his son to become a man for his sixteenth birthday on a school day, were only taken on special occasions. Morning appointments have never happened, but here I am, in the back of this vehicle with a man with whom I'm supposed to acquaint myself in the most intimate of ways before noon.

"Is there a problem?" Angel snapped as I wonder where he's finding his new clientele. "I said let's go."

Giving my new client a slight smile and keeping any words to myself, I slide into the seat. Besides, Angel likes me best when my words are few and far between. Having lived with the man since I was a child, there's never been a time when being around him or making these appointments becomes any easier. Angel didn't seem to mind when he found out that I had a legitimate job, but since that discovery, he's scheduling daytime meetings more often—even if the appointment is only with him.

The new client, a man of Middle Eastern descent, is only as tall as I am. His ample body sports a potbelly under a crisp button-up shirt, comfortable khakis, and a plain, golden band on his ring finger. His wife has to find him as unattractive as I do. Bless her little heart if she doesn't. His roving eyes draw the attention of every nerve in my body; the tickly touch of a millions spiders crawling over me causes me to shiver.

Angel sits silent in the passenger seat. The man doesn't introduce himself. Instead, he reaches for my face and I flinch—touching my face has not been a welcome move since the moment I answered Angel with my real name. The man laughs as I jerk and meet his wicked stare.

"She seems anxious, Angel," the man says in a thick accent that was a challenge to place. "I don't know that I can do anything with her."

Angel still doesn't say anything. The man touches my hair, gently manipulates a curl around his stout finger, and pulls it down to my shoulder. Beads of perspiration form along my hairline as my stomach tightens—nausea setting in. Slow deep breath in, slow steady breath out; my attempt to keep the advancing vomit from reaching my throat. Maybe breathing like this will keep me from crying too.

The new client's breath hitches, his heart beats through his white button up, his longer-than-professional-length dark hair sticks to his olive temples. Body heat leaks steam onto the windows of the truck. The man reaches for the top button of my blouse and carefully opens each button until my skin is exposed.

"Yes," he says, with eyes bright like he's found a treasure. "Beautiful."

As his gaze travels the length of my body, I do my own inspection of him—he's more than ready to get his appointment started.

"How much, Angel?" he asks, reaching for his pocket.

"Fifteen hundred, my man, for the next hour." The man pulls out a brown, leather wallet and counts out the specified amount. Lacing my fingers together keeps them from trembling, but nothing stops a wayward tear from dropping. Clients have had the "pleasure" of my company since I was thirteen and this never gets easier.

"Where to, my man," Angel asks sliding the payment into a jacket pocket.

"The Garland Hotel."

Angel nods and smiles.

My fingers fly, buttoning my shirt as if this isn't the prelude to our next more intimate encounter.

The driver takes us to the hotel that's nestled in downtown Cincinnati. All of this time and the man still hasn't given me his name.

"How much time do I have," The client asks, his gaze darting from my lips, breasts, then hips before returning to eyes that refuse to shed any more of the tears that glaze them.

"One hour, not a second more," Angel affirms, looking at the dashboard of the vehicle. "I'll be waiting."

The client, trying to be a gentleman, opens the car door on my side and extends his hand. Déja vu shifts to the day that a stranger came to whisk me away from my mother to an unknown place, leaving me for his next arranged encounter.

There hasn't been a day since Ryan took me from my home that I don't think about this sad life—my life—and the vise grip Angel has on me. The call never came where Ryan was to take me back to Dearborn, Michigan, back to playing in the yard with Nina, and to my place with a woman, despite her inability to show affection, was all the family that I knew. Sometimes I wonder if Mama's been looking for me or if she's even still alive. She was my whole life. That all changed with one meeting, one look out of the back of a car window, and the longest car ride I'd ever taken. A series of single well coordinated meetings that now bring me to the extended hand in the back of an Escalade.

Hooked arm in arm, I fake a smile as my client and I walk to the first floor room. He stands at the door, his arm stretched into the bright, modern decorated room, as I sashay past to the two cut glass champagne flutes, golden box of chocolates, and bottle of Rosé sitting on a clear acrylic serving tray on the king-sized bed, a small box of Trojans sit on the nightstand under a silver hoop lamp.

"Turn around," the thick accent demands.

Out of my periphery I see the man reaching for my shoulders. His delicate touch is a surprise. My past clients were rough no matter how fancy I dressed for the affair. He turns me in an about face to him and the fire that burns in his icy gray eyes says he's been starving himself for such an occasion as this. A new spark in his gaze ignites as he opens my blouse again, taking time to stroke the lacy material that holds the fullness of my breasts. Clammy fingers creep up my shoulder and make quick work of removing my blouse, revealing a brand—a tattoo of the sign of Gemini—on my shoulder, something Angel forced me to get when I was thirteen.

The man leans in and traces the tattoo with the tip of his tongue and follows with a kiss. He plants wet kisses down my neck and I gasp, a reaction that is contrived to make him believe that I'm enjoying his attention. Pulling away, he gives me a heated gaze as he inches back to the bed.

"Please, sit down," he requests, opening the bottle of champagne before pouring one flute half full. "You are one of the most exotic women I've ever met," he states, offering the glass. "Your features—light hair and tan skin … it's not a combination that is common."

"True." In twenty plus years of living, I have yet to see someone who looks like I do.

"Your eyes … they're green."

"Today they are," I say, sniffing the contents of the glass and trying not to sound sarcastic. "Sometimes, they are a shade of brown."

"They remind me of the eyes of a beautiful Persian woman that I loved when I was younger. Is your family Persian?" Silence falls between us as I consider his inquiry.

"Thank you for the compliment, Mr.—," I sip the bubbly contents of the glass, ignoring his question about my lineage.

"Bashir." He flashes a foxy grin.

A lean smile barely works its way across my face. "Thank you, Mr. Bashir."

Mr. Bashir sits on the bed and smooths the fluffy blue comforter with his hand—a familiar invitation. I move forward, he takes my glass, steals a sip, and sets it on the floor next to the bed. His hand travels up my covered leg until he reaches bare flesh. Mr. Bashir lifts my skirt, kisses my thigh, and my stomach twists. It could be the sip of champagne on an empty stomach or the overpowering odor of his cologne, but everything about this moment makes my insides churn.

Thoughts of blue skies and the ocean are the only things that keep my mind busy while the newest client satisfies what I can only describe as a voracious appetite.

* * *

Mr. Bashir rests like a man who put in eight hours of heavy labor while I collect the clothes that littered the room. With superman-like speed, I get dressed. Angel does not play when it comes to his time or money. One last check in the bathroom mirror shows the story of the morning; red cheeks, face glistening with perspiration so the curls in the front of my face stick to my forehead; eyes, which usually have more of a green hint of hazel, appear to be algae brown. My heart palpitates as if it's trying to escape the prison of my chest. With a wipe of my forehead and the tuck of a curl, I rush out of the room, down to the lobby, and back to the Escalade where Angel welcomes me with a wily smile.

"He wore the hell outta you, huh?" He laughs, however I don't find the humor in his comment. "Are you going back to work, Baby Girl?"

"No," I murmur. Glad that the appointment is over, a deep breath escapes as I close the car door.

"Take her home, man." Angel sings to the driver. "You want some water, Baby Girl?"

My throat feels like I swallowed a bag of cotton balls. The brisk spring air from the short walk between the hotel and the car didn't cool me off. Water would be great, but I won't indulge Angel's notion that Mr. Bashir "wore the hell outta me."

"No, thank you, *Sir*. I'm good." I say through a slim smile that causes Angel to snap his head over his shoulder.

He's met with a cocked eyebrow.

Angel's upper lip twists into his flared nostril, a look that is meant to scare me, but to no avail. Every class that is taken, every document that is completed, every project that is finalized at McFadden & Tate is a step closer to freedom. The only part of the plan I haven't figured out is how to get away. Alive.

"Don't forget about *our* appointment tonight, Gemini," he grunts as the driver pulls up in front of the apartment complex. "Get a nap in. You'll need the energy for what I've got for you."

The driver joins Angel in what can only be described as demonic sounding laughter.

"I know better than to forget that … *Sir.*" Contempt drips speaking louder than my actual words.

Angel suddenly stops laughing and glares at me as I exit the vehicle. I close the door and watch the Escalade roll out of the parking lot.

A welcome gust of spring air carrying the smell of freshly laid wood chips pushes me to my apartment door. Mr. Bashir's fantasy of banging his secretary, who is somehow off limits, left me feeling like I crawled out of a sewer. Hot water stings as it races from the top of my head to the rest of my body. Maybe the water can get hot enough to peel off every skin cell that he handled. The slimy touch of his tongue haunts me. The water is boiling hot, but shivers still race relentlessly through my body.

Beautiful, he said.

Baby Girl. Beautiful. Gemini.

Forever isn't long enough to never hear those names again. Water runs down over my ears but doesn't drown out Mr. Bashir's voice or his breathing. *Beautiful.* The pumice stone usually reserved for scrubbing, burns as I place it on my skin and wash as hard as I can. Droplets of blood smear the tattoo. Dizzying deep breaths don't stop the oncoming groan that grows into a wail. The water runs cold as I stand under the stream.

Still, I don't feel clean.

Chapter 6

Gemini

Not a cloud in the afternoon sky and the day was sadder than when my father and brother died. Tears streamed from my eyes as I craned my neck out of the back window to look at Nina as Ryan drove down the street and away from the subdivision. I sat back once she was out of view.

"Stop your cryin', Li'l Mama," Ryan's spoke as though he was speaking to a baby. His kindness encouraged me to a least try to do what he said—when my mother calls he'll tell her that I was being good. I wiped the tears with the back of my filthy hands—whatever dirt got into my eyes created more tears than my hand could dry. "Shhh ... We've got a long drive and you can't cry the whole way there."

The ride allowed for a nap long enough for the day to become night. I woke up to the sight of bright colored houses lining a quiet street. Ryan parked in front of a peach-painted, two-story brick house. Flowers and shrubs under the front window made the house look homey.

"You hungry, Li'l Mama?" Ryan inquired.

Hunger pangs racked my body. Nina and I ate an early lunch of peanut butter and banana sandwiches so I was starving. Though Ryan didn't look like he would hurt me, he was a stranger. I was too scared to answer his question.

"C'mon. I'll find you something to eat." Ryan opened the back door to let me out and we walked up to the front door where we're met by the scent of fried chicken.

"Hey, Ma," Ryan hollered from the entrance and looped into the cozy kitchen, where a short and hefty freckle-faced woman was standing over the stove. Dark circles under her amber eyes meant she hadn't slept in some time. Ryan kissed her cheek.

"Hey, sweetie." Her squeaky voice seemed much to small to come from her large frame. *"What took you so long? I was getting worried."*

"I got tired and pulled over to sleep a little bit."

"I'm glad you made it back safe." His mother smiled at him, but her eyebrows furrowed and nostrils flared as she peered over her shoulder at me. Ryan didn't seem to notice.

"What's for dinner?" Ryan asks looking over his mother's shoulder to the stove. *"I'm starvin' and so is Li'l Mama."*

"Li'l Mama, huh?" His mother said stirring a pot full of something white and creamy. *"Chicken, grits, and gravy."*

A smile broke wide on Ryan's face.

"Show your little friend where she can get cleaned up," she snarled, wrinkling her nose. *"You know me and Gillespie don't allow filthiness in my house."*

"Okay. Where's Pops?"

Ryan's mother dropped her head in the direction of a doorway across from the kitchen.

"C'mon, Li'l Mama."

I fell close in step with Ryan on the way into a living room where a dark-skinned man dressed in a white tank top and jeans sat watching basketball on the biggest flat screen television I had ever seen. His bald head shined like a bowling ball.

"Hey, Pops," Ryan greeted his father with what my friends and I

would call a secret handshake. "Here's Li'l Mama."

Ryan's father stood from the black leather couch. I tipped my head back in order to take in his enormous height. White teeth from ear to ear gleamed, but nothing about this man was friendly. He cupped his large hand under my chin and lifted my face up further, guiding my head from one side to the other, his eyes roamed my face until he looked into my eyes. Tremors danced from my shoulders to my knees.

"Hey, son. Go to Jimmy's Corner Store and get some beverages for dinner. Bring me back a forty."

He pulled out a wad of dollar bills and peeled off a hundred-dollar bill.

Ryan moved back through the kitchen, glancing over his shoulder before leaving me alone with his father. The man's creepy gaze returned to my face.

"Your eyes are beautiful," he said, his voice deep and dark.

"Thank you," I whispered.

"What's your name, Baby Girl?"

"Aish—"

Angel's giant hand swung and slammed into my face before I could get out my whole name. The force dropped me to the ground.

He crouched over me.

"Let's try this again," he said narrowing his dark eyes, his lips pursed. "What's your name, Baby Girl?"

"Ai- Aish," I stammered.

Again, his hand swung and hit the side of my face. The pain traveled from one side of my head to the other, causing my ears to ring.

"What. Is. Your. Name?" he asked, still crouched over me delivering one last hit. "If I ever hear you say that name ever again, little girl, I will beat you within an inch of your life. Do you understand me?"

Sobbing, I nodded.

Angel walked into another room while I clutched my head. A thousand questions swirled around my mind. Rocking back and forth on the beige plush carpet was my only relief until Ryan returned from his father's errand. He stooped next to me, eyebrows furrowed, he peered over his *shoulder toward the kitchen.*

"C'mon, Li'l Mama," he said helping me to my feet. A warm stream of liquid trickled down my legs and over my sandal-covered feet. Ryan shook his head. His large, warm hand took mine as he led me to a bathroom on the second floor.

"I'll get you some clothes."

Ryan took almost no time coming back and placed a small stack of clothes on the vanity. After getting cleaned up in record time, I slipped into the oversized Power Rangers t-shirt and black sweat pants. A glance in the mirror showed a handprint that covered half of my face and a red spot in the white of my left eye.

"Time to eat," Ryan announced from the hallway.

Eating was the last thing on my mind, but I didn't want to upset that man. So I followed Ryan back down the hallway, to the stairs, and to the kitchen. His mother was setting the table with places for four. Ryan pulled out a black padded parson chair for me to sit. I had hoped that Ryan's mother would sit next to me, but his father came from another room and plopped down while she placed the last of the food on the table.

"Hey, Baby Girl," he said, smiling at me as though he hadn't just tried to smack my entire face off my head. "You like fried chicken?"

Ryan plopped a spoonful of grits and slid a chicken wing onto the plate in front of me.

Persian mother, Sudanese Father. Fried chicken was not the kind of food we ate often. In fact, I didn't remember ever having fried chicken for a meal at home. None of that mattered at the moment. The aroma of the food on the table made my mouth water and my stomach growl a little louder.

"Yes, Sir," I whispered, afraid that if I said the wrong thing I'd get hurt again.

"Who is this little white girl and what's she doing here, Gillespie?" Ryan's mother spat, joining us at the table. "And how long will she be visiting?" Her bitter tone told a story of having unexpected visitors more often than she desired.

"She is who I say she is," Angel said biting into his chicken breast. *"All you need to know is her name. Gemini."*

No further explanation was given. Forks clinked on plates as everyone shoveled food into their mouths. Ryan's mother narrowed her eyes on me. She didn't have to hit me. That look was one my mother gave before she slapped me for talking too much.

"Gemini, huh?" she said, stirring the grits on her chipped plate, waiting for Angel to say something more. Maybe she wanted to talk about the name. I don't know what the lady thought of it, but I thought it was the worst name I'd ever heard in my life.

* * *

Snuggled in my king-size down comforter, the afternoon hours went by fast. Banging at the door disturbs the peace and my rest as slightly opened curtains shows the sun hanging low in the sky. Reaching out of my cocoon, I grab the cell from the nightstand. *6:07.*

"Aisha," Caren bellows from the other side of the door.

Cool air gives me a chill as I peel the comforter back to answer the door. Caren walks in past me with two bags of what smells like Chinese.

"I was thinking you needed some food. That ridiculousness I saw in your fridge this morning …" Caren unloads the food on my dining room table and pulls up a chair. *6:15*

"How did you even know I was home?" I ask taking in a whiff of the contents in the plastic containers. "I'm never home this early."

"I went in to invite you to my set tonight. You know Sasha—if she knows anything the whole department knows." No lies told, nothing in the way of information gets past Sasha. Her skills for getting dirt on people would be better used on TMZ and not as a receptionist for an accounting firm.

It's thoughtful for Caren to bring me something to eat—I hadn't had a bite all day. She's always looked out for me when we worked together. As close as we are, I've never told her about the rest of my life. With Angel's pending visit, our dinner needs to be quick. If Caren and

Angel cross paths, I could lose my friend when she discovers I've been keeping this secret from her or worse—Angel could hurt her for being around me.

"So, do you want Mongolian Beef or Sesame Chicken?"

I snag the Mongolian Beef and a fork. Caren hands me a fortune cookie and gives me a Cheshire cat grin. She knows how I love these tasty cookies and sometimes even the fortunes. Though none of the fortunes offer any encouragement for getting away from Angel.

"I'm gonna save this for later," I say, clasping the cookie in my hand.

6:35—the clock, the door, and the window are getting more attention than Caren at the moment.

"What's wrong with you?" she asks, slurping a bit of egg drop soup, her eyebrows crinkled.

"I'm just not feeling well, but thanks for hookin' a sista up, though." A tired smile and a little slang I learned from her is all I can muster.

"Listen, I can't have you withering away." Caren waves her spoon up and down the length of my body before plunging it into the cup of soup. "You know, Aisha, there's this trend that's really popular with people these days and though I usually advise against following the crowd, I think you should try it."

"What would that be?" I say sliding a forkful of beef into my mouth.

"I think it's called grocery shopping," she replies, pretending to think hard about her answer. "Yeah, that's it. Everybody's doing it. People go to these places called markets and load up carts with things to eat called food. It's so popular you might even meet other people while performing this activity. You might even find a man."

"Ha, ha." Laughter breaks free, a sound that rarely happens and only with Caren. And sometimes with Zephyr Gray.

"So, are you coming to my set tonight?" Caren asks, her penciled on eyebrows reaching toward her hairline.

Caren often asks me to come and watch her perform, but I have to be available when Angel calls and lately that's a lot. Any day I'm given to myself is spent between resting and planning to get out of Cincinnati so that I can leave Angel and this life behind.

"Yeah, I'll try," I say, knowing all too well that my priority appointment will keep that from being true.

"I think you'll like it tonight," she assures me as she grabs a fork and stabs a plump piece of saucy chicken. "I'll be singing some Anita Baker, some Jon Bon Jovi, and a little Etta James."

"What the hell kinda line up is that?" I ask, scooping a spoonful of rice.

"The kind of line up that pays two hundred and fifty dollars tonight," she exclaims around a mouthful of chicken. "I think they call it 'Mixed Tape Night'. There is absolutely no musical relevance between the songs I'll be singing tonight. They gave me a list and I just sing what they ask. Hell, I'll sing 'Jingle Bells' butt naked in July if they're paying me two hundred and fifty dollars."

Caren glance flickers between the fortune cookie on the table and me.

"Okay. Okay, I'll open it," I say, as a grin breaks wide across her face. Cracking open the vanilla wafer, the sliver of white paper with blue printing unfurls. I straighten it out and read it aloud:

"A thousand-mile journey begins with one step"

"Well, that fortune sucks," Caren barks a laugh.

"I'll keep it anyway." As cliché as it is, this time the message *is* for me. Step by tiny step moves are being made take control of my life. The crunch of the cookie is almost as delicious as the thought of getting away from Angel.

A quick glance at the clock makes my heartbeat take an uptick—*7:41*.

"You're gig's at nine, right?" I say with intention to rush her out. "You're gonna be late."

"But I need you to do my makeup. Please?" Sad puppy eyes are hard to resist especially when it's such a simple request.

Caren can't do make up to save her soul and I consider myself a semi-pro since it's a part of the night job.

"I've gotta look good for Dominic," she says. "Great sex and makeup means more gigs."

She brought her make up bag and I added to the party. Red lips, gold glitter eye shadow, and body glitter glow on her ebony complexion—all the fixin's for a girl who wants to look like a Nubian goddess. I pull her curly, shoulder length Afro back into a crown and she's ready to go to set.

8:25. Knots twist and pull in my stomach as Caren stands to leave and Angel walks in.

Damn. I forgot to lock the door.

Caren's eyes light up and her lips curl into a sly smile. She turns to me with a cocked eyebrow.

"Girl. You've been keeping *this* secret from me?" she asks, feigning surprise and placing a hand to her chest. "We will definitely talk about *this* later. Thanks for my makeup, sweetie."

In two blinks, Caren walks up to Angel and extends her hand. He dwarfs her petite four-foot-eleven curvy physique, but she takes the liberty of a sizing him up from head to toe. Angel loses no time drinking in Caren's freshly painted red lips and perfectly applied makeup before taking her hand.

"Caren Franklin," she announces, leaning back and tilting her head up to meet his eyes. "And you are?"

"Angel," he announces with a sly grin.

"No last name, Angel?"

"None that you need to know, Ms. Franklin."

Angel raises Caren's hand above her head. "Turn around for me."

Caren obeys the soft-spoken demand without hesitation like she's dancing for her man.

"A beauty as lovely as her name. Where are you off to tonight?"

Caren giggles as Angel releases her hand. She reaches into her ample bosom, pulls out a cell, and checks the time.

Tingles dance on my shoulders as Angel shows special interest in Caren. He still keeps his common law wife, Dane, around and has me as a bonus. Watching the two of them makes me sweat as I fight the need to throw up.

"I'm performing at The Millennia. It's downtown where Club Paris used to be." Caren holds up the cell and checks her face. "Maybe you and Aisha will come later? I'm singing until close."

A wily smile splits Angel's face as he licks his thick lips and leers at me.

"*Aisha* and I have some business to take care of." He stares into Caren's eyes, making her giggle. "If we finish early we'll come."

Caren's smile brightens and Angel shoots a glance and wink over his shoulder. "Good night, Ms. Franklin."

The sway in Caren's strut catches Angel's eye as she exits, leaving late for her performance, but every bit too soon for me.

Angel closes and locks the door behind her then turns his attention on me. He fixes his gaze on my face for a moment before slowly searching the rest of my body. A fast-moving hand grabs my neck and pins my back against a wall.

My breathing hitches.

"I thought I told you that I never wanted to hear that name again."

"I'm sorry, Sir." The slow tightening grip squeezes out a tear and leaves me just enough air to repent for my indiscretion. "You won't hear it again."

"I better not," he warns as he loosens his hold. "I've missed you, Baby Girl." He whispers and pulls a coil of my hair between his fingers. Even though I know how the night will be spent, I waver between initiating this transaction to get this meeting over with and waiting on him to commence. My indecision permits him to make this determination.

Angel paws my purple satin nightshirt and rips it open. A button bounces off a wall across the room. Large hands slide the remaining fabric off my shoulders as his gaze travels down to my perfectly painted purple toenails. A smirk slides across his face.

Angel backs me into the kitchen wall and dives in for my neck like the snake he is. He grips my fast pulsing carotid artery with his tongue and the roof of his mouth as he tries to suck the soul out of my body. Every painful motion reminding me that he's the client right now and he will be satisfied at any cost.

His hot breath fans my ear as he asks, "You know what I like, right?"

Without question. Having been Angel's personal concubine since the age of thirteen, I own the library of sex acts he enjoys.

Not one position will be overlooked tonight.

Chapter 7

Gemini

The not-so-plush carpet and my nightshirt for a cover made for an uncomfortable bed. Cold air woke me up at an ungodly hour.

Angel made up for lost time last night. Every hour spent, every position commanded, every drop of sweat that he bathed me in reminds me that I belong to him and to never forget.

A glance over my body shows bruises on the insides of my thighs. None of my new clients are as rough as Angel. Most of them contract me for a Girlfriend Experience to do the things that their wives used to do—listen to their problems and something more than missionary without making them feel ashamed about their desires. Companionship has a high price and there isn't one client that complains about the cost no matter how Angel inflates the amount.

For most, I'm the fantasy, a prize they have better chances at winning than the state lottery. For some, I take them back to a place and time when life was about sexual adventure, performing escapades in places that their wives have long decided were inappropriate. Not one of them is as forceful as Angel—he's the only *client* that is brutal enough to leave his mark like the dog he is.

No one wears turtlenecks when the day's high temperature is going to be seventy-one degrees and winter clothes are in storage. However, the hickey on my neck that's the size of a half dollar demands to be concealed.

Cover Girl, be a miracle worker.

* * *

A cheerful buzz from the news of McFadden's retirement echoes in the normally tense environment. Talk of Zephyr Gray being one of three candidates up for nomination to run the company is a hot topic. A smile works its way across my face as I stroll past the reception desk where Paul and Sasha are chopping it up about their hopes in Zephyr Gray as partner.

"They won't let him become partner," Paul's husky smoker's voice charges. "Look at my man. First of all, he's one of us. Then the brother is gonna need to cut all of that hair off and he ain't doin' that. And he's young. That old money won't let it happen unless Christ himself comes back and tells them it's him or hell, and we all know they'll choose hell."

"Could you be a little more hopeful, Paul?" Sasha flips her dark, back-length weave in Paul's face.

"I'm more hopeful for a date with you tonight. Ha!" Paul roars with laughter.

Sasha's hot pink lips pops open.

"That statement qualifies as sexual harassment. Don't try me," she warns, giving Paul and his tight-fitting uniform a roving stare.

The delightful aroma of cinnamon and herbs waft from my office. Once again, the door stands ajar. Zephyr's gifts are still where I left them, only with a sticky note attached to the smaller box. Next to it, steam puffs from a white oversized coffee mug with "This Might Be Wine" written in bold script filled with what smells like chai tea.

Good morning Ms. Mosley. I hope you're feeling better.
Zephyr Gray

One sip of the tea and I know the day will only get better. Handling the package with the utmost care, I peel off the tape of the large box—I'm not sure what I'll do with it, but the stunning mint green and gold paisley sheet needs to stay intact.

Upon breaking the seal on the plain cardboard box, a small gold box and a set of black studio style headphones are revealed. Removing the top from the slim golden box produces a thin, silky fabric of several shades of green. One tug and the fabric opens into a silk scarf. Curiosity burns as I unwrap the smaller box—a green leather-bound journal with an Aurora Crystal encrusted pen, a small bottle of Versace perfume, and an unpackaged iPod. I swipe the screen that brings up the passcode prompt.

Cradling the iPod in my hand, my thumb glides over the glass.

What's the passcode?

The four numbers on the card serve as the only clue.

It can't be this easy.

Four taps on the numbers on the screen and it opens. I chuckle.

Of course, it's that easy.

Eight songs titled "Beautiful" from Christina Aguilera to Musiq Soulchild to Snoop Dogg are set in queue on the playlist. Every song offering a glimpse into what he's thinking of me. If only he knew that *beautiful* is far from what I want to be.

What would he feel if he really knew me and discovered what I am? It's reasonable to believe that he would be professional, but I won't take that for granted. Every man I've ever known, with the exception of my father, has only been able to see me as a source of entertainment. It would be understandable if he didn't even respect me as a woman if he were to find out who I really am.

A relationship with Zephyr is out of the question and a dream I can't allow myself to have. It could ruin the only place I find solace. Thanks to Angel, work outside of McFadden & Tate means spending a great deal of time doing damage control.

Countless words come to mind as my thumb glides over the gilded edges of the journal. Further investigation finds random notes sprinkled through the pages with a message in the front cover in the most impressive script I've ever seen a man write:

To the gem in my life
-Z

"Gem"—How could he know? Gemini—the significance of the name Angel gave me is still a mystery. Only Angel and any clients he introduces me to call me by Gemini. My birthday is in August, the day after my mother's birthday, both of us born on the cusp—she's a Leo and I'm a Virgo—not that anyone has ever asked.

Add finding the reason for this name to the ever-increasing list of questions I need to have answered.

* * *

Preparing financial statements for multiple accounts takes up the early hours of the day. Aside from the occasional interoffice call, things were quiet. No one stopped by the office to give me more assignments and the best part was no calls from Angel for impromptu appointments.

Fatigue and the events of last night finally catch up with me on my journey to the coffee machine. Office chatter and the heavenly aroma of liquid joy are the only things keeping me from sleepwalking down the narrow hallway that leads through the maze of cubicles to the staff lounge.

"Good afternoon, Ms. Mosley." Charles Webber, the accounting department supervisor and son-in-law to Mr. Tate, stands in the entrance of the lounge rubbing his eyes, while wearing a thin, but crafty grin.

"How are you today, Mr. Webber?" The empty staff lounge is just steps away with coffee calling my name. He rests against the doorway, blocking me.

"Exhausted," he yawns, combing his fingers through perfectly trimmed dark hair. "Doing these audits is brutal even when everyone on the team is working at peak performance."

"I know what you mean." I chuckle. "That's why I'm here to get my second wind. Excuse me."

"Oh yes, pardon me."

Mr. Webber steps to one side, but follows close behind me to the coffee machine. Prickles shimmy down my spine as he watches me pour the brew into a company mug.

"Are you having any, Mr. Webber?" I ask holding up the carafe.

"Oh no, thanks." He snickers.

Rushed footsteps and keys chiming down the hall distract me from the current discomfort.

"Listen, Ms. Mosley, I need you to follow me to my office. There's something I need to discuss with you about your work performance."

Chills race from my shoulders to my neck. Mr. Webber, along with Mrs. Forrester, and Zephyr have always had good things to say about my work in spite of a lack of experience in the beginning and occasional tardiness. I work my ass off so I don't know what this meeting could be about unless he wants to offer me a raise.

When I arrive at an office near the file room, Mr. Webber's extended arm grants me permission to enter. He follows me inside, a little too closely for comfort.

"Please have a seat, Ms. Mosley."

He waves a hand toward one of the leather-tufted club chairs in front of a granite topped executive desk. Mr. Webber paces the length of the spacious office as I take a sip of coffee and settle in.

"First, I want to tell you that you've been a real asset to this company since your arrival. You have a great attention to detail that some of the more seasoned associates of this company don't have."

"Thank you, Sir. I do my best," I reply.

A variety of awards and plaques decorate the otherwise boring vanilla walls behind him. The light from one narrow window illuminates the silver-framed pictures of Mr. Webber and his wife, and a blue eyed, golden-haired baby girl showing all of her gums for the picture.

"That's what makes what I'm about to say so difficult," he says leaning on the corner of the desk. A sweeping glance at Mr. Webber discloses more of his intent than his words. "The company is doing some minor downsizing and your name is on a short list of people we have to let go."

Thinking about how my plan to get away from Angel crumbles before my eyes, ball my free hand into a fist. All I need is another ten thousand dollars; enough for a fresh start somewhere out of the state. It's a blessing that Angel has no idea what I've already saved—P.O. boxes are a godsend when you don't want bank statements found.

"I hadn't heard about any downsizing in our department, Mr. Webber," I say clearing my throat.

Hands clasped as if he were praying, Mr. Webber's tone goes from empathetic to distressed. "Ms. Mosley, this isn't my choice."

"I understand," I lie, trying to hold a brave face. "Is there anyone I can talk to about my position here? I really do enjoy working for this company."

Zephyr immediately comes to mind since I've worked on a number of projects for him. Mr. Webber slides into the chair next to me, gets into a comfortable position, and crosses a leg. The hum of the fluorescent light echoes in the otherwise quiet space.

"I can get your name off that list," he states, a little too cheerfully for my taste. "There is an associate that has a little more seniority than you, but I could be *convinced* to put his name on the list where your name should be," he winks. "If you catch my drift."

I narrow my eyes on the smirk that creeps across his golf-tanned face. "Come again?"

"*I* can ensure your position with this company if you don't mind *working* some extra hours. An hour or so after work once or twice a week …"

A mad dash from my seat wasn't quick enough—the hairy hand that touches the hem of my skirt shocks me as if the static electricity was a sure sign of his desire.

Mr. Webber presses his lips straight and stands. "Hey, I'm just trying to help you out. My father-in-law listens to what I recommend, and you wouldn't have any worries."

No worries? Is he for real? The eyes that roam over every part of my body say he's not joking. This is the life I'm trying to get away from and this is a condition of keeping my job? Never going to happen. Heat races up to my ears as only one word comes to me in my defense.

"No," I say locking my gaze on his. Mr. Webber grimaces, but nods.

"No? Just like that?" Mr. Webber closes the distance between us in a single step. "You'd be excused from any project that you don't want to work on. I could even arrange a nice raise and quarterly bonuses … Are you sure 'no' is your final answer?"

"*Hell no* is my final answer," I repeat reclaiming my space. "Also, you must not know how often Bethany and I chat when she comes to bring you lunch. There are advantages to having an open office door when a wife is looking for her husband."

Mr. Webber snickers at my threat, but glances at the voices that have stopped behind the door. One voice is recognizable—Zephyr.

Mr. Webber zips into the path of the closed door.

"Excuse me. What are you doing?" I ask, standing my ground.

Mr. Webber clears his throat while adjusting his flat navy polyester tie.

"You can say what you want, no one will believe you," he says, leaning into my space. "So let me cleanse your mind from any thought you have about reporting this."

Blood spikes through my veins like hot lava, as I stand speechless at his arrogance.

"And with all of this being said, empty your office. Good day, Ms. Mosley." Mr. Webber opens the door with all of the attention of a gentleman.

"Good afternoon, Miss—" The voice that has brightened my last few days fades fast as I brush past Zephyr and Derek on my way to clear out my office.

Swift footsteps meet me at the door of my office. "Is everything okay, Aisha?"

Without a word, my gaze flickers between Zephyr and the distance down to Mr. Webber's office before walking into the office claiming the chair behind the desk.

Zephyr's eyebrows crumple into the middle of his face as he blows out a sigh. "What's going on?"

"Why don't you go and ask Mr. Webber."

Chapter 8

Zephyr

Having a little sister and a strong mother has its benefits when it comes to understanding a woman's body language—just the tilt of Aisha's head as she walks let's anyone who's paying attention know a great deal about her confidence or how she's feeling in a particular moment.

Aisha had dashed out of Charles' office and didn't respond. She already doesn't make a big deal about seeing me, but she's always cordial enough to greet me in passing. Come to think of it, she makes a point to acknowledge anyone she comes across, even if the moment is brief, so this behavior is out of character for her.

"Are you okay?" I ask again, not wanting to make any assumptions about what I just saw. Sliding into the chair behind her desk, her posture not quite straight, the tears that glazed her eyes wouldn't fall.

To my surprise, her normally warm green eyes are a shade of brown that I've never seen before. The sadness in her eyes is a lot to witness, especially when she is the one who never fails to brighten my day.

"What's going on?" I ask hopeful that she'll trust me enough to tell me the cause of her distress.

"I said, why don't you ask Mr. Webber," her voice cracks sounding like the burdens of her emotions are too much to bear. She blows a gust of air loose as she fumbles with some papers on her desk.

Blood rushes through my veins as deep breaths help to keep my temper at bay. I don't need too many reasons to punch Charles in the face as he's an all-around asshole, but Aisha makes for a damn good reason right now. However, with my name in the running for partner I have to refrain from doing anything that will jeopardize the opportunity.

Fast and few steps take me back to Charles' office. A quick scan of the room shows that he's moved on from the space and the previous events. He's nowhere in the area so a visit to the company information center's in order.

"Good afternoon, Sasha," I say, as I'm greeted by a perfect set of pearly whites. "Have you seen Mr. Webber?"

"Yes, Mr. Gray," she croons. "He went in the direction of the men's room."

"Thanks."

"Is there anything else you need, Mr. Gray?" Sasha's voice fades as I pick up my pace to the men's restroom. "Can I order us—I mean, you something for lunch?"

Heat is trapped under my tie as I enter the restroom and find Charles washing his hands.

"Hey, Gray," Charles says, pulling from the paper towel dispenser. Taking a pause gives me time to calm down. "What's happening?"

"You tell me, Charles. Is there a problem with Ms. Mosley that I should be made aware of?"

Charles barks a hearty laugh.

"Problem? No. What did she tell you?"

He's not entitled to any answers from me, so I wait for an answer to my question. "Listen, Gray, she misunderstood a proposition that I offered her in order to secure her position. That's all."

"Well, as the lead on the major projects where Ms. Mosley assists, I haven't heard any news that her position is in danger."

Charles fixes his sight on me, still smiling.

"Now, what exactly did she *misunderstand*, Charles?" I ask. "And don't make this long. Two meetings and an emotional staff member mean I have no time for bullshit."

The smile that split his stretched orange skin is reduced to a slick grin.

"I just offered her some extra work, if you know what I mean."

I close the distance between us before he starts to the door. "Be clear so that I *do* know what you mean."

"C'mon now, Gray. I know you've had a tryst or two with some of the more attractive ladies in the building. I mean, Ms. Mosley has climbed the proverbial ladder so fast, she has to have given a favor or two."

My pulse quickens with the unfounded accusation. "Let's get something straight, Charles," I say, controlling the need to wrap my hand around his neck and pin him to the wall. "What I do in my personal life is none of your business, nor is it the business of the people in this company. But if you must know, I've *never* slept with anyone, man or woman, in this building … which is more than can be said for you."

"Do you think no one has noticed the preferential treatment you give to Ms. Mosley?" he laughs. "For crying out loud, as I understand it, she's taken every free and tuition- based class and seminar under *your* suggestion." Charles nods as he raises an eyebrow.

"What's to understand?" I shrug. "I suggest advancement opportunities to *all* of the staff members, especially to women and people of color. I think it's great that Ms. Mosley is motivated to enhance her skills to the point of rapid progression."

"Yeah, right," Charles snarls, trying to walk past me only to be blocked—his twisted lip meets his flared nostrils. We lock stares.

"What you fail to realize, Charles, is you've crossed the wrong one," I warn, leaning into his space so close he has to think I'm about to kiss him, "Or maybe the right one in this case. While you were noticing whom I'm helping, I've taken a few notes on who you're letting go, namely bright and promising Black staff members and women who must not have taken you up on any *offer* you have recommended."

Charles' face drops, holding the deep crease between his eyebrows.

"That sounds a lot like multiple lawsuits waiting to happen, doesn't it, Charles—I imagine your father-in-law would stroke out and the immense amount of stress there would be on Bethany, and she's what? Three months pregnant with baby number two? I don't think you want to play this game with me—Do *your* job: make sure your accounts are all balanced, keeping money in the bank, and not accidentally *slipping* into someone else's account or better yet, not into your own."

A step back gives a nervous-looking Charles some space and me some much needed air.

"Now, let's make this mess is easy to clean up. You *will* apologize personally to Ms. Mosley and clear up any *misunderstanding* she may have. Furthermore, any more communication about her position will not come from you."

He yanks the door open as I adjust my tie in the mirror. A glance at my watch shows that I'm about to be late for my meeting with a new prospective client. I'll check in on Aisha to make sure Charles did as he was told.

Somehow, I don't feel confident this is over with him.

Chapter 9

Gemini

Ryan's smile spread from ear to ear as he asked me to follow him into the basement laundry room when his dad left on an errand. There was no problem trusting Ryan—he was unlike his father in every way. He was kind, patient, helpful, and he looked after me a like an older brother.

I tiptoed down the stairs, scanning the dark but elaborately decorated space. A large projection television surrounded by dark wood cabinets covered the expanse of one wall. A black leather pit sectional sat in the middle of the basement in front of the television. A high bar and stools with a wall of liquor was nestled in the corner by the stairs. Ryan jogged ahead of me to the back of the basement. On a vinyl-topped card table sat a recycled vegetable can that held pencils, crayons, and a ruler. Another recycled can contained used popsicle sticks to be used as counters, a stack of paper, old math and science books, and some magazines for reading.

"Li'l Mama," Ryan whispered even though no one was around, *"I know you can't get to school right now. So I'll be your teacher."*

Having lost track of the days since arriving at Ryan's house, I had no idea that school was starting. Both of Ryan's parents preferred it quiet in the house so asking questions or any sort of talking around them meant a whack across the mouth. That part wasn't all too different from being at home. These rules didn't apply to Ryan.

"Nobody likes a dummy, Li'l Mama. Remember that," Ryan warned.

I'd never been a dummy or at least had never been called one, so his reasoning seemed sound. *"What do you know how to do? Are you good at spelling?"*

"I like to read. I'm not good at math—sometimes multiplication is hard for me," I explained.

"Okay. I'll teach you math and I'll get you some books to read. You have to read every day and find all of the hard words. I'll get you a dictionary."

Ryan couldn't have known how much it meant to me to have school. I loved to learn about anything and reading was a favorite past time. My curiosity was a blessing and a curse; my father adored and encouraged it. My mother shut down every question not answering even the simplest of inquiries. Thoughts of school back at home and the friends that were left behind overwhelmed the moment. I wondered if they missed me too, especially Nina. Salty tears fell. My heartbreak was written all over Ryan's face like he'd lived my life before.

"Listen, Li'l Mama. You're gonna be alright. You gotta be strong, okay. Stop all of this cryin'. Worse than a dummy, nobody likes a punk either and just 'cause you a girl don't mean you can always cry."

Ryan continued, trying to make me feel better. *"There's gonna be people in this world who gonna ask you to do stuff you don't want to do, say mean stuff to you, and treat you like crap—you can't always cry about it 'cause nobody cares. So stop bein' a punk, okay?"* A quick head nod was all he got from me as I wiped my face clean. *"We've got about an hour until Pops comes back. I'ma show you how to do this laundry so that when Moms and Pops are gone, you can be doin' this too. That way you'll minimize your troubles 'cause they're real strict."*

I guess that was the trade—Ryan taught me math and I did the laundry.

"Can I ask you something?" I said quietly.

"Whatcha wanna know, Li'l Mama?'

"How old are you?" I asked.

Ryan smiled at me, but I'm not sure why.

"Fifteen ... Well, I'll be sixteen in October."

Fifteen? I guess fifteen is old enough to drive to far places.

"How old are you?"

"I'll be ten August twenty-third," I piped up, excited to be turning double digits. "My birthday is the day after my mom's birthday."

"Well, I hate to tell you, Li'l Mama, but you're already ten. August twenty-third was last week."

"I missed my birthday? That means I missed Mama's birthday, too," Tears welled up and Ryan shook his head.

He raised both eyebrows, kind of thoughtful looking, pointed at me and said, "Look, quit bein' a punk, I'll go and get you something and we'll have a little celebration, just you and me, okay? But stop all of this cryin'— You makin' me mad."

One tear trailed down my cheek. It was hard not to cry, as there was nothing to be happy about. How did my mother not pick me up from here before my birthday? Why hadn't she called? The couch was where I got to rest for the night while everyone else had a bed. Talking was forbidden unless spoken to, not that I wanted to speak to people who thought it well to call me out of my name and slap me around.

Ryan telling me to stop crying about what made me sad was the hardest thing he could've asked me to do. Ryan had never punished me like his father did, but I obeyed him anyway. And Ryan made good on that promise; he bought one of those gas station pastries and put a candle on it and sang "Happy Birthday" to me. He was always thoughtful that way.

He was my teacher for nearly three years and the person I celebrated my birthday with each year. Ryan was a math whiz and figured out how *to help me understand the areas I struggled to grasp in school. He was so impressed with how fast I learned the concepts that he tutored me in higher levels of mathematics. We left off at college level Algebra—he said I didn't need to know anything more than that. African American History was Ryan's favorite subject, so we explored government through the Black Panther Party and the Civil Rights movement. He encouraged me to keep up on my reading and had me watch videos on how to write college essays.*

"Li'l Mama, you've been slacking on the writing. Write ten sentences everyday using words from the dictionary. Not just any words, big words. Nobody likes a dummy."

"Okay, let's recap these lessons," I said, pretending to write. "No one likes a punk, and no one likes a dummy. What else do I need to be cognizant of, Ryan?"

Ryan couldn't fight the smile that broke his serious attitude.

"Nothin', smartass." He chuckled.

Upon leaving the fourth grade I was reading at a tenth-grade level according to standardized tests, but none of it was useful for anything that I was there to do. Angel said I had to earn my stay in his house— like everybody else—so he gave me jobs to do. The assignments were simple—go to houses, sometimes abandoned, to deliver or receive packages for him. I was to say only one thing— "I'm Gemini"—and hand someone a package or someone would hand me an envelope, a box, or a bag.

Angel bought me a hot pink and black messenger bag decorated with rhinestones and satin ribbons. This bag was used on every run. No one questioned the fair-skinned girl with wide hazel eyes carrying the cute messenger bag no matter the time of day, no matter the time of year. My frame was tall and wiry, not curvy—no one should've mistaken me for an adult. I didn't look older than the almost thirteen years I'd lived.

School with Ryan was more like family time than real school—it was a pleasant distraction from missing my mom, which happened whenever I wasn't busy. Three years had passed and she still hadn't called.

Ryan was patient and fun and excited to teach me something new all the time, which I thought was odd for a high school kid. We were always good at keeping my studies a secret, being sure to put everything away in miscellaneous boxes in a remote corner of the basement after every session. With a laptop and a few other materials, Ryan was a better teacher than the one I had at school. Nothing that brought me happiness stayed that way for long.

Government was the subject the Friday before the Fourth of July and the good works of the Black Panther Party was the topic of the day.

"I've got something for you," Ryan said. He reached into a box of papers and produced a gold envelope.

"You're gonna need these someday, but never let Pops find them, okay?"

I nodded, as Ryan handed me a small blue card with my name and nine numbers on it and my birth certificate.

"Does Pops check your book bag?"

"Sometimes," I replied.

Ryan scanned the room, his gaze snapped to the dictionary on the desk.

"Keep these here for now," Ryan recommends, folding then stashing the papers in the book. "Don't lose them, okay?"

I agreed with the plan and continued my studies.

Angel had left on another one of his many errands just a half an hour earlier and we always calculated an hour and a half before his return. I started a load of laundry to wash and another load was drying which was probably the reason why neither of us heard Angel's unexpected arrival. Most days he announced himself in many sort of random ways— he asked if anyone is in the house, honked the car horn, or whatever. This day was different. He came in without notice. Angel walked down the stairs to the basement and discovered Ryan leaning over me trying to help me understand a passage that I had just read.

Time froze—I stopped reading, Ryan stopped talking, and Angel stopped and glared at the sight of our improvised classroom.

My mouth hung open, heart thumping fast and all I could think was that he was never supposed to see me studying. Angel turned his head to the side—*eyebrows furrowed, he gave us an inquiring look. His glance flashed back and forth between Ryan and me.*

"So, what's this, son?" The bridge of Angel's nose creased so much that it drew his eyebrows into the middle of his face. Ryan's breathing seemed so still, as if he were holding it captive. "Your mama interrupted my business because, according to her, she thought she heard you and Gemini down here having sex." Angel inspected the surroundings, his face getting tighter with every passing glance.

Ryan stood from his leaning posture stretching to gain an inch or two in his height, the air he was holding filled his chest.

"Nah, Pops. Nothing like that. I was teaching her some stuff about government." Angel ambled across the room to meet Ryan's steely gaze. Though it was only momentary, Ryan's reaction to his father was one that I'd never seen before, that same fear I always had.

"Who told you to teach her anything?" he asked, gritting his teeth. "I know I didn't."

Angel challenged his son's audacity. His nostrils flared wide enough that a train could run through them. Ryan stood motionless, breathing deep breaths and staring his father down, while his father scowled back. On any other day Ryan's mother, Dane, is gone doing whatever her business is. Today she's in the kitchen clanging pots and pans, but it doesn't smell like she's cooking.

"She's supposed to be in school, Pops. I'm teaching her so that she won't be a dummy. You always said nobody likes a dummy." The tone in Ryan's voice deepened as he took a stand against his father.

"Oh, I see, so that she won't be a dummy, huh? You trying to be her man?" Before either of us could blink, Angel flipped our makeshift table. Pencils, books, and papers flew.

Shaking in my chair between the two of them at attention, their eyes fixed in the early stages of a war, I covered my head. Without warning, Angel grabbed my arm, pulled me out of my chair and with his sights deadlocked on Ryan, he threw me to the floor.

My head hit a corner of the table on my descent to the tile. Angel, giving his son one final, deadly gaze, snatched the waistbands of my jeans and panties and jerked them to my knees.

Ryan's eyes widened as he became painfully aware of what his father intended. He stood stunned, at an apparent loss for words.

Angel's eyes glazed over as I wrestled butt naked on the floor trying to break free from the jeans that became my restraints. The back of his hand came down swift and hard on my left cheek, hard enough to make my ears ring. Ryan leapt to my defense and met with the barrel of his father's .357 magnum.

"So, it's like this, son—"

Angel pointed the gun at Ryan as if he didn't know he was his flesh and blood. "You so interested in what this one needs to learn, you gon' watch the real teacher."

Hot, hushed tears poured down my face. Angel yanked his pants down, dropped to his knees, and forcefully entered my body. My back jolted as the pain raced to every nerve of my body and a blood-curdling scream escaped.

"Open your eyes and look at me," he growled, covering my mouth to keep the screams in. Eyelashes hit my brow bone as I fixed my eyes on his cold-blooded stare. Lunch had rushed to the top of my throat, but I dared not vomit. He shoved into me, inching me across the frigid linoleum floor without regard, until he groaned and shuddered as though he'd become ill. Angel looked into my eyes, absorbed in the moment.

"Alright, son," Angel grunted still staring down at me. "Now it's your turn." His fear apparent, Ryan blinked in disbelief. "C'mon, nah, boy. I know you ain't no virgin." Angel adjusted his position and fastened his pants while waiting for Ryan to move.

He didn't.

Angel glared at his son, a hand on his gun. His face sent an unmistakable message about what the consequence would be for not following through on his command.

Ryan hesitated, glancing between his father and me.

I looked up at him, pleading.

Ryan peered at his father, then the gun.

Angel nodded with a menacing grin.

Ryan fondled himself with tears streaming down his face. He kneeled between my legs and took his turn. The aroma of sweat and cologne stung in my nose as I tried to fight him off.

"Shh, Li'l Mama ... I'm sorry," he mouthed as he obeyed his father's direction.

After watching Ryan perform until he ended in much the same way, Angel's lips turned up into a callous sneer.

Ryan lay on top of me, his body trembling. It took a while, but Ryan stood to pull his pants back up; he stepped back and turned away from me, but not in the direction of his father. Angel's glance slowly bounced between Ryan, who was standing a few steps away from me—struggling to hold his emotions to himself—and me who still lay on the floor in a painful, bloody heap.

"Now, that's all she needed to learn," Angel proclaimed pointing at me, his confirmation that he'd won that battle, if Ryan had any questions.

A month away from turning thirteen the only family I knew betrayed me a second time; Ryan was eighteen, and my mother—I didn't care to think about anymore.

Chapter 10

Gemini

Full-face glam makeup to hide the evidence of multiple sleepless nights this week is all the rage. I usually don't wear much makeup to the office—I have to wear enough of it for clients.

While throwing the contents of my desk into a box, he came to my office rescinding his decision and apologizing for any misunderstanding. There was no confusion on my part, but I accepted his words.

A glimpse over my desk shows the small pile of work I left at the end of the day hadn't grown. The gift bag feels heavier than before as I mourn the loss of a relationship I didn't even have. I take the journal out and flip through the pages, reading every message Zephyr left for me before placing it on the corner of my desk with the other gifts.

Today's email indicates that I'll be busy. Mr. McFadden wants to have a company webinar. *That should be glorious.* Mrs. Forrester needs balance sheets prepared for the Vivant account … *hmm*.

Zephyr Gray—no subject. I'm always pleased to hear from Zephyr even if it's just an email.

> *Good morning Ms. Mosley,*
> *I hope this message finds you well. My schedule today is rather light and I was wondering if you'd like to join me for lunch at Wesley's around 12:00?*
> *I look forward to your response.*
>   *- Zephyr Gray*
> *Message sent at 7:53 am*

Staring at the computer, smiling, rereading the short message, it strikes me as funny that he invited me by email. He's way too smart for a communication that isn't thought through. He has to know that the emails are always monitored. Responding to this won't look good for either of us.

For a little over a month, Angel was my only client. Every man who was a regular was taken off the books. I should've been ready for the proverbial boomerang— he never leaves me alone long enough for me to believe that life outside of him is possible. His little "time out" connected him with clients that had money and prestige. Fewer clients, more cash flow. To my disappointment, he never had any intention of freeing me. He said it— *I belong to him.* Thank God that many of his clients only need me for evening or weekend engagements, so messing up his money isn't a big issue.

Between hourly wage increases and a bonus, my bank account is finally looking like I can start my search for a new city to live in. While doing that, finding my mother is high on my to-do list. All of this madness began with her and I need answers. She has to know what she'd done.

"Good morning, Ms. Mosley," Zephyr chimes as he arrives unannounced and in a cheerful mood. The aroma of citrus and sandalwood follows him in the door.

Casual Friday brings out the fun for everyone, especially the executives who have to suffer wearing suits the rest of the week. Zephyr is wearing the hell out of his well-creased, dark denim pants and fuchsia seersucker button up. My heartbeat registers somewhere between pleasure and panic—staying levelheaded around Zephyr is no easy feat. Stuck in place, like a deer caught in headlights, I admire the structure of his muscular arms through his shirt. He shakes his head as he chuckles.

"Good morning, Mr. Gray," I say clearing my throat, diverting my gaze from him. "I wasn't expecting to see you this morning."

"Well," he asserts, "When I didn't get a response to my email, I thought I'd check on you."

I'm at a loss for words as we share the tight space. The challenge to keep myself together around Zephyr when working on major projects isn't a big deal because his attention is on other people and not just on me. In this space, it's pleasantly suffocating.

My concentration is at an all-time low while his jeans are hugging his sculpted ass just right.

"So, Ms. Mosley …" he begins.

"Ms. Mosley?" I laugh, turning to walk back to my desk. "Why are you addressing me so formally this morning? I've been Aisha all this time. What gives?"

We both laugh. I walk behind my desk and stand—the distance keeps my internal temperature from rising any higher.

"Okay, so let's start over." He laughs. "Good morning, Aisha."

"Good morning, Zephyr," I say, a smile breaking wide. "May I ask you a personal question?"

"Sure," he replies.

"Zephyr. What does it mean?"

"A zephyr is a gentle breeze," he explains. "Truth be told I think my mother named me after the car. It's her favorite."

A gentle breeze … he certainly is a breath of fresh air. "What about you?"

"Aisha means 'She who lives'," I declare. "My father named me."

"Nice," he says, nodding.

"Now that curiosity is fulfilled, is there something I can do for you?"

A sexy, but devilish grin splits his freshly trimmed face as he meets my gaze with a raised eyebrow.

"Well, my schedule is empty of appointments until this afternoon and I wanted to know if you would allow me to buy you lunch?"

Excited murmuring and hurried feet race past the door. Sasha on her way to her corner post.

"Thank you so much, but I'm going to have to pass," I say, shuffling papers on the desk. "And email? You don't see a problem with this type of communication while you're being considered for partner?"

"I'm not worried," he reassures me with a nod.

The gleam in his eyes dimmed and his smile faded as he stood waiting as if my answer was going to change.

"I'm sorry." Reaching for the corner of my desk, I pick up the gift bag. "Thank you for the lovely gifts, but I can't keep them."

Zephyr looks at the bag in my hand and confusion laces his expression.

"Listen," he explains, "I don't mean to be an ass, Aisha. Let me apologize for coming on too strong. It's a character flaw that functions well in my profession, but clearly is not working so well right now. I was out shopping and saw these things and I thought that you might like them."

One eyebrow flies up as a grin slides across my face.

"And you knew that I'd like *these* particular gifts from a few interactions?"

Zephyr relaxes against the door, looking as though he is entertained by the question.

"The journal and pen look pretty expensive, hundred-dollar bottle of perfume, two hundred-dollar headphones, hundred-dollar IPod, and those IPod selections took a little more than one short shopping trip."

Nodding, Zephyr's boyish grin returns, this time warmer and brighter than before. He playfully throws his hands up as if to surrender. I can only guess he's amused by my keen observation.

"That's why you work for this company." He chuckles, a bit of shame in his voice. "Just tear a brother down by itemizing costs of everything

… and the IPod did take a little time."

Laughing at his attempt to downplay the situation, I make another attempt to hand the gift bag back to him.

"These are very nice gifts and I do like them, but …"

"Then keep them," he says with a flick of his hand. "Please, enjoy them."

"Okay … Thank you … again."

Returning the gift bag to the corner of my desk, I then shuffle through the paper that covers the top trying to keep my jitters at bay. "Is there anything else I can help you with?"

Our gazes meet and I can't pull mine away from his. His eyes are like pools of ink and I want him to rewrite my story word for word.

"Are you sure I can't take you to lunch?"

Adriane whips the door open, out of breath.

"Mr. Gray, there's a woman at the reception desk insisting that she speaks with you right now. She's … very hyper."

Zephyr slowly focused on Adriane. "Did she say what her business is with me?"

"She only said that she wants to see you *now*. Security has already been called. She said she'll only leave after she sees you."

Zephyr takes off behind Adriane and my curiosity won't let me stay in my office. As we race down the hallway, Paul is trying to console a woman who looked like she's Naomi Campbell's younger sister. A little boy, dressed in his Sunday best, stood at her side. A few people are gathered around savoring the drama that's unfolding.

"Is he here?" yells the thin, statuesque woman.

Zephyr breaks through the small crowd.

"Vanessa," the whisper that was intended for her carries to several staff members. "What the hell are you doing here?"

Chapter 11

Zephyr

The last person I expect to see at the reception desk is Vanessa Fontelroy. We parted ways years ago under not very pleasant circumstances, so for her to come to my job is more than a surprise. Not a good one.

She played the crowd, tears and all—dramatic like I remember, which is part of the reason why we aren't together now.

"Babe," she squeals, throwing her arms around me. "I'm so glad to see you."

"Okay, everybody. There's nothing to see here," I say peeling out of Vanessa's Python grip. "There's only five minutes until the company webinar and we all need to be present online."

Aisha stands back as the crowd reluctantly clears leaving Vanessa staring at me teary-eyed and the little boy she brought with her standing in front of the reception desk watching us intently.

"What brings you to town, Vanessa?"

Boundaries have never been Vanessa's thing so crossing my arms maintains some personal space.

Long, red nails walk up my arm as she tries to coax me out of my stance. "It's been a while and I missed you."

"What did you miss most, Vanessa?" I snapped, ignoring Sasha's attempts to lean in.

A pearly-white smile spreads across her face as I speak into her ear. "Did you miss the way I took care of you and your mother with two jobs and a side hustle while I was in college? Or did you miss the look of utter joy on my face when another man showed up at the hospital while you were having what I thought was my baby?"

Sasha gasps, snatches up the phone and turns her back in a private conversation.

Vanessa's eyes bucked wide as her coppery cheeks turn scarlet.

"I'm sorry, Zephyr," she claims, batting her extended lashes. "That's part of the reason I'm here. I want to apologize."

Vanessa motions for the little boy to come closer. Dress-shoe-clad feet move carefully, all while his gaze is locked on me. Vanessa snaps her gaze to Aisha as she steps to my side.

"Excuse me, Mr. Gray. The web conference is about to begin." Aisha says, drawing me away from the madness of the moment as if she knew I needed help getting out of Vanessa's clutches.

"Thank you," I say, smiling. "I'll be right there."

Furrowed eyebrows and flared nostrils meet me as I turn back to Vanessa. Her gaze following Aisha's progression up the hallway.

"I hope that smile is for your son," she snaps.

My son? The pain that hits feels like she plunged another dagger in my chest.

"Pardon me? We established that your son is not mine." I challenge her, trying not to scare the little boy with my tone, but noticing Sasha's attention was back on us.

"All we established was that I was seeing someone else at the time of his birth." A sly grin lifts the corners of her mouth. "Nolan needs you in his life, Zephyr."

Gemini

Vanessa's glare is enough to lay me out on the floor if looks could kill.

My heart drops in the pit of my stomach as she asks Zephyr about his son loud enough for me to hear. In all the time we've been working together he's never mentioned a son or a crazy ex-girlfriend. Any glimmers of hope I may have entertained about future plans with Zephyr are now put to rest, but this is just the motivation I need to keep him off my mind.

The partnership, his son, and his son's mother—what he doesn't need is an undercover escort possibly ruining his future. It's a good thing she showed up.

"Good afternoon, ladies and gentlemen," Mr. McFadden greets from the desktop monitor, wearing palm leaves on a light blue button up for the webinar. "It's indeed a special occasion that I'm finally passing the helm onto another. Mr. Tate and I are excited about the candidates that we believe will carry this company into the future and make it a household name amongst the elites of the business world. Peter Wines, Keith Sanderson, and Zephyr Gray, good luck to you."

There were few people who thought McFadden should stay active in the company even as a founder of the business. The people of color couldn't disagree more—they're looking forward to Zephyr being a positive representation of the company, even though he isn't the favored candidate of the three.

"With that business aside, before this company is turned over to the next person a grave matter must be addressed. It has been brought to our attention that complaints have gone to Human Resources about possible misconduct between staff members of the opposite sex …" he says, the wrinkle in his pale forehead becoming more pronounced. "Matters of sexual harassment will not be tolerated."

My blood curdles as I listen to what vaguely sounds like the *misunderstanding* I had with Mr. Webber is played out for all of the company to hear. I didn't go to HR because I was sure no one would believe me—being Mr. Tate's son-in-law has given him undeserved favor. An investigation could uncover my other life and that would be a death sentence. Besides, he apologized for what he said.

McFadden zones in on dress code regulations, specifically aimed at women. Skirts are to be a professional length—nothing above the knees. Suit jackets and cardigans should be loose fitting. He drones on about the dress code for an eternal ten minutes before segueing into the new company handbooks that not only include the specific dress codes, but also the guidelines for fraternizing.

"There's to be no consorting between any member of administration and staff out side of work hours without expressed notification of the business being handled. Furthermore, any staff member interested in dating a co-worker will have to file a relationship contract with HR, notifying the company of your intentions. The document will serve as a written statement that the two interested parties are entering into a relationship that is voluntary and consensual. Any breach of these codes of conduct could result in termination."

As wrong as it feels, this is a blessing. If Zephyr has to do all of that just to go to dinner, I'll never have to involve him in the sordid details of my life, and shouldn't have any more problems out of Mr. Webber.

In all of the commotion surrounding the conference I missed a call from an unknown number and a text from Angel.

Angel- Bashir will be sending a car to pick you up tomorrow morning.

Be ready at 7:00 a.m. Don't mess up my money, Gemini. It will be the last thing you do.

If I thought for a second that I could bust this phone up in a million pieces and disappear, I'd do it. I need to get out—no, I'm getting out and locating my mother is priority one.

Twelve years is too long to go without hearing from my mother if she's not dead. She's the only reason why I'm here and she's certainly had enough time to have at least a lame excuse for leaving me with a monster who ruined every part of life since the day I met him.

Tapping the screen on the unknown number, I press the phone to my ear— a familiar, yet friendly voice answers on the other end.

"Is this Gemini Davis?" he asks. The baritone voice sounds professional.

"Speaking," I reply, still trying to place the voice. "Who wants to know?"

"This is Ryan, Gemini."

My heart stops, or at least it feels like it has.

When he left, I understood that he wasn't coming back and never thought about seeing him again. He betrayed me like my mother had— he left me in the hands of the demons who were his parents.

Heat burns my face as I hold the cell to my ear not knowing exactly what to talk about, though having so much to say.

"How can I help you, Ryan?" I ask, deciding to keep things as cordial as the office will allow me.

Ryan pauses as if he wasn't prepared to talk to me.

"Is there something you need?" Impatience colors my tone. "I'm busy."

"I'm sorry, Gemini," he finally speaks up. "We need to talk … or I need to talk to you."

"I disagree," I retort while tremors make holding the cell a struggle. "There's nothing that needs to be said."

"Now or later. Later won't be never," he says, obviously remembering how stubborn I could be. "When will be a good time?"

Ryan and Angel have the same attitude—everything has to happen when they say. Consequences aren't anything I have to worry about with Ryan, but I still feel compelled to do what he asks. Perhaps I can use this meeting to my advantage and get some questions about my mother answered.

"Fine, we can talk. Meet me at the Millennia at six-thirty."

"I can do that."

No sooner than the call is ended, a frantic knock at the door keeps me from getting back to work. A turn of the handle and Zephyr hurries past me, his eyebrows knit together so tight, his fresh lineup nearly meets them in the middle of his face.

"First, I need to apologize," he explains between deep breaths. "Vanessa is someone who I thought was in my distant past. Out of nowhere, she comes back and …"

"Listen, you don't owe me an apology or a report, Mr. Gray." His eyes flash to mine as if he's offended as I've returned to addressing him formally. "Were you able to catch the conference, Mr. Gray?"

"Yes … I did." Zephyr pinches the bridge of his nose as he sucks in a deep breath. "I heard that Tate was going to call for clearer guidelines on fraternizing. But filing documents in order to date someone in the company seems like overkill."

"Well, you have a lot to think about considering your candidacy for partnership, so I think it's a good thing to have some rules of engagement in place. You don't want to get caught up in any drama over the next few weeks."

"I'm not worried about drama, Aisha. Trust that."

"I respect that you're not worried about drama, and yet she showed up in six-inch heels, a red dress, and a five or six-year-old child clinging to her side. You should be a little concerned, even if you aren't worried."

As fast as he hurried in, Zephyr leaves without saying another word.

I guess something I said struck a nerve.

Gemini

Sinead Harnett's *Let Me* plays as I walk through the large ornate doors of The Millennia. A few couples take over the dance floor, and skirt hems float as ladies twirl out of the arms of their partners.

Ryan is easy to spot as his features haven't changed—his eyes are still warm, unthreatening, skin still clear, and he's clean cut. He's grown a few more inches—well-trimmed facial hair gives him a mature appearance. His massive arms show that he's been hitting the gym.

Being furious with him should be easy, but when he smiles, I don't see my attacker—he was as much a victim that day as I was. I see my brother, teacher, and friend who protected me for as long as he was in the house. At least until that day.

Ryan stands and reaches to hug me, but I draw back.

He lowers his arms and pulls out a chair.

Ryan stares, smiling as if he's dumbstruck. "You look incredible, Gemini," he says. "I've been thinking a lot about you."

"You can't be serious," I snap, giving him an incredulous glare.

Ryan sits across from me, perplexed with the bitterness in my tone. "Why can't I be serious?"

He shouldn't be surprised or confused if he recalls the day that he became an enemy.

One errant tear falls leading the way for more.

"You can't be serious. Because if you thought anything of me you wouldn't have waited so long to find me."

The corners of his mouth settle as he slouches in his seat.

"Do you have any idea what happened to me while you were gone?" I hiss. "Do you remember what you did before you left?"

Ryan rubs his hands over his face. "Um, yeah …" he sighs wearily. "I know I didn't say it before, but I'm sorry," he whispers. His eyes wander around the club, looking past me at the people on the dance floor.

"Look at me," I yell, causing a few nearby patrons to nearly break their necks trying to see what drama is louder than the music.

Ryan peers at the ceiling, remorse washing over his face. When his gaze finally returns, all I can do is stare.

"Do you understand what you did? To me?" I ask, my voice trembling, as he wrings his hands together, his gaze flickers to a passing barmaid giving us the eye. "I was twelve, Ryan. You were like my brother."

He shakes his head and bites his lip and for a moment it's like he stops breathing as tears stream down his face.

"I knew it wasn't right, Gemini. I knew. But … you know my pops …" his words evaporate as his Adam's apple shifts.

"You knew, and you left me there," I countered. "What did you know to be right? You watched your father rape me, took your turn, and then you left me there to pay the price for being the reason you abandoned him."

"You have to believe I didn't want to hurt you, Gemini," he pleads, his voice charged with grief. "But … I couldn't stay and I couldn't take you with me."

The attempt to explain his not-so-blind obedience to his father is infuriating. Although the sincerity of his apology isn't lost on me, I won't accept it—he doesn't deserve whatever closure or forgiveness he seeks.

"Why not," I ask, peering at the vent ducts and beams in the ceiling, trying to process his words. "What am I supposed to believe? Am I supposed to believe that you couldn't stay or you couldn't take me? Huh, Ryan? You could've stayed. Angel would've taken you to Ruth Chris', ordered the most expensive steak, and paid the bill in cash just for doing me," I rage, poking a finger in his chest. "So, what do you want me to believe? I might believe you didn't want to rape me, only because between the two of us *you* shed more tears than I did. But anything would've been better than staying with your parents. Do you want to know what happened after you left me? To call what happened, a living hell, would be an extremely gross understatement."

Ryan looks into my eyes as if he's trying to search for absolution. "What was I supposed to do with you if I brought you with me, Gemini?" he asks, throwing his hands up. "I didn't know where I was going, but I knew after what I did I couldn't stay there. Whether or not you believe it, I cared for you and still do."

"All I wanted to believe is that I had someone who loved me. Your father raped me repeatedly. Your mom beat the hell outta me because the sun rose or set. This god-awful name, sign, or whatever is tattooed on my shoulder. He said I belong to him and as badly as I want to get away, I can't see my way away from him. Oh, and here's the best part … wait for it … after your father started his enterprise with me, I got pregnant with his baby. I was sixteen. He made fun of me then blamed me—who'd never seen the inside of a doctor's office for birth control—for not being careful. Add insult to injury, your mother had me kicked out of the house. I guess she didn't like that I told her the baby was her man's."

Ryan does a double take, his eyes the size of saucers landing on my mid-section.

"Where's the baby," he asks, his voice quivering.

I flag a passing server and flash her my I.D. "Can I get a rum and coke, please?"

The server nods and hurries away. Ryan sits in silence while he waits for an answer to a question I'm not giving right now. Changing the topic of conversation, I probe about the one thing I need to know, the only reason for this meeting.

"Do you know where my mother is, Ryan?" I ask, tucking a loose curl behind my ear.

"Why would I?" he snarls, clearly disgusted that I would bring her into this dialogue.

"Wasn't it you who picked me up from my home and brought me to this hell?"

"So are you blaming me for all of this?" The server returns with my drink and sits it in front of me. "I'm sorry I didn't ask earlier, sir," she apologizes, a tray, pen and pad in hand. "Can I get you something to drink?"

"A shot of Patron with lime and a cranberry and vodka, please." The server leaves to fill Ryan's order as he levels a pitiful gaze on me—I figure it must be strange to overhear a conversation between a victim and her rapist.

"That puppy dog look doesn't work on me so you can fix your face," I say with a chuckle he doesn't find amusing. "I blame you for what you could've controlled. In the end, I wasn't worth an ass beating or a black eye and on top of that you left."

Silence ensues for a long while. The server sets Ryan's drinks down. He squeezes the lime wedge into the shot glass and tosses it to the back of his throat. He twirls the shot glass back and forth, which is the only thing that holds his attention briefly.

"I don't know where your mother is," he says still focusing on the shot glass. "But it might be a good idea for you to leave her wherever she is."

The pain of Ryan's words hits me in the chest and for a moment I can't breathe. Finding my mother will answer every question I have about my life and if he couldn't save me from his father before, the least he could do is tell me where I can find her. There's no way he doesn't know, and he owes me at least that much.

"What happened to the baby?" he questions, his gaze returning to mine as I take a sip of my drink.

Ryan's interest in the baby strikes me as strange and it's nothing I ever cared to talk about once the baby was gone. I should've kept my mouth shut about it.

"She was stillborn," I say, offering him nothing in the way of emotion because I have none. "Why is it important?"

Ryan sets the drink down.

"Stillborn," he repeats as if he doesn't understand the word.

"I'm not sure what you know about your parents, but they're horrible people. It's one thing that they dabble in everything illegal, but the events that followed after you left proved that they're monsters on a level you must've never experienced," I say gauging his expression. "I hid the pregnancy, kept the appointments, and assignments that Angel made for me. Your mother walked in one day while I was getting dressed and saw my baby bump. I was about eight months pregnant then."

Ryan shifts his gaze as I take another sip of my drink. His light-brown eyes grow darker and his eyebrows furrow as his mouth slowly turns down.

"She beat the hell out of me ... kicked in my stomach. I tried to defend myself, but the one thing you never taught me was how to fight."

Ryan searches my face.

"After I walked six blocks to the corner store, bleeding so damn much I nearly passed out, somebody called 911. I told EMS that I got jumped by some girls from the neighborhood. I delivered a baby girl that night, but she was dead ... with a bruise to her face."

A tear trailed down his cheek as he shook his head.

"God knew. I mean, what was I gonna do with a baby ... your father's baby ... your ... sister."

The longer I look at Ryan the more I want to sock him in his face, for old shit and new. He shifts in his seat as if he's somehow uncomfortable with where this conversation has gone. His eyes glaze over as his gaze flickers to a few people moving to the dance floor—being shifty eyed, something he taught me to look for in dishonest people.

"I- I'm sorry," he whispers, stammering, never letting his gaze rest on mine. "I didn't know. I- I ..."

"I'm not sure why you wanted to meet or how you even found my number," I say pulling cash from my wallet, "But this wasn't going to be a happy reunion. I want to know where my mother is because she's the only one who knows why I'm here and I think you know where she is."

Ryan finally looks up—his unshed tears brimming on his eyelashes.

"Please excuse me, but I have to get ready to meet with a client tomorrow. It'll be my ass if he doesn't get his money's worth."

I throw ten dollars on the table to cover my tab, but Ryan throws up his hand.

"Put that back. I've got you."

Reaching in his back pocket, he pulls out his wallet to pay the bill. Ryan's gaze follows me as I get up from my seat and turn in the direction of the exit.

"We still need to talk," he declares. "There's something I need from you."

As often as I try to forget about the last and most damaging memory of Ryan, it's the only one that prevails. "I'm sure there's nothing you need from me. And keep the money. I don't need to owe you something too."

"We need to talk about my father," he admits. "When will be a good time for us to talk?"

Another rum and coke would hit the spot, but I've already given this meeting too much of my energy and time. Shrugging, I simply look at him and offer three words.

"Make an appointment."

Chapter 12

Gemini

Gray skies and early morning thunderstorms make for good rest, but not when you oversleep for a paid appointment. Mr. Bashir enjoys simple elegance, so a minimal make up and a little black dress will do the job for him. What he really wants is to see the Louis Vuitton stilettos propped over his shoulder.

The driver, dressed in formal black suit and tie, is at the doorstep with an umbrella in hand as I leave the building. A quick yank of the door handle reveals the same foxy grin that I met a few weeks ago.

"Good morning, Gemini."

"Mr. Bashir," I greet, offering him a wan smile. "It's good to see you this morning."

His gaze glides from head to toe, his eyes stopping at the location of a fading passion mark.

"I see Angel marked what he thinks is his territory," he says, twisting his lips with disgust. "Such a beast."

A gentle touch caresses the area on my neck where Angel placed his brand. Mr. Bashir leans in and delivers a tender kiss like he's kissing the pain away.

"James, take us to the airport," he insists, his gaze locked on mine.

Bashir gently runs his hand under the hem and squeezes my thigh. Even though this is our second interaction, this one feels different than the last.

"So where are we going, Mr. Bashir?" I ask, hoping that my smile masks my anxiety about my first full weekend with a client.

"Have you ever been to Miami?"

Wait … Miami?

* * *

Monday. I already miss the blue skies and even bluer waters of Miami. The weekend went by too fast and even getting back to work and seeing Zephyr was not enough for me to want to leave, but in all of that something isn't sitting right with me.

Mr. Bashir asked me not to say anything to Angel about our trip out of town. He told me he assured him that I would return on time.

I'm not sure what kind of relationship he thinks that I have with Angel beyond being the favored trick in his small harem, but I never have a desire to discuss anything with him. However, I'd be lying if I said this doesn't worry me.

We met with several of his friends, namely Peter Vanders, Miranda Lester, and Jupiter—owners of JLV Video Productions. The extent of our time was spent over lunch at a fancy ocean side restaurant, where I did a great deal of smiling and nodding while Ms. Lester did a great deal of ogling. When she wasn't making intense eye contact with me, her almost-see- through-blue gaze roamed the length of my body, paying a great deal of attention to the way my legs looked in the glass slipper style stilettos Mr. Bashir purchased for the occasion. Mr. Bashir and Peter talked while Ms. Lester kept passing looks between Jupiter and me, smiling while whispering in his ear.

Mr. Bashir kept me close, his hand on my thigh. The only time I spoke during the entire meeting was to place my order. At least the seafood was great.

* * *

Exiting the elevator to work, the tension in this place is so thick, even Stevie Wonder could see it. The joyous buzz that inhabited the office just a couple of weeks ago is gone in exchange for fast-passing greetings with eyes fixed to the floor and quiet murmurs about who could've gone and complained to HR about being sexually harassed. Things were so hush-hush that even Sasha hadn't heard anything. Despite what she didn't know about that situation, she spared no change on what she knew about the current state of affairs between Zephyr and Vanessa.

"This isn't a good look for Mr. Gray, that woman showing up ... and with a child," she exclaims, eyes as wide as half dollars while Paul and Mark rub their foreheads simultaneously.

"I like Mr. Gray," Mark says scratching in his flaxen hair, "I would've never thought he'd be caught up in any kind of drama. He's so cool."

"Man, what I wouldn't give to have *that* kind of drama?" Paul pipes up with wide-open eyes. "Did you see the legs on that woman? She can wrap those golden gams around me all night long. I'm sure my kids wouldn't mind another brother or sister."

Sasha's pink lips drop apart, disbelief written all over her face.

"First of all, she'd have a hard time getting her legs around your wife and that eight-month-pregnant beer belly you're carrying. Second, were you not paying attention to anything Mr. Tate said? Are you looking to get fired?"

Paul adjusts his pants and stuffs his hands in his pockets, bending then shaking a leg before correcting his posture.

"At any rate," Sasha continues, glancing over her shoulder and peering at Mark, who is talking with another staff member. "That woman could be the very reason Mr. Gray doesn't become partner. You know how much harder it is for a Black man to get ahead in life … damn near impossible."

"I don't think she'll be that big a problem," I say, joining in the gossip. "As long as he focuses on his job, he should be fine."

A tilt to Sasha's head and furrowed eyebrows let's me know that my opinion must be misguided as it comes to the facts in this matter.

"Do you think the order of child support isn't going to be a problem?" Sasha's glare lands smack on my eyes. "Oh, I know … her calling Mr. Gray out of meetings to address a crisis with the little boy won't be a problem. She showed up out of nowhere and caused a scene and then served him with papers. That sounds like a major issue for a company with old money, old White men, and traditional family values. He was in a better position for serious consideration before that woman set foot in the building. And now who knows what's gonna happen."

Sasha's right. All I want to feel is relief because between Vanessa and the new guidelines, Zephyr is safely out of my world. It never occurred to me that the situation would turn his life upside down.

The rumor mill lulled to talks of lunch orders as Zephyr and Derek greet the small group of us standing around.

"Ms. Mosley," Zephyr snaps. "I need you to meet me in my office in ten minutes."

Wrinkles in his forehead and red eyes give the impression he hasn't slept in days. The stress of the office has Zephyr's normally calm mannerism in flux.

"Yes, Mr. Gray," I say, hurrying to my office to get my tablet for notes.

These impromptu meetings are getting to be too much even if this one is with Zephyr.

* * *

The breeze that I make moving toward Zephyr's office keeps me from sweating. It's easy to believe this meeting will be more professional than with Mr. Webber, but I can't hold any faith in it. Mr. Webber took me by surprise and now everyone in the building is paying the consequence of his actions.

"Thank you for meeting with me," Zephyr greets me turning from the computer monitor, his boyish smile and sparkling eyes making me weak. He struts to the door and closes it as I slide into one of the club chairs sitting in front of his L-shaped glass desk.

"I brought you here so that I could bring you up to speed on some things and inform you of some others." Zephyr returns to his chair, puts up a hand, and chuckles as I open the tablet I brought for note taking. "That won't be necessary for what we have to talk about."

A glance around the office shows degrees from Hampton and University of Michigan hanging proudly on a wall next to a purple and gold fraternity graduation stole framed in a shadow box. A wall-sized sepia painting of African villagers hangs among a few colorful masks. A dark wooden figurine of mother and child lives on the corner of the desk opposite the monitor and the aroma of sandalwood causes heat to rush to my center. Though no pictures of his family are on display, Zephyr's space is welcoming.

"Do you have any questions about any of the new guidelines that are being implemented by the company?" he inquires breaking the fleeting silence between us.

"No, I don't."

Zephyr locks his gaze on mine, still beaming. I, however, won't let a smirk part my lips as my self-control weakens.

"I'm not good at beating around the bush—a character flaw, I guess," he confesses. "So, I'll be straightforward … I'd be honored if you would allow me to pursue a friendship with you outside of the office, Aisha," he says tenderly.

My heart plummets into my stomach as thoughts of being seen in public places with Zephyr swirl in my mind. Every word I want to say is caught in my throat while threats disguised as reminders taunt me—Angel's voice is as audible as if he were standing in the room. *You belong to me.*

"With the partnership at stake, lots of people are watching, especially Mr. Tate since McFadden is retiring. The thing is … though I understand the benefits, I don't agree with the guidelines about fraternization. Respectable adults shouldn't have to check in with a third party to be friends with other adults. I want to be able to see whomever I want outside of the office without reporting to Big Brother. With all of that being said, I'm going to follow protocol because I don't need anymore negative attention."

"But the guidelines do prevent any confusion between parties … Mr. Gray," I argue. "And if things go sour, I could be the one out of a job."

Zephyr draws in a long breath and laughs.

"Wow. Back to *Mr. Gray* … " he repeats, shaking his head.

"Yes, the guidelines will keep any perception of indecency at bay," I say, knowing full well that indecent is what I'd love to be with him. "So, I see it as a good thing."

"Point taken."

His warm glance flickers, searching my face while the sounds of Kem playing from his computer barely drown out the patter of feet and chitchat outside his office door.

"Is that all you need from me," I ask, preparing to leave.

"Yes, Ms. Mosley," he says walking to open the door. "That will be all."

Only now do I realize that with all of the time we've spent together working on projects Zephyr has taken up a space in my heart no one has ever occupied, a consequence I didn't foresee.

I want him in every way imaginable and I'd give to him what every other client has to pay for, but the boundaries have been set.

Besides, he has Vanessa to think about and thanks to Ryan's sudden reappearance, I have the same issues.

Gemini

The five o'clock exodus is in full swing as I make a mad dash from Zephyr's office to mine. Time is flying and one of my higher-paying clients is expecting to meet me for his weekly sexual healing session by six o'clock— emotions have to hit the backburner for a five-thousand-dollar evening.

A tall crystal vase filled with blush-colored roses sits on my desk as if to welcome me back to my work. This has Zephyr's lovely, yet cocky hand written all over it. Delight builds while I dig into the arrangement and pluck a small, unaddressed white envelope from the fragrant bouquet. A smile breaks wide as quick fingers open the package.

Gemini,

There's no apology great enough that can make up for the hell you've gone through, but hopefully these are a start.

Signed, Ryan

Stunned doesn't begin to explain how I feel. Palpitations pound inside my chest as I bolt to the reception area, catching Sasha, as she's packing up for the evening.

"Hey, Sasha," I say, hoping my panic isn't obvious. "Would you happen to know who left the flowers in my office?"

"No, Ma'am," she pipes up while sifting through some papers. "A delivery service brought them, and I took them to your office."

It's common knowledge that nothing gets by Sasha and she holds gossip like water in a slotted spoon so it's hard to believe she has no idea what the name of the service is or at least of a description of who left the flowers.

"Are you sure you have no idea who could've sent these?"

A smirk tells more than she's willing to say.

"Ms. Mosley." She stops shuffling long enough to meet my gaze with a smile. "I told you a delivery service dropped them off. Why can't you accept the gift? I'd think a beautiful bouquet of flowers is something to be excited about."

A wonderful surprise if it had been from Zephyr, but not from Ryan. My best guess as to how he even knows where to find me is that he's back in contact with Angel.

"They're just flowers. It's not a big deal," I lie checking the time on the computer monitor.

Of course, the flowers are a big deal, but I don't have any more time to interrogate Sasha. A quick turn, my feet pointing me to my office, puts me in the face of Mr. Webber's sneer.

"Ms. Mosley, I'll need to see you in my office."

Without waiting for my response, Mr. Webber leads the way down the hall.

Back to the last place I want to be in this building and I'm late for my appointment. I hold my position in the doorway as he hurries to his desk.

"Please come in."

"No thank you, Mr. Webber," I answer folding my arms across my chest. "I'm late for an appointment. Do you mind making this brief?"

He frowns. "I have a client that has an account that needs special attention," he discloses. "I need extra hands on deck and Mr. Gray mentioned that you were good with finite details. You and Winfree will be leading a few staff members on this project, starting in the next hour."

What I know is that Zephyr would never throw my name in what will only be a three-ring circus with this project. This feels like Mr. Webber taking the backdoor to that earlier offer.

Angel is priority—I won't die trying to please Mr. Webber. I'll quit this job first.

"I'm honored that you want me to work with you, Mr. Webber, but starting tonight isn't possible. I'm already late for an appointment."

One eyebrow flies up on his sun-exposed forehead. His eyes roam from my crossed arms to my fancier-than-office-purposed high heels.

"This will definitely be a write up, Ms. Mosley."

I clench my teeth so that my jaw doesn't go slack behind this threat.

"You'll need to get with Winfree and discuss when you'll be available."

The minutes tick away as I stand in the doorway trying to think of what to say next. I'm the only one aware of the reason behind this impossible arrangement and that it'll get my ass beat, or worse, if I consider doing it.

"Is there anything else, Ms. Mosley?" he snaps. "You said you had an appointment. You can leave."

Livid. It's the only word that comes close to how I'm feeling, but taking this matter to Zephyr again isn't a great plan—clearly, the last conversation with Mr. Webber only made him angry.

Among the sea of cubicles, Zephyr is chatting with Winfree and if the smile on her face is any indication, things are working out for him. I reach my office, grab my purse, and lose no time working my way to the parking structure. The phone rings and I pray it isn't Angel.

"Caren," I pant. "I can't come to your show tonight. I hope that's okay."

Caren sits silent on the end.

"Hey. What's wrong?" Caren sounds like she has a bag of marbles in her mouth. "Where are you?"

After listening to her mash up and stir her words together for what has to be the longest two-minute conversation we've ever had, I decipher that she's at The Millennia.

Her timing is usually impeccable. Not so much right now.

* * *

The energy it took to entertain a client while trying not to seem preoccupied with Caren has given way to a migraine. The client's loud and less-than-pleasant cologne didn't make the two-hour appointment any easier.

The club's parking lot is empty except for Caren sitting outside away from her white Prius, her black sequined dress glinting under the dim parking lot lights. Black tears stream down her cheeks as she forces a smile.

"Thank … you," she says as I pull her nearly dead body weight from the ground. "See? *You* love me."

Her emphasis on *"you"* makes me wonder what happened with Dominic. I'm sure she'll tell me all about it later.

The cell rings as Caren slides down and finds her sweet spot in the passenger seat. I shake my head as I read the caller ID.

"What do you want?" I roar, my annoyance measuring somewhere between utter confusion and irritation.

"Hey," he says. "Did you get the flowers I sent?"

The day's activities have my body pleading for rest and it's clear that I'm not going to get any—I should've ignored this call.

"The question isn't did I get the flowers. The question is *how* did you know where to send them? I mean, is there something wrong with leaving me alone? I deal with enough crap from Angel."

"I need to see you. It's important," he claims, his calmness nowhere near matches how infuriated I am. "Finding you wasn't all that difficult— if you don't want to be found don't get a job using your real name."

The phone, that I thought I held securely against my face, slips to the car floor while Ryan's inaudible voice is rambling. I haven't allowed my picture to be taken and haven't attended any of the company's events, but it had never occurred to me how easy even a client could find me.

Caren moans as she shifts in the seat, rolling her head side to side. I hope she doesn't soil my car. There wouldn't be enough words to explain what happened to Angel since I'm not supposed to have anyone in the car that isn't a paying client.

Having a friend is something new for me and she's the only one I have, but I'm questioning if I can deal with her emotional lows, Ryan's sudden and relentless return, and my daily constant demands.

* * *

The usually quick walk to the building takes ten minutes to get from the parking lot to the apartment with a very inebriated Caren. Getting her to the couch is the last duty of the day, before reporting to Angel.

"Hey, Baby Girl," he answers as if he was waiting for the call. His mellow timbre puts me on edge—the voice of the calm before the storm.

"Yes, Sir?" I answer, feeling like I'm unprepared for what's coming next.

"What's going on with you and Bashir?"

I nearly choke on my spit, surprised by the question.

"Um ... wha- what do you mean?" I ask, peering over my shoulder as though Angel is close.

"You're not dumb and I'm not stupid. He pays to fuck you and that's it. Nothing more," he retorts, his normally gruff tone returning. "So ... I'm a bit disturbed that Bashir is now attempting to make a week-long appointment with you. And even though I tripled the cost from the first appointment, he was cool with whatever price I gave him. The way I see it, the money is beside the point right now. Something isn't right about this.

Wait, did he really just say something isn't "right?"

"So, I'll ask again ... what's going on with you and Bashir? Where did you go and what did you do for the weekend?"

I tighten my grip to keep the phone from dropping to the floor from my shivering. Mr. Bashir told me not to talk to Angel about anything that happened this weekend.

"We had sex," I say slowly, trying not to divulge all of the details of the trip. "We took breaks and had more sex."

"And that's all? He's acting like he's caught feelings or something."

"I'm sure you, above of all men, know that I'm a good fuck, Angel." Sarcasm tears from my lips unapologetically, as I choose to forgo my feelings of fear and trade them for a pair of brass balls, if only for a minute. "It's quite possible he's in love with all that my brand of attention has to give. Clearly, I'm worth every penny and more. You've made certain of that."

Silence.

"Okay," he says, breaking the lengthy pause. "Where'd you go?"

A dull pain hits in my chest as I put my face in my hand, trying to quickly think of something between the truth and a lie. Defeat chokes me because I realize he already knows the answers to the questions he's asking.

"We went to Miami," I declare.

The pause Angel takes after my confession is unbearable—it's never good when it happens.

"Any future appointments with Mr. Bashir have been cancelled," he barks, ending the call abruptly.

I'm not sure whether to be relieved or worried. I'm inclined to worry. Angel
never walks away from money, no matter the amount, but thirty grand? How does he expect me to make up that kind of cash?

What is he not telling me?

Zephyr

Three weeks and the new company regulations on fraternizing are already in effect, and frankly this is some bullshit. This mess smells of Charles' hot garbage, mad that Aisha declined *his* brand of overtime.

Working with Aisha was something that I could look forward to with every project. Her presence alone makes everything easier. She has an attention to detail that surpasses the laziness brought on by nepotism in this company. She loves this job, loves knowledge and it shows. I was unaware of how many supervisors coveted my interaction with her, which might be the reason for Charles' major misstep in judgment. The unwarranted write up he gave her is a first step to getting her terminated, which won't happen if I have anything to do with it.

And then there's Vanessa.

I don't know what game she trying to play. The most humiliating moment in my life was when she sent me out of the room while she was in labor because another *friend* showed up. The next was that she didn't ask me to return. The way I see it, she knew then who the father was, and it wasn't me.

The glint Vanessa had in her otherwise cold, brown eyes when she personally served me with the petition of child support, spoke of the kind of evil I'd never wish even on Charles Webber.

She went to the courts to order child support and visitation prior to finding me, though I'm pretty sure that isn't the order of the process. I think her modeling contracts have slowed down or the boy's natural father bailed. At any rate, this is about money. If the boy were *my* child we'd have no issue. After telling her that I had my lawyer file a motion for an emergency lean until a DNA test showed that her son was also mine, she hit me with an invitation to go on Maury, all while she's dropping the boy off at the office in the middle of the day. Unfortunately for her, security has become my own personal protection force and she's been banned from the building.

The office phone rings, breaking me from my thoughts of Aisha or Vanessa.

"Good morning, Mr. Gray," says the crackling voice on the other end.

"Glorious day to you, Mr. Tate. How can I help you?"

"McFadden and I would like to have a word with you in conference room A12 in ten minutes."

Ten minutes. Meetings with McFadden & Tate are commonplace, but in my soul something doesn't feel right about this one.

* * *

Under normal circumstances, I'd turn every bit of this three-minute walk to the conference room into five. This doesn't seem to be the time to take a leisurely stroll and I make it to the office with time to spare.

There's something to be said for gut instincts and mine are never wrong. The entire board of directors, including my right hand, Adelaide Forrester, is sitting in the well-lit and suffocating room when I arrive.

"Welcome, Mr. Gray," Tate says, greeting me like I've won a prize. "Please have a seat."

I scan the grim, pale faces while I sit next to the only woman and other person of color, Adelaide, in the meeting.

"Gentlemen and Mrs. Forrester," I retort with cheer. "What's the cause of celebration? The last time the whole board showed up, I was being promoted."

"Mr. Gray," Tate begins in a more somber tone. "To cut to the chase, we are taking your name out of the running for partnership."

I lean back and lace my fingers as I examine each face. Even Adelaide's normally golden and freckled complexion appears faded, and wrinkles across her forehead tell another story from the popular vote.

"The matter of this woman who has recently found her way into the doors of this company is shining a bad light on us and a number of clients have caught wind," McFadden explains as his sunburned skin tightens. "They're threatening to part ways with us if this issue isn't resolved immediately."

"The last thing I want to do is make the company look bad," I reply. "However, as per prior communications, I'll need to see formal letters signed by those clients that are being negatively influenced by my personal affairs."

"We thought you might ask, Mr. Gray," Tate says extending three letter-sized envelopes in my direction.

Taking the papers from his hand, I open and unfold each one, careful not to show the shock on my face. One seven-figure client I brought to the company added a personal, hand-written note stating that she won't have a man represent her company while he is actively denying the paternity of a child.

"Well, Mrs. Forrester and gentlemen of the board, your concerns are off base. If you had called me into inquire rather than accuse, the situation would have been made clear. This matter is being investigated and will hopefully be rectified very soon."

"Additionally, Mr. Gray," Mr. Tate continues. "We have reassigned and distributed the bulk of your accounts to Wines, Sanderson, and Webber."

Sitting among the closed mouths around the large slab table, I made no effort to fight the smile that slides across my face. If I didn't know any better, I'd think they were waiting for me to fight about this, but I won't give them that satisfaction.

"Gentlemen." I salute them with a chuckle. "I thank you for lightening my work load and I'm grateful for the opportunity to represent McFadden and Tate. Good day to you all."

Standing, I adjust my tie, happy this wasn't an issue of my termination. They have no idea that I'm always three steps ahead.

Decreasing my responsibilities has given me a new opportunity, and motivation to get my own business established.

Chapter 17

Gemini

"Glorious day, Ms. Mosley." My breath hitches as Zephyr stands in the doorway of my office with a smile that doesn't quite reach his eyes. His locs fall over one shoulder of his raspberry plaid Armani blazer. He looks like he's about to dazzle the hell out of whichever new client he has on his schedule.

"Mr. Gray, this is a surprise," I say, taking a break from the data charts I'm creating for a presentation with Ms. Forrester.

"Yes, there have been lots of surprises this morning," he retorts, his gaze locking on mine. "I'd like to take you out tonight?"

"Didn't we talk about this," I ask, tilting my head in confusion.

He leans against the door as other co-workers pass, looking into my office. "Did you file the appropriate paper work for this meeting?" I ask, laughing at his blatant disregard for procedure.

"No, Ms. Mosley, I didn't," he claims. "It's a yes or no question. I understand that you're a model staff member and you don't want to rock the boat, so to speak. I also don't want you to feel obligated. This dinner isn't in exchange for your position in the company. I just want to get to know you."

That's exactly what I don't want. Keeping my composure around Zephyr isn't easy—just a hint of sandalwood in the air made my heart race and between my thighs moist, something that has never happened with any other man. Working on assignments with Zephyr gave me the pleasure of his presence without the pressure of an intimate exchange of knowledge. What he doesn't know won't kill either of us.

"I've missed working with you too, Mr. Gray," I confess with a grin, my heartbeat galloping like a wild horse. "But we talked about you following protocol, remember? The partnership?"

"Yes, I remember," he replies, not bothered by the reminder. "If memory serves me correctly, I told you that I'm not worried."

Twirling a pen between my fingers, thoughts of a free schedule dance in my mind while my imagination revisits the idea of life away from Angel and a future with Zephyr. His grin widens while I fight to keep a straight face.

"A night out with you would be nice," I say, sticking the pen behind my ear. "What time shall we meet?"

"I can pick you up," he declares, his eyes sparkling like diamonds have been dropped in them.

"I'll meet you, thank you."

He sighs. "How about we meet at the Museum of Contemporary Art at six?"

"Sounds good."

Zephyr stands away from the door, smoothing his suit jacket, pulling tiny ropes of hair behind his shoulders. "Let me know if you need anything," he offers, as he adjusts his sleeves. "My workload was suddenly lightened. So, I've got time on my hands."

Dismissing his last comment, I get back to work. I don't want anything holding me here when I have the chance to be with Zephyr.

* * *

The museum was the setting for an event that one of Angel's wealthier clients hosted for some important people. He was a bachelor in need of an escort—one of my easier jobs. All I had to do was look pretty and keep quiet. A job where at the end of the night I went home untouched. I thought that maybe he was one who preferred the company of a man, but didn't want anyone to know it. I wonder how much he paid for that night.

I park my car and walk to meet Zephyr at the corner of East 6th Street and Walnut to the entrance of the enormous gray building. I'm not expecting to see him since I'm early, but he's there, already waiting, wearing that I-just-won-the-lottery smile again. My insides melt the closer I get to him.

"Good evening, Ms. Mosley," he says, embracing me.

"You can call me Aisha … after five," I say.

"Okay … Aisha," he sighs, peering behind me before settling his gaze on mine. "Let's see what other beautiful things we can set our sights on tonight."

No sooner than I hook my arm inside of Zephyr's to walk through the museum doors, the cell rings. One press of a button sends the call to voicemail.

"You're not going to get that?" he asks, "It could be important."

Not yet. I'm almost certain that it's Angel and all I want to do right now is be in this moment with Zephyr. I don't know that there will be another time that I'll be able to spend with him. "I'm sure it wasn't important."

My heart races as Zephyr holds his hand out for me to take it. Placing my hand in his send electricity coursing through my body. His touch is everything I imagined it would be.

Zephyr gently brings my hand up to his luscious lips and kisses it. "Thank you for spending your time with me," he whispers. "I know that you could be doing anything else."

Yeah … about that.

"Do you like art?" he asks as we stroll through the first floor stopping at a large board with nails and colorful threads.

Before I can answer his question, the cell rings again.

"I don't know much about it," I admit, reaching into my purse to stop the ringing once more. "Honestly, it's not something I've ever thought to study. Some of it's nice, I guess."

"Hmm … okay," he smirks as I fumble with the cell, trying to sneak a peek at the screen. "Are you going to answer your phone this time?" he asks. "Someone is being persistent."

"Not now," I explain though at this point I know who's calling. "Like I said, it's probably not important."

We continue to walk through the building, stopping at a few exhibits while he tells me about each of the pieces and the artists who created them.

"So you've studied art?" I ask, impressed with the information that he has shared.

"I always study beautiful things," he says while searching my face, "and beautiful people."

"Really now?" I say, cocking one eyebrow.

Zephyr brings one hand to my chin—I snap back, the only response I've had since Angel first touched my face.

"Are you okay," he asks, "Aisha, relax. I'm not going to hurt you."

My mouth falls open, and I'm rendered speechless as I get lost in the depths of his gaze.

"Um … no," I say just above a whisper. Zephyr's eyebrows furrow as my words get caught in my throat.

It's quiet enough in the area where we are that we both hear the cell as it vibrates again.

"You're a popular girl tonight," he says.

"I suppose."

"You should answer that. I'll wait."

My heart pounding, I concede to his request just so he can stop being concerned. Zephyr moves away from me as I pull my phone from my purse and take the call. As I do my skin tingles with dread.

"Yes," I whisper. Angel's silence has always scared me more than his words. All I can hear is his heavy breathing. "Yes, Sir?"

"Where are you?" Angel says, his voice dripping of rage. "You're fuckin' with my money."

"I decided to go for a drive," I lie. "You didn't have me scheduled for an appointment."

"Oh, you decided? Okay. So, you're going to *decide* how you're going to get me the five hundred dollars that I missed because of your sightseeing."

My record with Angel and his clients is impeccable—I've never actually missed an appointment and I'm always available whenever he calls.

"Are you good?" Zephyr asks while studying my face, not hiding that he's listening. His eyebrows furrow in response to my expression and he shrugs as if to ask a question.

"Is everything okay?" he mouths.

My gaze flickers to the various artistic pieces and the floor trying to avoid eye contact with Zephyr as I think of a convincing lie to tell while responding to Angel at the same time.

"Get your ass home now. I'll get my money out of you and I'll get it tonight." I feel like he just punched me in my chest as Angel ends the call.

"I'm sorry," I apologize trying not to show the panic that's consuming me. "I have to go. You were right. There's an emergency."

"Is there anything I can do to help?" Zephyr asks, his words thick with worry.

I can't look at his face—I'll break thinking how close I was to a dream. Turning on my heels, I move like my feet are on fire.

"No, I'll see you at work tomorrow," I yell, having made the distance to an exit.

This couldn't be a bigger mess. Going forward with Zephyr is already complicated and we haven't spent more than a couple of hours together.

* * *

The twenty-minute drive it took to get back was too long only to find that Angel isn't even here—the Escalade that normally waits for me isn't anywhere to be seen. Resting my face in my hands, I let out a gust of air.

I can't keep living this way and I sure as hell am not going to die while I'm in this life. There's got to be a way out.

Leaving the car, I'm confident there's time before dealing with Angel. Opening the door is a challenge because my hands are shaking and sweating. After all of the fidgeting to get the key in the door, I get the door open.

"This is good reading, Baby Girl," Angel says, lying on the living room sofa holding a copy Shakespeare's Twelfth Night. "No wonder you're so smart."

If I thought for even a second, I was going to move away from my front door, Angel's cold glare gives me cause to believe otherwise.

"Well, why don't you come in?" he requests in his signature easy-going, mellow tone.

The fact that he doesn't sound as angry as he did on the phone scares me more than the call itself. Angel stands and struts over to me. "Now, let's talk about how you're going to get my five hundred dollars to me."

Gemini

I should've called into work today but coming in means a dollar and a step closer to my freedom. Angel had his way in every position that pleased him, and then some strange man joined us. He got every penny of his five hundred dollars out of me plus interest, as far as I'm concerned. No breaks until three in the morning. It'll be at least a week before I have no physical reminders of last night.

"Good morning, Ms. Mosley," Zephyr greets me, walking across the lobby area. He glances over his shoulder, doesn't look like his usual happy self.

It's all that I can do to hold myself together.

He peeks over his shoulder before bringing all of his attention to me.

"What's going on with you?" he asks, searching my face.

Sucking in a deep breath, and calm myself, keeping my thoughts or confessions to myself.

"Is this about the call from last night?" he whispers.

I can't find it within myself to lie, so I don't respond at all.

"Listen, I'll call Adelaide and—" he envelopes me in a welcomed embrace.

"That won't be necessary," I say, a little insulted that he keeps trying to save me. "I just need to throw some water on my tired face. I'm exhausted."

"Your face is gorgeous," he says, peering into my watery eyes.

A quirk of the lips is all I can muster as he murmurs more kind words. A short pause in our conversation finds me lost in the rhythm of his heartbeat. "I'm going to visit my folks in Detroit in a couple of weeks. Would you like to join me? As a friend?"

Detroit? My heart skips a beat as he mentions the city that's only twenty minutes outside of where I lived before Angel. I haven't been anywhere near home since the day Ryan showed up. This could be my one opportunity to get away from Cincinnati and Angel for good, and find my mother.

"What about the partnership?" I ask, scanning the area, where other eyes were already focused on our interaction.

"I told you, I'm not worried," he whispers, his smile beaming.

The pain in my body reminds me that I'm going to die living for Angel if I don't get away.

"In that case … I think I do," I say, taking in one last deep breath, catching the familiar and soothing scent of sandalwood, which is becoming a thing of comfort. With his arms casually wrapped around me, I've never felt so safe.

"Okay," he says pulling me closer, his strong hand still stroking my back, "I'll get the dates set up for the Fourth of July weekend. I'll arrange hotel accommodations for you because I don't want you to feel pressured to meet my folks. After the work day is over, I'll go home, get the car, and we'll drive to the D. Maybe we can stroll the River Walk or something while we're there. I hear they've built up the riverfront quite nicely. There'll probably be a concert or something we can check out at Chene Park … how does that sound?"

"All of that sounds wonderful."

I need this get away. Fourth of July weekend is usually slow because all of Angel's clients are busy with their families—even he'll be busy with Dane.

Zephyr pulls away and a chill snakes up my spine as I miss his warmth. My tears stained the shoulder of his crisp teal broadcloth button up, though he doesn't seem to mind. His gaze glides over my face, rendering me speechless. He's unlike every man I've met in my life.

"Are you going to be okay?" he asks, his face filled with concern.

"I'll be okay," I say, tucking a loose curl behind my ear. "Thank you … for everything."

"Just in case you want to talk, here's my cell."

I pull the cell from my bag, input the numbers he rattles off, and call. He smiles as he pulls his cell from his pocket and taps the screen.

"Locked you in," he exclaims.

In this moment, I know that my life with him would be everything I've ever fantasized about, but I have to find the courage to tell him who I really am.

After updating the contact, I drop my cell in my purse. Zephyr gives me a squeeze, then flashes his I'm-a-fat-boy-that-loves-cake smile. I guess nothing gets him down.

"If you need anything, give me a call. I don't have any meetings today, so I'll be getting caught up on paperwork. Maybe we can get some lunch."

"I'd like that a lot," I reply, noticing Sasha passing, flickering her gaze in our direction. Some damage control might need to happen with her.

Walking to the bathroom, I think how I'm unexpectedly closer to my freedom than a few hours ago. The happiness that has been elusive for so long is now a reality that will happen much sooner than even I expected.

Chapter 19

Zephyr

Accounting 101—Opportunity cost; the decision to give up something by not going with a particular plan.

The company thinks that redistributing my accounts is a consequence for disgruntled clients. I see it as a gift. I've been working on a plan to break away from McFadden & Tate for the last year. Securing clients is top priority and highly qualified employees are a must.

A real estate appraiser assessed the condo at one-point-two million dollars while I continue to do research for a property in Detroit's Financial District to put one of my dreams into action.

"Good afternoon Zephyr," says Adelaide with a warm, but tired smile, knocking on the open door. "You needed to see me?"

"Come in," I reply, getting up to offer a chair and close the door. Adelaide has been my right hand since my promotion despite being here longer and being older than myself. "What does your work load look like?"

"Just finished up presentations for the Janowik and Chandemere accounts." She sighs, her brown eyes looking up at her imaginary schedule. "Meetings with a few others by week's end. What do you need?"

"I'd like for you to make a list of staff members that you feel are not only capable, but competent for a new project I'm planning."

Fatigue fades as Adelaide narrows her gaze on me and her tired smile brightens.

"What are you up to, Mr. Gray?" she asks quirking an eyebrow.

"I've got a thing or two up my sleeve," I admit. "I'm leaving out of town again soon and would like the list as soon as you can put it together. And while you're doing that, I'd like to know—how do you feel about relocating out of state?"

Chapter 20

Gemini

Between a light workload, what seemed to be an endless search for my mother, and fantasizing about new possibilities with Zephyr, the day flew by. Thoughts about the upcoming Fourth of July weekend and that feeling of him holding me in his arms cycle through my mind with no desire to stop the spinning.

A group of staff members murmuring around Sasha's desk give me the side eye as I pass them, not giving them a word or second thought. I make my way to Zephyr's office to thank him once more for helping me get through the day. The cell vibrates, and I change directions toward the elevator as I see Caren's name on the screen. I haven't seen or talked to her in weeks.

"Caren," I say, trying not to sound worried. "Where have you been?"

She left my apartment before we could talk about what happened to her that night and hadn't been answering my calls.

"I've been at my place doing a lot of thinking," she begins, "I don't have a set tonight. We need to talk."

She doesn't sound drunk or anxious, so I feel safe in honoring her request.

"Sure. Where do you want to meet?"

"Meet me at Wesley's."

"I can be there in fifteen minutes."

"I'll see you there." Caren never asks to talk, so I can only imagine this is something serious.

* * *

The sunny evening and clear skies brought out the crowd at Wesley's as I wait in the bar area. Going longer than a few days at a time not speaking to each other hasn't happened since Caren and I met so I'm hoping that nothing serious has transpired.

Caren swiftly moves into the lobby of the restaurant wearing an urban regal style that befits her superstar persona. A metallic gold head wrap exposes the crown of her ever-growing Afro. Large wooden bobble earrings swing with her sway, nicely complementing a black and Kente print blouse and torn faded blue jeans. Greeting her at the door, I throw my arms around her short, thick body, but her hugs noticeably stiff.

"I've missed you, girl," I say, studying her face.

Her gaze flickers around, never meeting my eyes.

"Hey, Aisha," she responds, her tone dry and unwelcoming.

"Caren, what's going on?" I ask, seeing the tears brimming on her eyelashes. "Why are you so ... not you?"

"Everything, Aisha. Just everything," Caren's voice shakes with her vague confession. "My dad is in the hospital with stage four lung cancer and my family is a wreck. The doctors are only giving him a few months to live. He's already spitting up blood whenever he has to cough." Tears trail down Caren's round rouged cheeks.

"I'm so sorry, sweetie."

Pulling her into another hug, thoughts surface about my own father and brother, the sudden loss, and not having time to think about them since I've lived with Angel and Dane. I was never allowed to miss my father and Malik and hearing this news makes me sad.

Caren watching her father die must be overwhelming, but as she stands before me so fragile, I can't help but think about my own.

"That's what had me so caught up that I didn't get a chance to thank you for saving me from myself that night," she says with a tearful laugh. "But there's something else I need to tell you … " Caren steps away from me, turning her gaze to the floor.

"What is it?" My heart flutters as her pause sends my imagination reeling.

"So you know the night you picked me up from the club?"

I nod, surprised she remembers anything.

"Well, Dominic and I had a falling out of sorts. I mean, that night we had sex and it was great and everything, but then he told me that he couldn't schedule me to perform any more and I lost it."

I'm not totally surprised by her admission of sleeping with a club manager for gigs, nor am I surprised that he dropped her after sex, but I am surprised that it drove her to get drunk.

"I know how much your music means to you." I can't help but feel bad for her, but the knots in the pit of my stomach are telling me there's something more to this story. She looks up at me momentarily, her eyebrows meeting in the middle of her forehead making one long brow.

"But that's not all."

"What else is there to know?" I say with chuckle, "I'm just glad you're alright."

Tears rush down Caren's face as she wrings her hands.

"I need to know that you're not going to hate me," she pleads. "You're the only friend I've got these days."

"I don't think it's possible to hate you," I reply, trying to be patient, "But what's wrong with you?"

Caren peers up at me, her face etched with remorse, like a child who just got caught taking a cookie out of the cookie jar without permission.

"I … I had sex … with Angel," she stammers, just above a whisper.

Pain races through to my chest almost as fast as heat rushes to my face.

"What did you say?" I ask, nausea quickly approaching my salivating mouth.

"I didn't mean to," she claims. "I … just …" her words die as she turns her face away from me again.

"Did he rape you?" I whisper frantically.

"No. It wasn't anything like that," she says turning back to me.

"Then what the hell happened?"

Patrons at the front of the restaurant turn in our direction.

"Listen, I know you and Angel have a thing," she says her voice shaking, "And this has been bothering me since I left your apartment that day, but …"

Hands over my face, I hold back a scream.

"I'm sorry, Aisha. I really am."

I don't know what Angel could be up to. Caren is not very street savvy. Her parents were very strict and kept her sheltered, so she wouldn't recognize any tricks he's tried to pull.

"And he didn't rape you?" I ask again, my thoughts racing a million miles a second, still in disbelief.

Caren tilts her head to one side as her mouth goes slack.

"Why do you keep asking that?"

This is as good a time as any to tell her my secret. Not only has she slept with someone who she thinks is my man, but she still talks to Sasha and I can't be sure my secret will remain that way.

"I'm really sorry," Caren cries.

"How did this happen?" I ask, sucking in a deep breath.

"I guess you went to work because you weren't in the apartment when I woke up. I was lying on the sofa, crying, when I heard someone come in. I thought it was you. He asked me what I was doing there and …"

Pain radiates in my head as her story unfolds.

"He saw me crying and he asked me why …"

I tune out her recounting the events that led to her sleeping with Angel until a smile slowly slides across her face. The sight of her pleasure disgusts me.

"Is there something funny?"

"I'm sorry, but he was such a gentleman and so kind," she says, her explanation making her smile wider. "I started telling him about how Dominic and I broke up and how my gigs had pretty much dried up because of it and he placed one finger on my lips, wiped my tears, and kissed my cheek. And then he called me Baby Girl and…"

Wait! What the hell? Baby Girl?

"Stop! What the hell did he call you?" I growl. Caren's usually shimmery dark-cocoa skin is now a shocking shade of crimson. Tears, fast and free, blaze hot streaks down my face.

"I'm sorry," Caren pleads, "I mean, he kissed me, and I couldn't help myself. Everything he did just felt so damn good. Every fiber of my being needed that attention and …"

"Shut the fuck up," I roar as patrons snap their attention to us. "I can't believe you. You … have no idea what you've done."

I don't even think I have any idea of what she's done. I don't know if that was an invitation to be in his business or easy access sex because I wasn't there. He called her Baby Girl? I'm offended, but I don't know why.

"Caren," I say, trying to regain some shred of composure. "You can't ever let this happen again."

Anger and confusion replace the shame as Caren looks at me.

"Really? He said he isn't your boyfriend, so what's the problem?"

"I'm telling you, don't do it again, okay?" I snap. "You don't know Angel like I do. That is not a relationship you want."

Caren's confusion morphs to all-out anger. "If he's not your man, why should I listen to anything you say? Why am I even feeling bad about this?"

"Believe me, he's not your perfect guy. Promise, I wouldn't steer you wrong about this. Just listen to me, please."

Nothing I'm saying is registering. I didn't think she would have a problem with leaving Angel alone. "I need you to trust me on this."

"Why am I listening to you? He isn't your boyfriend."

"Angel's my … He's my …" I choke on the words that will save her from a disastrous decision, but certainly saves me from her judgment or having her repeat anything I said.

"Your what, Aisha? Who is Angel to you if not that?"

I still can't bring myself to say the words *my pimp*.

"He's just a bad person. If I didn't have to deal with him, I wouldn't."

"And why is that?"

I stand in front of Caren unwilling to offer any more information than I've already given her.

She narrows her gaze on me but doesn't say another word before she storms away from the restaurant. Watching Caren walk away, my heart twists as the only person I've called a friend walks away.

Another betrayal to embrace.

Chapter 21

Zephyr

Disappointed faces meet me as I leave the elevator and walk past the maze of cubicles. My only guess is that news that I was no longer in the running for partner has gotten around. What they don't know is none of this bothers me in the least. White men tend to believe that they are the be all and end all, especially when dealing with Black men of a certain level of intelligence.

"Good morning, Mr. Gray," Sasha greets me, sounding melancholy.

"Good morning, Ms. Brown," I reply. "Any messages I need to address before getting my day started?"

"No, Mr. Gray, she says, her eyebrows raised. "I'm sorry about everything. I was rooting hard for you."

"Thank you. I appreciate that very much."

With no further adieu, I take a detour toward Aisha's office before going to my own.

There's no answer to the tap on her door and she's usually planted firmly behind the desk by eight o'clock.

In the time it took to walk to Aisha's office and back to the reception desk, Vanessa managed to make it into the building.

Standing in front of the desk, wearing a white maxi dress with her long hair pulled into a bun, she looks like an angel, but all I hear in my head are the lyrics to Poison by Bell Biv Devoe—all curves and smiles can't be trusted.

"I'm sorry, Mr. Gray," Sasha apologizes. "I don't know how she got past security."

"Hi, Zephyr," Vanessa sings, the corners of her red lips turned up into a Cheshire cat grin.

"How can I help you today?" I ask, looking at my cell for the time. "Weren't you served notice not to come within a thousand feet of me, my property, or my job?"

"We need to talk about Nolan's care," she explains stepping into my space. "We need to re-enroll him for the upcoming school year and tuition is due for the fall quarter."

As I cross my arms, she reaches for my chest, then pulls back.

"D ... N ... A, Vanessa," I say, reiterating the last thing my attorney said to her. "There will be no money coming from me until you can prove to the courts that he's mine. How old is the young man? Six? Seven? We haven't been together in eight years, easily."

"There was that one night after we ran into each other at Burke's house party, Zephyr," she brags, speaking about a rebound night between relationships. "I sent a picture to your sister," she says as if she's confident that her statement will move me. "She seems to think that Nolan looks just like your school pictures."

At one time, Vanessa was everything I thought I wanted in a woman and a wife. However, between her need for multiple partners outside of our relationship and this type of manipulation, she was a hard lesson learned. I'm thoroughly convinced that the boy isn't mine. And as far as what my sister thinks, she believes Taye Diggs and Tyrese look like brothers. She's wrong about them—and this.

"So, what you're really saying is that you want me to have you arrested for stalking and harassing my family," I warn. "And … your antics have cost me a higher paying position."

Vanessa's grin fades as she looks over her shoulder at Sasha, who isn't hiding that she was listening to every word being said.

"I wonder how Mr. Tate would feel if he knew that you and what's her name? Ms. Mosley?" She snaps her fingers and speaks loud enough for not only Sasha to hear, but also for Sanderson and Webber, who walk to the desk at the moment, to get an earful as well. "Did you enjoy your night out on the town Wednesday night?"

I say nothing to confirm or deny the accusation as Sanderson and Webber slow their progression to the boardroom.

Sasha's jaw dropped far enough to fit a whole sandwich her mouth.

"I hear fraternizing is against *company policy*," Vanessa says, crossing her arms and raising an eyebrow.

"This is what's called extortion," I say, leveling a steely gaze as I step into her personal space. "I know you're not a lawyer, but I know a few and I'm sure this qualifies. You've been avoiding this subject of bringing the boy in for a DNA test, which only leads me to believe you know he's not mine. So do me the kind favor and leave me alone before you get slapped with a lawsuit of the kind from which you'll never recover."

"Just know I have people watching your every move, Zephyr," she informs me. "Make no mistake, this isn't over."

Nostrils flared and red lips twisted, Vanessa turns on her six-inch wedges and storms back to the elevator.

Sanderson and Webber share a telling glance before walking away.

Chapter 22

Zephyr

I wanted to marry Vanessa.

In college she matched me on every level—one of the best and brightest in Eastern Michigan's architecture program, loved to cook and travel, the fact that she had a budding modeling career made for some exciting weekends away from home every once in a while.

She told me she was pregnant—ecstatic doesn't begin to describe how I felt even though it was far from planned. My parents were disappointed, as they didn't like her much. My mother told me often she thought she looked like a witch. I guess they saw something I didn't want to see. But then they came around to the idea of being grandparents and they made the best of the situation.

"Zephyr," she said over the phone, her voice shaking. "I think it's time."

It wasn't often that I left Vanessa once she was close to her due date, but I had a meeting with a real estate agent to put a down payment on the purchase of our first home as a surprise to her.

"On my way," I replied, moving like my feet were on fire.

The room was dark with only Vanessa and her mother present.

Vanessa looked beautiful and comfortable. Her mother's twisted lips, however spoke of a different sentiment.

"Hey Babe," I said to Vanessa, kissing her forehead. "How are you feeling?"

"She's feeling fine," Ms. Fontelroy snapped. "She's been here half the night with me."

"With all due respect, Ma'am, I just got Vanessa's call. I got here as soon as I could."

Honestly, taking care of Vanessa and her mother was stressful. Vanessa is her mother's only child and I wanted to make sure they each had what they needed. Classes and two jobs was a lot of work, but I felt like Vanessa was worth it. We had a good history and I was looking forward to our future.

Twelve hours had dragged by and Vanessa was only dilated to six centimeters—I had no idea one baby could take so long to make his entrance. I kept checking the monitors, excitement building with every visit from the nurse.

A knock on the door changed my whole world in a matter of seconds.

"Wassup, Van?" asked the man, who entered the room dressed in video game playing sweats. Flowers in hand, he kissed Ms. Fontelroy on the cheek and handed her the bouquet. He strutted over to Vanessa and kissed her on the lips.

"Wassup, my man?" he asked, turning to me and extending his hand.

"Wassup," I retorted, gripping his hand. Every muscle in my face drew into the middle.

Heat rushed up my neck like someone had lit a match to my body. I recognized him to be el Gentry, star starting forward from Eastern's basketball team. My gaze snapped back to Vanessa, where I was met with a tilt of her head and a shrug.

"I'm so glad you could make it, son," Ms. Fontelroy crowed.

"So, Vanessa—" I said, not knowing what else to say.

"Is this the friend you were telling me about, Van?" Michael asked.

"Yeah, he's a good guy," Vanessa explained, smiling at me. "He's been helping me and my mom out with some of our accounting for my modeling and stuff."

And stuff?

"*That's wassup,*" Michael replied. *Ms. Fontelroy gave me a once over and smelled her flowers as Michael pulled up a stool on the other side of Vanessa's bed.*

"*So, Vanessa—*" I repeat.

"*Zephyr, do you mind stepping out of the room, please?*"

I glanced at Ms. Fontelroy, whose smirk made me want to do a thing I was taught to never do, and with that, I left the room without saying another word.

I sat in the waiting area for another three hours before the attending nurse arrived, only to tell me Miss Fontelroy wanted me informed to go home and she'd call me later.

* * *

That call never came. If her son were mine, he would be older.

Now she's saying this child is mine because of one night when we were both on the rebound. I can't say I'm not nervous—mainly at what this would mean for Aisha and me. Then she mentions she has people watching me. This is a bit much to process. I don't know what she wants other than money, but my lawyer will put a stop to this madness.

* * *

My attempt to have a working lunch is interrupted with questions from Charles, who's apparently heading a personal investigation into who I spend time with away from the office.

"Gray," Charles says, standing in the doorway, a sly smile cracking his face.

"What can I do for you, Charles?" I ask, as I continue researching office buildings in Detroit.

"Are you enjoying your time with Ms. Mosley?" Charles inquires as he leans on the doorway. "Word around the office is you two are being rather ... *cozy*, shall we say?"

"Have they now," I reply, staying focused on my task, though heat building under my collar is making this a challenge.

"HR doesn't have any documentation on file," he sneers. "My father-in-law won't be pleased to hear about your defiance."

"Really now?" I ask with a chuckle, not addressing the question or the statement.

The sly smile that beamed just moments before, fades.

"So what has you and Ms. Mosley so close these days?" Charles grunts as Winfree and other staff members walk by as if he's rallying to go and tattle to big brother. "We know that you aren't cuddled up with your baby mama, the lovely Ms. Fontelroy."

Taking a deep breath, I tear my attention from my research and level a narrow gaze on Charles.

"What should be understood is keeping tabs on me and my personal affairs in no way increases your bottom line," I inform him, as his face grows red. "According to a brief overview of the accounts that you've taken over for me, there are a few glaring discrepancies that not even nepotism is going to help if not corrected. I'm not sure how you'll explain away funds missing to the tune of sixty grand over five accounts, funds that weren't missing even one day before you took over those accounts. Tell me, Charles, what kind of crib does the new baby need?"

Twisting his lip, Charles adjusts his tie and marches away as I return to my research.

My time with Aisha, at this point, is sacred and I won't have Charles, Vanessa or office politics messing that up.

Besides, Charles doesn't have long before the company finds out about his special *offers* for overtime to female staff members or the money that's mysteriously leaving affluent accounts—it's beneficial to have good working relationships with people who can be your eyes when you can't watch things yourself.

Filing a personal protection order against Vanessa has kept her quiet while she's getting the DNA results for the child—paternity needs to be established before any further discussion will be had about money and I'll need as much as possible to make this next move.

Gemini

Sleep was traded for worrying about Caren—about Angel and Caren. Going into work is out of the question.

What is Angel hoping to gain by sleeping with Caren? She was vulnerable, just the way he likes his women, but I can't wrap my mind around the two of them finding any pleasure with each other. She made everything sound like it was a romantic evening.

She's a little city girl with big city dreams and Angel can destroy her on every level. At twenty-five, she's older than his other recruits so I'm confused about his purpose.

The cell rings from the nightstand and one look at the screen makes the day better already.

"Good morning, Zephyr," I say, trying not to sound as weary as I feel.

"Hey," he says, his pleasant but troubled voice calms my racing heart, "Is everything okay? Sasha told me that you're not coming in today."

A smile edges across my face at his concern for me.

"Not today. I had a rough night and just couldn't find the energy to go into work. Besides, I probably would've spent my whole day trying to take a nap under my desk."

"Well, I'm taking off for the day at lunch. I have to meet a client. Want to meet

and then grab a bite to eat?"

I'm not passing up this opportunity no matter how exhausted I am.

"That would be great."

"Awesome," he says. "I'm meeting my client at the gun range."

"Why the gun range?" I ask, thinking that's an interesting place to hold a meeting.

"He owns the range," Zephyr explains. "I need to let off steam anyway. The week has been stressful."

"Actually, I'd like to learn to use a weapon," I declare. "Could you teach me?"

"Sounds like a plan," he replies. "Can you be ready by one? I'll pick you up."

Angel doesn't know I've taken off from work, but he could have his people watching or just pop by at any given moment. My pulse takes an uptick as I imagine the worst that could happen.

"I think it would be better if we just met somewhere. I know we've never had the occasion to talk about it, but I'm not big into surprises."

Hopefully my declaration keeps him from wanting to plan these impromptu activities for me again. "This isn't a problem, is it?"

"No, not at all," he concedes, "We'll do it your way. I'll meet you at the Hollow Point Gun Range at two."

We say our goodbyes and end the call.

"Please let him be real," I whisper, speaking a prayer to a god that I never talk to especially since this life hasn't given me a reason to believe in one.

I take in a deep breath, grateful that he doesn't force the issue.

Everything is so easy with Zephyr—he's too good to be true. There has to be something I'm missing. Every man I've ever encountered since the age of thirteen only wanted what I could offer him, usually in the way of sexual favors. So how can he be so different?

No sooner than I utter my prayer my phone rings again, this time it's Ryan. Deciding whether or not to answer the call is easy—I don't.

Whatever he has to talk about can wait.

* * *

Parking in the lot of the Hollow Point Gun Range, I slick my eyebrows in the rearview mirror.

"Hey, Zephyr. I'm here," I announce with a call.

"Great," he replies. "You'll need to leave your phone in the car. They aren't allowed beyond the lobby."

"Alright. I'll be right in."

Holding the cell, I stare at the screen, apprehensive, but glad to throw it in the cd compartment for a moment's peace.

Guns and rifles, hanging like art on a pegboard, decorate the lobby of the range. Arriving in my favorite red jogging pants and a fitted black t-shirt, I hope I'm easy to find, but the area is empty except for a few people.

Zephyr is chatting with a man who looks vaguely familiar. The man, whose back is turned to me, is shorter and stockier than Zephyr—built like he may have played some football in his heyday, but maybe hasn't seen the inside of a gym lately. Zephyr has taken off the business side of the day and already changed into faded denim and a fitted neon orange t-shirt, he'd be hard to miss if there was a crowd.

The two banter back and forth about their favorite vacation spots and best times of year to travel. Zephyr offers several places that he's visited that he'd like to visit again, even saying that he'd love to get married on the beach in Bali.

Sparkling eyes peer over the shoulder of his conversation partner and the scene fades to nothing but Zephyr's million-dollar smile. Stepping aside from the man, his arms open wide. He wraps me in an embrace that doesn't last long enough.

As his chest presses against me mine, the rhythm of his heartbeat causes mine to dance.

"Hey, I'm glad you could make it," he breaks contact long enough to peer into my eyes, his beautiful black diamonds glinting as he searches my face.

"Thank you for the invitation."

The smile that stretches a mile grows wider. Zephyr tears his eyes away from me long enough to introduce me to his acquaintance. My energy pools quickly to the floor as the man turns around, his sly grin takes center stage as I try not to pass out.

"Aisha, I'd like for you to meet Anwar Bashir."

The sudden weight of my hand is making it difficult to stretch it to meet the man who broke me into the next phase of Angel's business. Mr. Bashir gently takes my hand in his and kisses it while drilling his icy green stare into my eyes.

"Enchanted to meet you, *Aisha*," Mr. Bashir sneers, his reception sending chills zipping up my arm. My eyes sting with the tears that I can't let fall. Drawing me into his side, Zephyr doesn't seem to sense anything wrong—in fact, he laughs.

"Anwar thinks he's a charmer," he brags. "He owns an oil field back home and several gun ranges in the state."

"She's quite heavenly, Gray," Mr. Bashir declares, never taking his eyes off me. "You'll have to tell me where you stand under the sky, so I can catch a beauty like this one." Scanning the area behind Mr. Bashir, I avoid eye contact and fake a smile.

"Yeah? What would your wife and kids say, Anwar?" Zephyr chides.

"I'll send them on vacation somewhere and they'll never have to know," Mr. Bashir laughs and winks at me again.

I drop my gaze as Zephyr turns to me.

"I'm not feeling well," I lie. "Can we go, please?"

Zephyr finally ends his conversation, thanking Mr. Bashir for suggesting vacation spots they talked about.

"Would you like a free membership, Miss," Mr. Bashir inquires as Zephyr opens the door for us to leave.

"No, thank you."

Even though I was forbidden contact with Mr. Bashir, it doesn't mean he's not in contact with Angel. If he is, just seeing me with Zephyr is going to mean trouble, possibly for both of us.

* * *

Breathing becomes easier and the tension in my shoulders wanes once we leave the building. Zephyr's hand warms mine as we stroll to the far end of the parking lot.

"I'm sorry that we had to leave," I say with as much sincerity as I could muster.

Zephyr gently drapes his arm around my waist and pulls me into his side. On impulse I place my hand on top of his. He slowly draws in a breath and smiles.

"No worries. You seemed rather uncomfortable, so I was good with leaving."

I whip my head in his direction so fast that I hear my neck crack. "You noticed," I ask, surprised to hear his assertion. "You played that off quite well. I didn't think you picked up on anything."

He nodded with quiet confidence.

"Yeah, you got pretty tense. Anwar can be a bit much for some. I just wanted an uninterrupted opportunity to spend time with you and I can do that anywhere today."

He gently pulls me closer. "We can get that bite to eat if you want."

"I'm not really hungry."

"So then? What shall we do?"

I don't care what we do as long as I can be with him.

"You said that you wanted to blow off some steam," I remind him. "What else do you do to relax?"

He looks up above his head as if waiting for the answer to fall from the sky.

"I find cooking relaxing."

"Nice." I reply, imagining that he'd be good at it. For a moment, all concerns of Mr. Bashir escape me as I get lost admiring his beauty and savoring his aroma.

"May I prepare something for you for dinner," Zephyr asks.

If my heart was a runaway train a moment ago, it just jumped off the track. The twinkle in his eyes begs me to say yes and I surrender to his unspoken plea.

"I'd love for you to cook for me," I say, unable to control the smile that splits my face.

Zephyr releases his breath like he was waiting for good news. "So … shall we go to your place or mine," he asks.

"Yours."

In the time I've known Zephyr, he's helped me advance within the company and made me feel safe in ways that no man has made me feel.

In this moment, he has my heart and there isn't anything that I'd change about it.

Gemini

The drive is wet and pleasant as light rain falls at a steady pace. As Zephyr talks about growing up in Michigan, I can't believe I'm sitting with him, in his car, going to his place. My excitement to be with him keeps my words to a minimum, but he doesn't seem to mind. He's looking over at me and smiling every few minutes. Or maybe he, like me, was just glad to be in that moment.

I'm dumbstruck following Zephyr into his home—his condo is more like a palace. I can easily fit two, maybe even three, of my apartments into his fifth-floor residence. The scent of sandalwood that meets us at the dark wood entryway is pleasingly overpowering.

"Hey, Aisha," he calls with a laugh, breaking my attention from perusing the vast space, "Have a seat at the island."

I look across the space to the stately island of white quartz flanked with tall red parsons chairs.

"Do you drink?" he asks.

"Not often."

"What's your poison?"

"Rum and coke."

Zephyr's face is thoughtful as he considers my choice of beverage. "Do you like wine?"

My thoughts are suspended as I think about the times I've actually had wine.

"It's okay, I guess," I say, trying not to sound like I have no experience with wine drinking, even though the middle-of-the-road answer may have given that away.

"I have some Moscato D'Asti," he says searching the giant side-by-side refrigerator. "That should be tasty with some smoked salmon and garlic buttered green beans."

Zephyr takes out two salmon fillets and fresh green beans and sets them on an empty portion of the countertop to prepare for our dinner. He removes two goblets from the wine rack under the espresso-stained cabinets and puts them on the island.

Pots and pans clang as Zephyr searches for the right equipment to prepare our meal while I move to the wall of windows that separates his condo from the gorgeous river below.

Pulling open the sliding glass door wall, the sounds of the traffic rushing, the river whipping along the shore, the familiar and comforting scent of sandalwood wash over my tense body and peace creates a home within me. The wind caresses my face and I feel the love that abandoned me long ago. A dull ache wells up in my chest making it hard to breathe. The lump in my throat that feels like the size of a fist grows, making it difficult to swallow as I reminisce on a time gone by.

Trips to the ice cream parlor, weekend rides to the park, all-day shopping trips to Fairlane Mall or visits to the Detroit Zoo, cuddling and reading with Malik before bedtime. I miss the way my father would pick me up to get a hug from me. I miss Malik's big brown eyes and long eyelashes—his eyes were beautiful and sparkly no matter if he was happy or sad. I miss my mother, even though our relationship wasn't the best. I miss the picture window seat in my room where I would read all day if I weren't daydreaming or playing with Nina—I wonder where she is and what she's doing.

In all of my wanting and wondering, I don't hear when the clanging of the pots and pans stop. Gentle hands trace my waist and pull me back into Zephyr's warm body. I grab his hands as his hips gently rock us back and forth.

"Hey," he sings a whisper, his mellow timbre completing my serenity, "What's going on with you? No one as beautiful as you should always be so sad."

I lean my head back toward his voice—tears fall without apology.

"There's so much about me that you don't know," I whisper.

"There's so much about you that I want to know," he retorts.

I turn to look into his eyes.

Tenderly, he cleans the tears streaming down my face with his thumb.

"I don't know that I can … " The rest of my words are choked by the mere thought of baring that part of my life.

Zephyr searches my face, and then places a soft kiss on my lips. His tender touch sends a fiery tide through my body that I have never experienced. He's everything in this moment—the view, the wind, his smell, his touch, and his kiss.

Zephyr pulls me closer. Even with our clothes separating us, I feel as one with him. His heartbeat is mine and his warmth soothes my soul all the more. His warm, sweet breath fans my neck and I can't control the vibration that courses through my veins. He lifts his head, his gaze glides across my face.

"Aisha," he whispers, "With everything you think I should know about you, all I want to know is … will you let me love you?"

Gemini

Peering into my eyes, Zephyr waits for me to answer.

"Please, love me," I whisper.

Luscious lips trail kisses down my neck. His touch feels so damn good. Breaking contact, he searches my face once more before crushing his warm, soft lips against mine. I receive his passion with some reservation, but without resistance. I want to know what it is for him to love me. Zephyr bathes my collarbone with kiss after kiss then a final one behind my ear sends shivers down my spine. His erection strokes my torso.

"Let's go," he whispers.

Dizziness overwhelms my ability to say the words sailing through my head. Zephyr takes my hand and guides me through his palace to a massive master bedroom that looks like it comes straight from a page of Veranda Magazine.

The cream, tufted wall panels and side mirrors serve as the headboard and backdrop for the dark wood nightstands floating on either side of the California king bed. Zephyr stops short of the edge of the bed and turns to me, his breaths deep and steady. I lay my hand on his chest—his heartbeat pounds like this might be his first time to this kind of rodeo.

"What's wrong?" I whisper, unsure of what else to say.

Zephyr lowers his head and touches his forehead to mine. Sandalwood mixes with his sweat, drifts into my nostrils and massages every nerve in my body.

"Aisha," he murmurs, "This isn't why I brought you here. We don't have to do this."

His confession rings so sweet that it brings tears flooding back.

I peer into his eyes and read his heart. Cradling his face, I draw his to mine, and capture his lips with a gentle kiss.

"Love me, please." I whisper.

Pulling me into his firm body, he presses his soft lips against mine. His large, strong hands slowly glide underneath my t-shirt. Heat from his hands warms me to my core. He lifts my shirt over my head and crushes another kiss, the faint taste of chai tea on his lips.

Helping Zephyr out of his shirt exposes his perfectly chiseled form. My hands tremble like a leaf in a breeze as I trace his taut abdomen. Zephyr laces his fingers with mine and guides my hands around his waist. Reaching for my hair, he pulls down the tired ponytail and runs his fingers over my scalp, sending shivers zipping down my spine to my toes. A pleasant kind of suffocation takes hold as Zephyr's strong arms embrace me.

Loosening his hold, he kisses me while he unhooks my bra, and then sliding it off my arms. Every single touch sparks a new impression as though he's burning his fingerprints onto my skin. Cupping my breast, he dips down for a taste of my hardened nipple.

Waves of pleasure ride my body as my fingers tangle through his spongy ropes. Zephyr caresses one nipple with his thumb while he softly sucks on the other until my knees get weak. The roots of delirium dig themselves deeper with each loving touch. Every delicate stroke sends me higher until I feel like I'm flying.

Zephyr slowly stands and offers me a heated gaze that fans the blaze under my skin, and then crushes his lips on top of mine. He comes up for air and lifts me off my feet. I wrap my legs around his waist and return his affections, capturing his earlobe in my mouth and sucking it while I hold tight to his neck.

He moans full and sweet, lays me down on his pillow-soft bed, and delivers a kiss to my navel as he's pulling off my pants.

He raises one eyebrow, giving me a devilish smirk.

"So, you came prepared for this, I see," he slyly approves of the lack of even a lacy undergarment.

I've spent most of my life getting naked and giving myself to strangers, never once desiring to do so. I hardly know this man, yet with him everything feels so right.

He disrobes, exposing a hearty erection, and crawls into bed and kisses my forehead. He props himself up on his elbow, studies my face, and smiles.

"You're … ravishing," he says caressing my face, "I wish I could think of a better word." Zephyr rushes a heated kiss to my neck that turns into a gentle sucking on the same place that Angel left his mark just weeks prior. The pricks of a hundred cold needles suddenly run up my spine. The nerves that were once wrought with pleasure by Zephyr's touch now twist with the reminder of Angel's contact.

"Not there, please," I beg, squirming to gently push him away. "Please … Stop." I plead louder and push his shoulders back.

Lifting his head, he examines my eyes. My pulse races and I can't catch a coherent thought to save my life.

"What's wrong?" he whispers frantically. His tender voice brings me back to where I am—in his house, in his bed, in his arms, but I'm too shaken up after suffering the image of Angel to appreciate this moment. I want him to love me, but I don't know how he'll feel if I tell him what's really wrong.

He strokes my cheek and tucks a loose curl behind my ear.

"Can you just hold me, please?" I whisper.

Zephyr's concern and disappointment are written all over his face and in his now nonexistent erection. I feel bad that I doused the fire between us, but I need to get the vision of Angel out of my head. Lying in Zephyr's arms is the only thing I think will help.

He kisses my forehead once more and pulls me into the warmth of his body. I burrow into his chest as he cradles me. In the sound of his heartbeat I feel safe. In the sound of his heartbeat I find what I think may be love.

"Whatever you need, Love," he whispers.

Love. A name I've never been given before, an emotion I haven't felt since my father died. He called me "Love."

Zephyr sweeps his hand up and down my back. "I've got you. Whatever you need, I've got you."

* * *

I wake, realizing I'd slept from late afternoon into the early evening, but it's the best sleep I've ever had.

Peering over my shoulder, I see him sitting on the floor clad only in loose pajama pants. His legs are crossed and both hands rest on his knees, with his palms open. Eyes closed, he's meditating.

Scanning the minimally decorated room, I observe an incense burner and smoke rising from a stick that's placed in it.

Turning over to sit up, I watch him—the cadence of his breathing, the stillness of his limbs. I try to match the rhythm of my breathing to the rise and fall of his chest. Even at rest, his corded upper arms give the impression he'd be ready to fight a war with his bare hands.

"Are you gonna just sit there and watch," he asks, tone rich and serene.

My heart jumps into my throat, as I was sure he didn't hear me move.

He takes in a deep breath and faces my direction. I'm taken aback by the sternness of his features until a closer look into the impish sparkle in his eyes reveal his trickery. Slowly the corners of his perfectly plump lips turn up and let out a laugh.

I blow a sigh of relief and laugh along. I didn't realize I was holding my breath. I regret stopping what maybe the only time I'd know what it is to be loved by him, to make love to him. But what's worse is to fall asleep … after all of that.

"I'm sor—"

"Please, don't apologize," he replies. "I need to apologize to you. It wasn't my intention for any of this to happen. I just wanted to spend some time getting to know the gorgeous woman who crosses my path every morning and doesn't pay me any attention unless we're in the throes of a project," he admits. "But then you were crying, and I wanted to hold you and let you know that you're safe."

Safe— that's exactly how I feel.

"I- I don't know what to say," I stammer.

"Just please accept my apology."

"I appreciate your kindness. Most men wouldn't have stopped when I asked."

"Men can be jerks, but Helen would kill me if she knew I treated a woman that way."

"Helen?" I ask, tilting my head.

"Helen is my mom," he explains, standing from his position on the floor. "She'd strangle me with her bare hands, dig my grave in the backyard, and my grave marker would read, 'The Lady said no and his ass ignored her'. I'm too grown to have my mother whip my tail."

Zephyr gathers my clothes from various places in the room.

"Here," he says, handing me the bunched fabrics, "I'll go get dinner started." I keep his comforter pulled up over my body as if he hadn't just seen all of me.

"Thank you."

Turning on his heels, Zephyr struts out of the room.

The sun hangs low in the sky outside his bedroom window, so I know

I couldn't have slept that long, even if I feel like I've slept a full eight hours. Taking time getting dressed, I scan Zephyr's room to see what I can learn about him.

A large, picture of a nude man painted in shades of plum and midnight blue embracing a woman rendered in red and gold and covered only by a white sheet. *Interesting*. Another glance around the room reveals some religious paraphernalia—an ankh and a Bible sitting on the table where ashes from his still burning incense float onto the table.

"Are you okay in there?" Zephyr calls from the kitchen.

"Yeah," I say, hurrying to pull on my pants. "On my way."

The heavenly smell of garlic and salmon drift into the bedroom. My stomach rumbles in expectation of a good meal. I still don't see a clock in his room. "Zephyr, what time is it?"

"Six-thirty-ish."

Rushing my time with Zephyr will be a big mistake. I hope no one is looking for me tonight.

Chapter 25

Gemini

Zephyr cooks like he has his own show on the Food Network, only better because he prepared the whole meal without a shirt on.

The smoked salmon with lemon garlic butter sauce melts in my mouth. The green beans and rice pilaf perfectly marry the Moscato D'Asti and it's at this point I know I've died and gone to heaven. I've never had a meal this good.

We forego eating in the dining room and enjoy the sumptuous meal at the kitchen island. I can't take my eyes off him. Exchanging a glance, he smiles as I sip my wine.

"What?" I ask around a small taste of salmon and rice.

His grin grows wider.

"I can't believe you're here." His eyes sparkle with his confession. "Can I tell you something?"

"Sure." I turn my gaze from him to my nearly empty plate and move some rice around with my fork, bracing myself for almost anything.

"Hey," he says. Zephyr uses his index finger to guide my chin until our eyes meet. My heartbeat takes an uptick with the tenderness of his voice. "Please, don't think I'm strange when I say this ..."

The knots in my stomach grow a little tighter with each soft-spoken word.

"I don't think you're strange, Zephyr," I say, lifting a green bean to my mouth.

He pauses for what seems like infinity.

"I'm going to marry you," he whispers.

My heartbeat hitches and I choke on a grain of rice that hadn't been swallowed.

The knots in my stomach dissipate only for it to drop to the floor. Flashes of past events and wished-for imaginings race through my mind at top speed—my first day at work, the day Angel called me for a random day time appointment, writing spelling words with Nina, the journal he gave me, making love to him on Pink Sand beaches, him kissing my pregnant belly, being in the hospital with my baby and Angel, Miami and Mr. Bashir, him and Mr. Bashir talking at the gun range.

Zephyr is all I can ask for or want, however I can't help thinking of what will be the cost for happiness.

"I've loved you since the moment I laid eyes on you. Something in my gut said you're the one I've been waiting for and my heart has been fixed on you since that day, Aisha."

The intensity of his gaze causes butterflies to take flight in my stomach that's still making its way from the floor. "I'm going to marry you."

A nervous giggle bubbles up.

"You're not strange—you're crazy. You don't even know me," I say, diverting my gaze. I twirl the stem of the wine glass between my finger and thumb, hoping he won't notice my hands shaking.

"I know I haven't met a woman who matches your beauty—not just your face, not just your body, but your soul is radiant. You have a quiet confidence—you don't have to turn cartwheels to get anyone to notice you. And then when you speak, you have a fresh perspective on life that I don't hear from most people—optimistic. I know there's a story behind those mysterious green eyes and I want to be a part of that story. I want you to be a part of mine."

Optimistic … If only he knew.

My heart sinks as a lump rises in my throat.

"You belong to me. You're mine. You'll never belong to anyone else." Angel's gruff voice words echo in my head.

Our gazes locked, neither of us dares to look away. Studying his warm expression, I feel remorse for having ever shown up in his life, for falling in love with him.

"You don't know what it will mean for you to be a part of my story, Zephyr," I declare.

"I'm going to marry you," he whispers. Zephyr leans in and places a deliciously soft kiss on my lips. I look over his shoulder into the kitchen. The clock reads 8:03 and I haven't heard my phone ring—all day. The sun has gone down, and headlights and lampposts have taken center stage as the primary glow for the city. My head pounds as I remember that I left my cell in the car back at the gun range.

"I have to go," I say, hopping out of the tall chair, voice shaking, "We should be getting ready for work in the morning."

Zephyr's face drops and becomes wrought with confusion. "Did I say something wrong?"

"I just need to go," I snap, running my hand through my hair, "Can you take me back to my car, please?" I cross my arms underneath my breast and walk to the door.

He doesn't move as he watches me pacing a hole in the floor in front of the door.

"Zephyr, I need to go."

Sliding from his seat at the island, Zephyr slowly walks toward me, not uttering a word. "What are you doing, Zephyr? I need to go," I roar.

He arrives at the door, reaches for me and I recoil.

"What's wrong now?"

I know Angel has tried to call at least once, if not a hundred times, looking for me and I got the beat down of a lifetime for missing his call a couple of weeks ago.

Zephyr folds his beautifully formed arms across his chest, mirroring my stance. "I know something is going on. This behavior is not like the woman I see every day."

I run a shaky hand over my forehead. "You don't know me, Zephyr! I keep trying to tell you and you're not listening. Can you please just take me back to my car?"

Zephyr narrows his gaze as if doing so would give him answers to the sudden change in my behavior.

"I'm sorry you're so upset. I hope it wasn't anything that I said or did." The heartbreak in his eyes smacks me in the face, but my mind can't stop thinking about the consequences this day might bring. I thought spending time getting to know Zephyr might be worth any reprimand from Angel, but it's not worth dying for.

He turns on his heels and stalks back to his bedroom.

Angel is going to kill me.

Chapter 27

Gemini

Dead is not how I plan to get away from Angel.

Zephyr's hardened expression gives me pause, enough to keep me from apologizing for my actions at his home. The millions of words I could use to explain everything are suspended in the vacuum of my mind. He won't understand anyway.

He doesn't know he's in love with a prostitute and I'm not ready for him to know. I don't have enough money saved to leave and not be found. Then he'll be caught in the middle or worse.

The road stretches past streetlights, strip malls, and restaurants. We zip by other vehicles on the road, and yet the ride to the gun range seems longer than the drive to Zephyr's place.

The silence between us is flagrantly thick. My gaze flickers between Zephyr and the road, as I wonder why I didn't remember to get my phone out of the car. He sucks in a deep breath and releases it in a rushing wind.

"I know whatever's bothering you can't be so much that we can't talk about it," he says. His gentleness conflicts with his rigid appearance.

I'm clear on one thing—we can't talk about this. Ever.

Every minute that passes is a minute added to Angel's fury.

"How do you know, Zephyr? How do you know it's anything I can talk about, especially with you?" I say, staring straight ahead.

Taking his eyes off the road for a few seconds, his face twisted, Zephyr shot a look at me that was more hurtful than any words he's ever spoken. "Why couldn't you talk to me about what's going on with you?"

"You don't know me, that's why," I snap.

"So that means you're not important to me? Because I don't know everything there is to know about you? Is that what you're saying?"

I slowly face Zephyr, leveling a hard gaze on him. "There are some fairly significant things about me that I don't want to tell you … for your safety and mine."

His furrowed eyebrows draw in deeper. After passing through a yellow light of an intersection, Zephyr pulls his car into an empty shopping center parking lot.

"What are you doing?" I ask, terror about to strangle me. "Why are we here? Take me to my car."

Zephyr turns to me, hurt and confusion arrest the twinkle his eyes held earlier in the day.

"You say something cryptic about not sharing information about yourself for our safety and I'm not supposed to be concerned? For either of us?"

All I can think about is getting back to my phone and my phone log. "You wouldn't understand."

"Try me," he says, his gaze daring me to speak my truth. "Let me decide if I understand what you're going through."

"Zephyr, please," I say, folding my arms across my bust while tapping my foot. "I'll tell you later, but I need to get back to my car now."

My gaze moves over his worried face and then I see resignation in his eyes.

Zephyr turns away from me and puts the car in gear. It's now that I realize he hasn't raised his voice at me—not once, not even in protest. Not a hand raised, not a threat has been issued during his appeal to know my secret, to understand who I am and the pain I endure every day. This makes me love him enough to keep my secret for his protection.

Leaving the parking lot, he resumes driving in the direction of the gun range.

"Do you live in a dangerous neighborhood?" he asks.

"No."

"Gun toting roommate?" He flashes a weak smile.

"No," I snap, annoyed that he's trying to force the issue. "Please stop … I'll tell you when I'm ready."

* * *

Flashing blue and red lights, caution tape, and trucks from Channels 5 and 19 halt our entrance into the parking lot of the gun range.

Zephyr pulls over a block up from the chaotic scene. We both step out of the car, joining the small crowd of onlookers.

"What's going on?" Zephyr, asks a bystander.

"I don't know, man, but I think somebody got robbed or something," states the pale-faced guy. I'd swear he actually witnessed a crime—his face is nearly as white as his platinum-blonde hair.

Zephyr stalks toward the army of police cars as I examine the parking lot. The balmy night air turns against me, as breathing becomes challenging. Beads of sweat form, trailing down my forehead. The gun range and adjoining store closed at 8:00 p.m. The only car still parked in the lot is a late model Cadillac bearing Mr. Bashir's name on the plate. Zephyr returns with just this information:

"Anwar is dead."

* * *

Dim lights stream in, begging my eyes to open. Zephyr's handsome face and weak smile are the first things I can see clearly.

"Hey, Gorgeous." Zephyr's voice rises above the random chorus of beeping and murmuring. My heart drops to my stomach when room comes into full focus and I realize where I am.

"Why am I here?" I ask, bolting up from my relaxed position. My head aches as soon as I'm upright. Zephyr picks up my hand that isn't connected to the IV and kisses it.

"You passed out," he explains. "I went to talk to the police and when I told you Anwar was dead, the color drained from your face and you fell to the ground and we couldn't revive you."

I slowly loosen my hand from Zephyr's grip to rest my head in it.

"Angel did this, I know it," I mutter, not thinking Zephyr is listening. "I need to get out of here."

The room spins as I yank the thin hospital blanket to swing my legs out to the edge of the bed. Zephyr catches my feet and gently guides them back to the bed.

"You're not going anywhere," he commands. "You got a concussion when your head hit the sidewalk so hard. You'll be here at least twenty-four hours for observation."

Panic sends shockwaves to every nerve in my body.

"He's gonna kill me," I whisper, the floodgates pouring open as I lean back. Thoughts of Angel and his retribution swirl in my head. "I've got to get out of here," I plead. "He probably knows I'm here."

Zephyr's eyebrows inch deep into the middle of his forehead.

"What are you talking about?" he asks, his inquiry soft, yet demanding. "Who is this 'he' and why do you think he's going to kill you?"

Zephyr's patience knows no end. However, the fire in his eyes tells me he's ready for combat if necessary. Even in Ryan's weak-willed attempt to protect me from his father, his stance was not one of a fighter. I owe Zephyr an honest explanation, even some regret for everything, but I don't know which I'm more afraid of; telling him who I really am or getting him caught up in my world knowing Angel will kill him, too. His blazing, dark eyes lock on mine, waiting for an answer. Swallowing past the lump in my throat, I prepare for whatever may come next.

"Don't leave me when I tell you the truth," I whisper, dropping my gaze, thoughts racing back to the conversation I had with Caren, where she begged the same "promise me." I wasn't as kind as I want Zephyr to be, but then I didn't actually promise.

"I'm listening," he says coolly.

"Zephyr, please, promise me … I need you to promise me."

One hand wipes his face as he sighs.

"I promise … that whatever you say won't change how I feel for you right now," he declares.

Peering into his eyes, I dare to trust his words.

"Anwar's death wasn't random," I confess, my mouth drying out as I try to explain what I know. Zephyr reaches under his locs and rubs his neck.

"How do you know this?" he snaps under his breath.

"Angel … he killed Anwar."

Gemini

"Who is Angel?"

I can't speak fast enough for the urgency that radiates from Zephyr's eyes. A golden-skinned woman comes into the room to check my vitals, which gives me enough time to collect my thoughts.

"Is there anything that you need while I'm here, Ms. Mosley," asks the soft-spoken attendant.

"No, ma'am."

"Be sure to press the call button if you need me."

She gives Zephyr a quick once over and winks at me. In exchange I give her some semblance of a smile as she leaves the room. Without hesitation, Zephyr's gaze finds mine and the temperature in the room turns up to hell.

"What's going on, Aisha?" he asks, his patience visibly leaving. "Who is Angel and how do you know he's involved with Anwar's death?"

"What you already know will get us both killed," I warn. In the short time I've known Zephyr, little seems to bother him, but this information has him on edge.

"So, if what I know is enough to get me killed, I definitely should know enough to make dying worth the while."

My heart crashes against my chest, as I peer past him to avoid eye contact.

"Angel is … my pimp," I say.

The whisper sliding past my lips echoes and bounces off the walls as if the room is haunted.

Zephyr's mouth goes slack. Stony silence hangs in the air as he wipes his hands over his face.

"I forgot my phone in my car," I continue, shame from my admission smothering me. "That's how he alerts me to any appointments. That's why I was in such a rush to get back to my car. I knew he probably called but I couldn't be certain until I got to my phone."

Zephyr's gaze grips me; my humiliation is on full display. His Adam's apple moves as he swallows any words that he might have.

"And the reason I got sick when you introduced me to Anwar is because he was a client."

Zephyr closes his eyes, bows his head, and raises praying hands to his lips as his chest rises with his slow, deep intake of air.

"If Anwar called him to mention I was there he would've come looking for me," I say shaking my head. "My car wasn't in the lot when we got back, so I—"

Without any a warning, Zephyr whirls away from me and storms toward the door. "Wait. Where are you going?"

"Aisha." His shaking voice stabs me in the chest as he reaches for the door handle. "I need some air. I'll be back … I promise."

* * *

The hours of the night stretched into the sunrise and Zephyr hasn't returned. With the constant alarm of medical staff waking me up every two hours, I feel like a Mack truck hit me.

A light rapping at the door announces an early morning visitor. My heart skips a beat in hopes that Zephyr has returned from wherever his travels took him. The door slowly opens and a captivating blond man with happy blue eyes enters the room sporting nurse scrubs over his toned physique.

"Oh," I say, speaking my disappointment.

"Oh?" Stanley, my night time nurse, chides, "I take care of you all night and all I get is an 'Oh'?"

A slight smile is all I can muster.

Stanley wraps the blood pressure cuff around my arm and pushes some buttons to get the machine started. Reaching for the thermometer, he snags a cover from a box.

"Open wide, Diva." The slight movement of my jaw to receive the thermometer drives a dull pain through my head. "How is your head feeling?"

"Like shit," I say around the metal stick.

"I bet." Stanley laughs.

He reads the machine after it beeps. "One hundred point three." The blood pressure machine announces its job done as well. "One-forty over eighty. I might just see you here tonight."

The idea of staying one more day in the hospital twists more knots into my already tight stomach. "I have to go. I can't stay here."

"I don't know if that will be up to you," Stanley warns. Sitting down to the computer in the corner of the room, he records my vitals. "Dr. Owens is on duty this morning and should be here in another hour or so. He'll let you know how soon you'll be able to leave."

After quickly completing the data entry, Stanley crosses the distance to the door.

"I'll go and get you some pain meds for your head. Do you want a popsicle or something to put on your stomach?"

I don't feel like eating anything, but a popsicle to eat has to be better than starving.

"Are there any red ones?"

Stanley leaves with a promise to find at least one red popsicle for me. I turn on the TV for some background noise and slowly lean back on the bed, careful to adjust my pillow for comfort. My eyelids are heavy. Getting some sleep is finally in order.

* * *

Slow, heavy footsteps come to the side of the bed. Keeping my eyes closed, I avoid the pain the lights will bring. Hoping the doctors will just say what they need to say and keep it moving.

"Good morning, Gemini," Angel's deep, smooth voice shatters my sense of safety and a moment's peace. Icy shockwaves charge through my body and draw a well of tears that fill my eyes that I squeeze closed.

"Well, Baby Girl, it seems you haven't learned your lesson about fuckin' with my business. Now what do you propose I should do about that?"

Pain hammers my head and even with my eyes shut tight, I feel the room spinning. I don't dare breathe.

"So, what should I do, Baby Girl?" Angel's husky voice mocks. "Because you didn't answer your phone, I missed out on a few grand yesterday. So… I guess what I'm gonna have to do is put your girl in training after I collect the money from the life insurance policy I put on your ass. I think she'll be a good addition to my workforce. She auditioned well … almost as good as you … almost. Some practice with some well-to-do clients will get her right."

Tremors shake me from my shoulders to my toes.

"Now, how do I make this look like an accident?" he murmurs. "You're worth two million if your death is ruled an accident …" No longer able to hold in my terror, I set free a guttural howl as he laughs.

"I thought I raised you better, Baby Girl."

Saliva fills my mouth and spills out with the flow of tears.

"I'm really sorry that it has to be this way especially since I promised your father I'd make sure you were a good girl …"

I feel his eerie shadow looming over my trembling body, his hot breath on my face.

He touches my hair.

I jump, and the most horrifying scream I've ever heard breaks free from my lips.

"Aisha." The frantic voice calls, sounding nothing like Angel's ominous tone. My body shakes like I spent the day in the arctic. A soft hand pushes my hair back from my face and wipes the perspiration from my forehead. "Aisha … wake up. I'm here."

I shake my head and snap my eyes open to find my hospital gown wet, and Zephyr's worried face, his eyes feverishly searching my face.

Still wearing yesterday's clothes, Zephyr sits on the edge of the hospital bed, and lifts his feet, gym shoes and all, into the bed. I scoot over to make room for him and he collects me up in one arm and passes his other hand over my hair.

"It was just a dream," he whispers.

After a few moments pass, a light tap on the door alerts us to the entrance of Dr. Owens, a short, middle-aged man with salt-and-pepper hair. He walks in with some fresh-faced residents dressed in white coats at the tail end of my collapse.

Lying in Zephyr's arms makes calming down easy, but not so quick. Wrapped in his embrace, listening to his full, steady heartbeat, my head rides the easy ebb and flow of his breathing. This is what I need: to have my mind at ease and feel that no one can harm me. The only thing I think would be better is him making love to me, but at this point it's a goal, not what I need. Without maneuvering out of my cocoon of safety too much, I turn toward Dr. Owen and his audience of academics. Not one of them looks a day older than my twenty-two years.

"How are you feeling, Ms. Mosley?" Dr. Owens inquires with an intense smile at Zephyr, who doesn't relinquish his spot. Pencils and clipboards stand at attention, awaiting my reply.

"I'm fine," I lie, but for real my head is about to explode—I must've hit the ground really hard.

Dr. Owen moves to the computer and fiddles with the mouse. A few keystrokes later and my chart appears on the monitor. He quickly reads the information Stanley entered.

"So, you came in last night with a concussion," he asks, eyes still scanning the monitor.

"Yes." I look up at Zephyr who's engrossed in what is on the television, but I've learned he's pretty good at looking like he's checked out when he really hasn't.

"You have a pretty bad contusion, but that's about it. Your MRI didn't show a fracture which is good, but your blood pressure is concerning, Ms. Mosley. One forty over eighty is high, especially for someone of your age."

If he only knew that my blood pressure is the least of my problems.

Pencils fly while each resident takes notes.

"Has your nausea eased up?"

"I guess. It's been a few hours since I've eaten anything."

"We'll get you something to eat to make sure you hold it down. If you can't keep anything down, we may look at you staying for further observation."

Every muscle in my body draws up at the thought of staying one more night. Every knock on the door, I think Angel is on the other side. Zephyr glides his hand up and down my arm, reassuring me that he's with me.

"I can't stay, I can't afford to be here," I explain to the room full of ears. I remember a technician coming by for me to fill out billing information, but I couldn't complete any paperwork since I was so out of it. Besides, I wouldn't even know what address to give them—I don't need Angel to know about where I've been. He already has my car and my phone, so at this given moment I could just never go back, but I don't know where I'd go where he wouldn't find me.

It's a good thing I deleted every call and text between Zephyr and me.

"Ms. Mosley, your health is important and releasing you too soon might not be in your best interest."

Zephyr sits up a little straighter, his body a little more rigid, but still involved in whatever programming is on.

Dr. Owen's voice starts sounding like the teacher from the Peanuts cartoon specials as I focus on what has Zephyr riveted to the screen.

"Excuse me, Doctor," Zephyr pipes up with a sense of urgency, "My fiancée and I have a flight scheduled to return to Detroit for an extended stay with family." He peels his eyes away from the screen to give Dr. Owen his undivided attention. His face is hard to read; he's cool, no signs of worry, no indication of stress, but this sudden suggestion to go to Detroit is unsettling. "I'll have my doctor keep her under observation. She needs to be released now."

"Mister—"

"Gray," Zephyr replies with a dryness I've never heard part his lips before.

"Mr. Gray, I understand your choice, however I don't think this is in Ms. Mosley's best interest considering ..."

"If you understand my choice, don't delay the process. Our plane leaves in a couple of hours."

Dr. Owens raises an eyebrow and scratches his temple.

"I'll have a clerk send her file—"

"I'll carry them myself. Thank you."

Dr. Owens' eyebrows draw inward with the slight tilt of his head.

"Alright. I'll get her documentation prepared."

The only African American female resident leads the way out for Dr. Owens and her colleagues. With some trepidation, I stretch my neck in the direction of the television and can't believe what's on the screen. A selfie that I had taken for Mr. Bashir, per his request. A picture of me, that isn't in the least bit flattering is plastered on the television monitor: no makeup, uncombed natural curls, and my hazel eyes appearing that melancholy, algae brown they turn when I'm sad. The caption reads:

"Missing- Gemini Davis, 5'9", 145 lbs., 22 years of age, curly auburn hair, and hazel eyes. History of mental illness and does not have her medication. $5000 reward for her safe return."

Angel has always had a knack for making sure I didn't get to far out of his reach and it wasn't hard since he scared the hell out of me. However, this move was beyond anything I would've ever expected. My mouth dries out with a deep, silent gulp of air—I can't pull myself away from the screen as easily as Zephyr had just moments earlier although a commercial is playing. I remember taking that picture for Mr. Bashir after our first meeting because he wanted a souvenir, or at least that's what he said.

Zephyr swiftly moves to his feet and stands at the bedside. My head is killing me so I can't move that fast. Extending his hand, I receive it with a weak grip. He gently guides me to my feet and holds me. With a headache and kneecaps that feel like they've been replaced with gelatin, steadying myself is a challenge. I wrap my arms around his neck, rest my head on his shoulder, nuzzle my face into the smooth curve of his neck, and enjoy the faintest fragrance of his signature scent. Zephyr hugs me next to his warm body until I no longer wave around like a rag doll.

"What's this all about, Zephyr?" I barely get the words out; I've never felt so weak in my life.

"Listen … we're leaving," he whispers, quietly revealing his plan in my ear. "We're driving to Detroit tonight. We're ending this now."

Lifting my head high enough to look into his eyes, I shudder. I've only read this look in Angel's eyes—the look of a killer.

"Zephyr … don't," I warn, guessing what he may be thinking.

The normally warm eyes with a boyish sparkle have been replaced with fiery caldrons. "Don't do anything that's going to ruin your life. I'm not worth that life."

Zephyr tightens his embrace. The most tender forehead kiss from his warm lips eases my anxiety about his unfamiliar, hardened disposition. "You're worth everything in my life," he breathes.

At that moment, Stanley rushes in through the door.

"At least two of the floor nurses were in the lounge and saw the news segment of you and remember seeing you," he declares. I turn to peer into ocean-blue eyes that are filled with worry, then snap my gaze back to Zephyr.

"How do you feel about getting a cash bonus today?" Zephyr asks.

Stanley's blue eyes grow wide.

"Get a wheelchair," Zephyr snaps.

"Right away," Stanley says, dropping papers on the bedside tray. "This is a copy of your documents."

Three minutes later, Stanley returns with a wheel chair and helps me into the seat.

"Take her and don't let anyone see you," Zephyr commands collecting the papers and shoving them in his pockets. "I'm going to get the car. I'll meet you at the loading dock."

Stanley grabs the handlebars of the comfortable wheelchair; the breeze that's made from the speed of the walk is refreshing.

Scanning the hallways, Stanley dips in then out of the "staff only" elevator and drives me down isolated hallways of the hospital until we get to the loading dock where Zephyr is waiting.

"Thank you, Stanley," I say, as he helps me out of the wheelchair while I try to keep my hospital gown from blowing in the wind.

"No problem," Stanley replies. "Be careful."

Zephyr grabs the clothes from my lap, throws them in the car, reaches for his wallet, and slides him a small stack of bills.

"This is a grand," Zephyr informs Stanley. "I appreciate your help. I'm trusting that you'll forget that you ever met us."

"This message will self-destruct in thirty seconds," Stanley says with a nervous laugh.

Sliding down into the passenger seat, I say goodbye to Stanley as Zephyr shuts the door.

He slides behind the steering wheel and pulls out of the driveway into the overcast light of day. Next, he pulls out his cell and taps the screen.

"Hello, Nora. This is Zephyr Gray," he says to the head of Human Resources. "I have a family emergency at home in Detroit. Please inform my staff that I won't be in for the rest of the week. I'll keep you abreast of any changes."

He wraps up the conversation, then ends the call.

"You'll need to call into work in about an hour so they don't immediately think you're with me," he advises putting his phone in his pocket. "When we get to Detroit, scan the hospital records to Nora."

I nod and watch the street as we drive past people walking near the hospital.

"I don't know why he would say I have a history of mental illness," I wonder aloud after a long pause.

"He doesn't have any idea where you are." Zephyr rationalizes the insanity of a madman's thinking. "If you have a mental illness, people will be on high alert to find you. And that's incentive? He wants you back in a bad way."

The silence between us stretches for an infinite minute before he tries to lay my mind to rest.

"You're not going back," he counters quietly, "Not if I have anything to do with it."

Chapter 29

Gemini

A shooting pain assaults my neck and isn't kind about waking me up from the best sleep I've had in forty-eight hours. I roll my head in Zephyr's direction.

From the driver's seat, he greets me with soft eyes and a slight smile—he's a pleasant sight to wake up to, no matter what pain I'm in.

The ride didn't seem long at all. The day I was taken from my childhood home, Ryan picked me up in the late afternoon and we didn't reach Cincinnati until the next morning. This trip took only a few hours. All I can think is that Angel isn't far enough away that he can't get to me.

"Was that nap good for you?" Zephyr teases.

"Yes, it was." I sigh.

His gaze floats over my face to my hair then meets my eyes once again.

"How are you feeling?"

My head throbs, but only slightly—there's a more pressing issue than my headache.

"I'm starving," I exclaim as my stomach growls.

"I thought you might be," he laughs. "I'm surprised you didn't wake yourself up earlier, as loud as your stomach was growling."

"Really, Zephyr?" I fuss. "My stomach is practically touching my spine and you thinks it's funny?"

"I want to get you home first," he says, handing me a small pack of graham crackers from his pocket. "I'll make you something when we get there."

"We aren't going to a hotel?" I moan in protest, "I'm not ready to meet your family."

"I understand, but I don't know how far your boy's reach is. If the segment that aired in Cincinnati has aired in Detroit or he's sent any information this way, someone might recognize you and five thousand dollars is enough incentive for anyone to make that call."

True.

If Angel knew where to send Ryan to get me, he might still have those connections. I nod and turn my head back to my window.

"I didn't choose this life, Zephyr," I defend a question he hasn't asked. I figure it's better to start the conversation because he's going to ask sooner or later.

Zephyr doesn't respond, and I take his silence for permission to continue.

"I was taken from my home just before my tenth birthday …"

"You were kidnapped?" he snaps.

I open up and tell him my story.

Rubber running over I-375 pavement and cars whizzing by is the only sound to be heard until we exit onto Lafayette.

A few turns and we're riding on E. Jefferson Avenue. My heart pounds as we pass the Motown Pancake House three lanes over. My father took me on several daddy/ daughter dates there. I always ordered the chocolate chip stack of pancakes and my father ordered a Farmer's Omelet and waffles with some type of gooey looking fruit compote. We spent Sunday mornings there while we let my mother and Malik sleep in, talking about everything from him coming to America from Sudan when he was a young boy, to his work at the Detroit One building, to my desire for a dog, two cats, a Scarlet Macaw, a white Arabian horse, and riverfront mansion for us all to live. One of our last conversations was about how he and my mother met. He kept stories short and sweet, just enough for my nine-year-old ears.

Theirs was a fairytale romance without a happy ending.

"So, no one has ever come for you?" Zephyr breaks my trot down memory lane with one simple question. "I mean … you didn't have any family searching for you?"

I want my silence to speak for me; I don't want to think any more about the fact that no one came for me—that thought is with me every day.

"My father and little brother died in a car accident the spring before I was taken. I never knew of any other family members on either side. My mother was all I had." Zephyr's eyebrows lifted toward his freshly trimmed hairline at my account of the lack of a family tree.

"Wow," Zephyr says as he takes a left onto Burns Avenue.

The quiet tree-lined street reminds me of every lovely scene you see in a horror film before you find out that there's a neighbor killing the residents, picking them off by sin, and burying the bodies in the backyard. Sprawling branches create arches over a tidy, narrow street and manicured lawns. Every majestic brick building lining the street looks like a castle.

Zephyr pulls into the driveway of one of the estates and parks behind the house where another much smaller two-story abode is hiding in the shadow of the mansion.

"Welcome home," he chimes as I look around the immaculately groomed yard.

Zephyr jogs around to my side of the car and opens the door. The familiar smoky smell of neighborhood backyard barbecues drift through the air.

My mouth waters as my stomach twists at the delicious aroma.

Zephyr helps me out of the car and once I'm on my feet, what's left on my stomach beats its way to my throat faster than the throbbing returns to my head.

"I've gotta throw up," I whimper.

"C'mon."

Zephyr guides me as quickly as he can inside the smaller house to the first floor bathroom. The bitter sting of stomach bile gushes from my throat, into the toilet as I make it through the bathroom door. Sliding onto the cool ceramic floor, I appreciate its refreshing effect for me.

Zephyr scoops me from the floor and carries me to a main floor bedroom. He flips the fluffy, white-on-white comforter, lays me down, and takes off my shoes. I don't know what I did to deserve this kind of attention from him, but the white flag is raised and this stupid struggle I keep having with myself is over.

I love this man and there's no more fighting it.

Gemini

Days have gone by and Zephyr has been a better caregiver than the hospital nurse. He bribed his sister to go shopping for me so I'd have clothes to wear during my stay. Every morning I wake up to a hot bath. While I'm bathing, he changes the sheets on the bed. He's treated me to his five-star, chef-status culinary skills, making the most delectable red velvet waffles and fried chicken one morning, fried fish and grits another morning, and today, a grilled turkey breast omelet with all of the fixings—each meal served with fresh fruit and flowers cut from his mother's garden.

Today's breakfast came with a small envelope addressed to me.

> *"You embody absolute perfection. I love you"*
> *Signed,*
> *-Z*

I'm far from perfect. I'm damaged—a result of abandonment and abuse—but Zephyr sees perfection. All men have called me beautiful, but he calls me "Love."

"Good morning," a slim woman with a mocha complexion quietly chimes.

I'm at a loss for words as the tall, slender figure standing at the door with her arms crossed across her slight bosom stares at me. I didn't hear anyone come into the house.

"Good morning," I reply. The woman leans on the doorframe with a slight smile and twinkling eyes like Zephyr's.

"I'm sorry to disturb you, but I needed to see what has my son running back and forth to the carriage house." Zephyr's mother closes the distance between us and extends her hand. "I'm Helen."

Gravity must be working overtime because I can hardly lift my arm. I had no intention of meeting his mother, especially this way. With a great deal of effort, I stretch my hand.

"I'm Aisha."

"So … you're the one," she says, wide grin and a cocked eyebrow accompanying a nod.

Not knowing what to say, I don't even attempt a conversation, though my loss for words doesn't seem to surprise her.

"May I sit next to you?"

After I shift to make room, she sits on the edge of the bed. Her soft, dark eyes glide over my face and pulled back hair before meeting my gaze. "He said you were beautiful … and this time I can agree with him."

Catching wind of what his mother thinks of her son's usual taste in women, I chuckle.

"Don't get me wrong," she says. "My son has a good heart, but in the past that translated into him choosing someone who may have been a decent person, but not so pleasing to my eyes. Zephyr is handsome and has good genes, but I shouldn't have to worry about what my future grandkids will look like."

Before I can stop myself, I let out a hearty laugh at his mother's cheeky statement.

"I'm sorry we're meeting under this circumstance," I say, almost asking for forgiveness for my presence.

"No worries," his mother stops me, "I knew something strange was going on. We only keep the carriage house for our guests and he seemed anxious, watching the back door and all. Then I'd see him go out the back and didn't return for a while. Mother always knows."

My eyebrows shoot up and I shake my head, panic setting in.

"Ma'am, we weren't doing anything."

His mother laughs. "Honey, Zephyr is thirty-three years old and has been doing what you call "anything" since he was seventeen. As long as I don't have to hear or see it, I'm fine."

I imagined that she would be more proper, even prudish and uptight, but she seems pretty cool. With her smooth cocoa skin and plump cheeks, she doesn't look old enough to have a thirty-three-year-old son. "But, I am curious, Aisha … what brings you here unannounced?"

As if he has bionic ears and heard what his mother asked, Zephyr bounds to the door out of breath, like he was being chased by something.

"Hey, beautiful!" He waves and gasps as he lays eyes on Helen. "When did you get here?"

His mother crosses her arms and angles her eyebrow at her son's dramatic entrance. "The better question, son, is when did your *houseguest* get here?"

Zephyr dances to his mother and kisses her cheek, which she returns with a swat.

"Boy, get off me," she says with one last hit.

"Mama, Pops said he needs you to help him pick out his suit for tonight."

"Mercy, I forgot about this thing we're supposed to go to this evening."

"Where do you kids think you're going anyway?" Zephyr says, putting extra bass in his voice as if to inform his mother who the boss really is between them.

Helen quickly leaves her seat on the bed.

"Boy, get out of my way." She shoves her son to the side and he drops to the floor with all the drama of a Broadway performer.

"Geez, Mom. You didn't have to use all of your muscles to get by."

Helen cut her eyes so deeply at him he should be bleeding.

It's all I can do not to laugh out loud.

"I'm gonna use more than my muscles if you don't get off the floor. Anyway, all you need to worry about, Zephyr Jewel Gray, is the talk that we're going to have tonight about Aisha," she says looking over her shoulder. "No matter how pretty she is."

A smile cracks my face from her compliment as she travels toward the front door laughing.

"Don't you and Pops be out there fooling around now," Zephyr yells down the hallway. "We don't want any babies up in here!"

"Boy, hush," his mother's distant voice calls back, "Your father is my man. I'll do him any time and any place he wants."

Zephyr twists his face, feigning disgust, then turns my way. "She didn't need to go there."

"You asked for it." I laugh. Zephyr picks himself up, dusts off his pants, and claims the seat his mother just left.

Although it's a pleasant seventy degrees outside, it feels like a hundred and ten degrees with him sitting next to me. My heartbeat shifts into overdrive and I turn and wrap my comforter over my shoulders and curl into its warmth.

Every time he looks at me, I swear he takes a part of my soul with him. With all of his running back and forth, I haven't actually had to give him more than a glance all week. The awkward silence that always seems to find us hangs thick in the air.

"Can I be honest with you?" I ask.

"I'd hope that you're always honest with me."

Well, it's pretty clear that I haven't been. So many thoughts about me, about him, about us, I don't even know where to start.

"I really don't understand what you see in me," I say after a brief pause. "I mean … you don't know me and I don't think I deserve … "

"Stop … Look at me," he commands, suspending the beginning of a soliloquy that was going to, at the very least, give him more of an idea of what I think I deserve.

Staying curled up in my newly found safety blanket is a challenge. His voice invites me to turn over and uncover myself enough to finally take the first good look at him since we arrived. His gaze meets mine as

I turn to him. He scoots down from his seated position until we're face to face.

Zephyr kisses my forehead and pulls me close.

"I wish I could tell you that I'm not trying to prove anything to you, but that would be a lie. I've been trying to prove to you that I want to you in my life since that first glance." He draws me into a tighter embrace. "I'm no good at hiding my feelings when I'm feelin' a woman. I really tried to keep my cool when I first saw you," he confesses, pulling the locs that laid between us back over his shoulder. "I really wanted to impress you, but I didn't want you to think I was strange. You don't know I'm kind of sensitive."

"I have to admit I thought your approach was … different. I only receive gifts from … never mind," I stop short of bringing up *that* life.

Zephyr reaches under the cover, his splayed fingertips dance in rubbing my back. Bursts of tingles race around my head as he buries his warm hands at the nape of my neck.

"After I worked with you on the Woodson account and you caught that ten-thousand-dollar error on a line item balance, I knew how I was going to spend more time with you," he says, smiling. "I went to work on securing your position in the company. I wasn't giving the company any reason to let you go after the assignment was over. Classes will always show that you want to be an asset to a company. The instructors were impressed with how fast you caught on to concepts."

"I had a good math teacher," I say thinking back to my *school* days with Ryan.

"But you never paid me any attention outside of projects," Zephyr complains.

"If I paid attention to you, I wouldn't be able to get work done," I explain. "I'd think *you* would understand what a work ethic is. I needed to get the promotions to get more money."

"And ambitious—one more thing I love about you."

"Besides, I don't want anyone to know anything about me. At this point you know too much."

"I'll decide if I know too much."

Zephyr's gaze slowly scans my face like he's trying to read my story on my face word for word. His sweet breath tickles my nose and I almost forget this heaviness in my spirit about exposing any more of my life to him.

"What's your favorite color?" he asks changing the subject.

"Red."

A smile cracked his face. "You have something in common with my mother."

"Best childhood memory?"

I think about the father/daughter dates I'd have with my dad on Sunday mornings.

"Let's talk about that later."

Zephyr lifts both eyebrows.

"Okay … Do want children?"

My breath hitches as tears sting my eyes. Another part of the story I left out. There isn't a day that goes by that I don't think of the baby I lost or experience the random throes of purgatory that have me wavering between wishing I could hold her or celebrate a birthday and being glad she never saw this side of heaven with her own eyes.

"I want children," I whisper past the lump in my throat.

Zephyr graces me with his beautiful smile and his eyes grow glassy.

"I'll stop … for now," he says.

I bury my face into the curve of his neck and soak up the attention he has to give. His warmth has me floating in and out of consciousness. He feels like home, like … love.

"Hey," Zephyr whispers and draws me from the peace of his embrace. "You haven't been out in a while. Do you feel like going to this event with my parents tonight?"

"I don't have anything to wear," I say reminding him of my lack of a wardrobe. "And what about Angel? He could still be looking for me."

"I've got you …"

There isn't anything I'd say no to if it involves him.

"Yes … I'll go anywhere you're going," I say, my face still buried in paradise. His 'thanks' is given with a deep sigh and a single kiss to my temple.

Chapter 37

Gemini

Zephyr called the office and arranged to take the rest of his three-week vacation time and also had his family doctor examine me for the concussion I sustained. He recommended that I stay away from work for the same amount of time.

I'm pretty sure we're subject of company gossip by now, but this buys me a little time to figure out a plan to stay free.

Zephyr pulled out all of the stops for me to attend this gala fundraiser his father organized to benefit the Cancer Unit of Detroit Receiving Hospital.

He arranged a spa day complete with a full-body massage, hair and makeup, and a mani-pedi. Every inch of my flesh had been kneaded and pulled until I hardly remember what my own body feels like. Every nerve still sings its appreciation hours after that part of the day is over.

Concerned that someone still could be looking for me, he drove me to my appointment and waited for me like he was my personal bodyguard.

"I'm going to get dressed," Zephyr says, walking me to the door. "A driver will pick us up at eight."

With a kiss, he struts off to the main house.

The stillness of the air is laden with the perfume of flowers as I glide from the entrance, through the house, and to the bedroom. The room that has been my sanctuary for the last week has all of the drapes open, allowing the evening sun to pour in. Blush-colored roses and bright-orange tiger lilies greet me from every corner. Three boxes wrapped in black glitter, embossed paper, and a card sits on the bed. I open the envelope and admire the enclosed card. A small piece of paper falls out of the card.

> *"Thank you for accepting my invitation to this event. As your personal security guard, I've arranged for a car to pick us up at eight. I hope you enjoy your gifts as much as I enjoyed picking them out for you."*
>
> ~ Z

A smile quickly splits my face as if I were sitting at my birthday party and getting that last big gift.

Starting with the smallest box first, I rip off the paper and open the gift. My heart pumps a mile a minute as the sparkle of a ruby and diamond necklace set jets a million tiny rainbows across the room.

What makes a man want to love a woman the way he does? I've never known what it's like to be in love or to be loved the way Zephyr says he loves me. I've never done anything to make him love me and he seems to love me in spite of it.

The medium sized box—a pair of silver diamond-dusted, open-toed stilettos and matching clutch that sparkle nearly as much as the jewelry. Snatching the largest box, I tear the wrapping.

Eyes watering and hands trembling, I lift the one-shouldered, red cocktail dress out of the box, where there is also a red strapless bra and panty set that lay underneath. Turning to a cheval mirror standing in a corner by the bed, I behold a woman I've never seen before.

Holding the dress next to my body, the woman in the mirror surprises me. Grassy-green eyes travel the lines of her face, the graceful curve of her neck, the power in her shoulders. I'm spellbound by the sun-kissed honey complexion as she pulls long straightened hair over her shoulder.

I've never met this woman.

She's triumphant and free. I look forward to knowing her.

A car announces its arrival with the toot of a horn. A quick glance at the clock shows me I've been involved with the woman in the mirror for nearly twenty minutes, more than enough time to be dressed and ready to go.

Peeling out of my clothes, I quickly pull on the undergarments, slip on the dress, then put on the shoes and jewelry.

One more cursory glimpse in the mirror leaves me with one thought—*I see what Zephyr sees.*

* * *

Streaks of orange and pink blaze across the sunset sky painting a perfect backdrop for tonight's event. Tuxedos and gold, black, and silver designer ball gowns decorate the foyer as the guests enter and mingle in the grand ballroom of the convention center. Outside the ballroom doors, vendors from all over the tri-county area present their wares. Some potential customers meander around the mall of entrepreneurs. Some ogle the Cadillac that will be raffled. We enter the bustling affair, Zephyr looking GQ sharp wearing his tailored black suit and red jacquard tie, perfectly coordinating with my ensemble.

Women glide by in their sparkling floor-length gowns giving me side eyes, pointed glances, and up and down gazes.

As the only woman wearing red, I understand why all eyes are on me, but this kind of attention is not needed. With all of the eyes peering at me, one pair follows me across the room, making me uneasy.

The thick-bodied blonde takes up residence in my periphery as she keeps me in her line of sight. She doesn't look familiar; I catch her gaze as Zephyr and I make our way to the ballroom. She takes no time closing the distance between us in rushed steps.

"Aisha?" The woman says, stopping in front of me.

Breathing becomes restricted as I pivot in the direction of the voice. The watery eyes of the blonde who has been watching me, meet mine. "Aisha?"

"Yes," I reply. The woman throws her arms around me. She stands at least four inches shorter than I am in her stilettos. I don't return her affection, but her sentiment isn't lost on me. "I'm sorry, but how do you know me?" She slowly releases her grip and steps back.

"Aisha … it's me, Nina," she claims, her voice thick with emotion.

The last memory I have of Nina is of a scrawny, summer sun-tanned brunette. Even her grey eyes seem to be fainter than I remember. If this is Nina, she looks different, more different than the natural maturation process should look on any person.

"I'm sorry, but how am I supposed to know that you're really Nina?"

"I know I might look a little different, but remember this?"

In the middle of a swarm of the elite exchanging laughs and business contacts, Nina lifts the skirt of her black floor-length gown up to her thigh, revealing a faint scar the span of her hand. I do remember.

She got it when we climbed to the top of a crab apple tree in her back yard. On our descent, Nina missed a limb and fell out of the tree, but not before the tree gave her a good whipping for climbing up there in the first place. She needed forty stitches behind that fall.

Yeah, I remember.

Nina's expectant eyes await my response.

I open my arms and she falls into them.

"I thought you were dead," she whispers. I guess that's an appropriate thought since I left and never came back.

"No, I'm very much alive," I say, a lump forming in my throat, the thought crossing my mind I'm not sure how long that will be a true statement.

"Where have you been? I asked your mom every day for months when you were coming back and she'd never tell me. She'd always find some way to avoid answering the question."

"She wouldn't answer the question," I ask, shaking my head. "She knew who she sent me with and she had no answer?"

Emptiness consumes me as the noise of the event fades. Squeezing Nina tighter is the only thing keeping me from passing out.

"It might be a good idea for you to leave her wherever she is," Ryan's voice echoes.

"Have you talked to my mother lately," I ask, finding the strength to sidestep her question, pressed to know if I can get to my mother as soon possible.

Nina steps out of our embrace and peers around the room as if she's looking for someone.

"I haven't talked to your mother in years, but we see her around from time to time."

Heat builds in my cheeks and I dig my heels down into my shoes. "She's still here?" I ask, speaking loudly enough to make a few nearby guests turn in our direction.

"She still lives in the old house, I think. We moved to Ann Arbor a few years back, but we've run into her on a few occasions. She seemed to be doing well considering."

"Considering what?" I ask, my attention on people walking around Nina and I as we stand in the display area of the Cadillac for raffle.

"Well, with your dad and Malik dying and you missing, we thought she'd be in a psych ward somewhere." Nina's gaze shoots behind me, as she looks past my shoulder.

"Good evening," Zephyr says extending his hand around me to Nina as her smile stretches from east to west. "I'm Zephyr Gray,"

"Nina Downing." Nina's cheeks go from pale to rouge with the touch of Zephyr's hand.

"Are you a guest or a vendor, Ms. Downing?"

"I'm here with my fiancé. He's here promoting his personal food preparation business."

"Nice, I'll have to check him out."

"I'm sure he'd appreciate it," Nina says, blushing.

Zephyr stands next to me, his eyes glide down my side, then he glances back and forth between Nina and me.

"Well, Ms. Downing, I'm sorry to interrupt, but I need the attention of this lovely lady, if I you don't mind." I meet his gaze and the smile I try to fight back inches into being.

"If you don't mind, Mr. Gray, I'll be with you shortly," I say as I hold his gaze. "Don't go too far."

"I won't. I have my eye on you," he says with a wink.

Zephyr struts to a nearby vendor peering over his shoulder once to flash that million-dollar smile again. When I turn back to Nina she's got one eyebrow cocked and wide grin plastered on her face.

"I'm not even gonna ask," Nina says with a chuckle. "I need to get your number. I don't want to lose touch again."

"I lost my phone last week and I haven't replaced it yet," I say, finding a story between the truth and a lie. "Do you mind writing your number down?"

Nina shuffles through her wristlet-sized purse and hands me her fiancé's business card.

"I take all of Damien's appointments, so you can call any time."

I glance at the card and place it in my clutch.

Glancing over my shoulder in Zephyr's direction I see him watching me, peering around one of the men he's talking with. I wrap up the impromptu reunion with Nina and give her the hug I couldn't give her the last time we were separated.

"Be sure you call, Aisha."

"I will," I say, making a promise I don't know if I can keep.

Turning on my heels, I pass the throng of people at the ballroom entrance and walk toward where Zephyr is standing.

Separating from the group, Zephyr meets me, takes my hand into his, and leads me on a walk to the main-floor bar.

Smooth jazz melodies play as low as the ambient lighting while bustling conversations about politics, sports, or the evening's occasion rise above the music. Wide eyes from the barstools and low-seated tables follow, giving me their all too familiar glares. I often wonder if I have the "look" of someone who's for sale.

Zephyr chooses a spot with two comfy chairs tucked away in a dark corner. We don't have to wait long before a server comes whizzing by.

"Excuse me, Miss, do you mind getting a rum and coke for my lovely date and mojito for myself, please." The server quickly writes the order, flashes a smile, and moves in the direction of the bar.

Zephyr takes his seat next to mine and a smile slowly spreads across his face.

"I'm glad you agreed to come tonight," he says.

"Thank you for a wonderful day. I've never seen this side of life," I say, not able to express my gratitude more than words will tell.

For some reason the two of us sitting here, makes me think about that movie where the client falls in love with the escort and shows her a better life. No particular scene, just the thought that any man would love someone in my line of work.

"I want you to see how much I love you," he says.

My gaze locked with his, as the server returns with our drinks and sets them on the table in front of us.

"I want to know you," Zephyr declares. "Let's start easy. Where did you go to school?"

"I homeschooled," I admit. "I like to read, and math comes easy. I had to sneak to neighborhood libraries to study for my GED and take the test. I passed that, so I decided to see if I could test out of college and took online classes for what I didn't pass. I have a certificate in accounting."

Zephyr's eyes sparkle, as a smile splits his face.

"So then, how did you end up at McFadden and Tate?" he asks taking a sip of his drink.

"Walking into a temp agency was probably the dumbest smart move I've ever made in my life. I needed a way to get out of the business. Angel didn't catch on for a minute. He trusted that I would always be scared. I figured as long as I made it to appointments he had no reason to bother me. But then he found out …"

Zephyr leans forward. "And then what happened?"

"He started making more appointments during the day time, sometime spontaneous appointments," I explain. "Like the day you stopped by to see me and I told you I wasn't feeling well."

Zephyr's handsome chiseled face melts into a grimace. "Was that a lie to get out of work?"

"No," I reply as a live band queues up, a saxophone solo playing. "Angel called, and I actually got sick at the thought of having an early morning appointment while I was supposed to be working at the office. That was the day I met your friend."

"Bashir ..."

"Yeah. I think he had other plans in mind. For one weekend appointment he—"

"Weekend appointment?" Zephyr's eyebrows shot up like he was surprised.

"Yes. He took me to Miami to meet some people who I guess were business partners..."

"Miami? Wow..."

"Why 'Wow'?" I ask.

Zephyr's gaze lowers as if he's looking at the floor for the words to articulate his thoughts.

"He was about to set you up," he informs me, his gaze meeting mine, "However, I don't know how good it would've been for you."

"What do you mean?" This is when my lack of experience with the outside world is obvious.

"Anwar was a shrewd business man and had lots of money tied up in investments and businesses. He didn't look like it, but he was treading on billionaire status ..."

"So?"

"Well ... he had a large share in a family-owned oil field. He owned several gun ranges as well as a few other companies, one of which he was a partner in—a porn video production company." My heart drops into the pit of my stomach and my mouth opened wider. "He was probably scouting when he booked you the first time. He even liked to star in some of the productions ... you know that position comes with perks."

Zephyr scratches his temple and shakes his head.

"So how do you know so much about Bashir's business dealings?"

The uncomfortable pause that comes answers my question in a way I hope Zephyr doesn't confirm.

"He was one of my wealthiest clients, but he also wanted me to be a partner in the porn company," he admits.

My eyelashes hit my brow bone and my vocabulary leaves me. The weight of an elephant sits on my chest.

Zephyr leans in and takes my hand. With his gaze locked on me, his usual warm smile sends a chill through my body.

"I declined the offer, Aisha," Zephyr confesses as he covers my hand and strokes it with his thumb. "You know that woman you met this morning? Helen? My mom? I'm not doing anything she can't brag about."

"But … you thought about it."

"I love and respect women and knew I wasn't going to scout for the girls. I didn't want my name associated with a production company of that sort. I have a younger sister and a mother who would've whooped my grown ass no matter how many millions it would've brought in."

"I like your mother," I say, sipping my drink as I watch his eyes dance over my body.

"I'm trying to find the words that can eloquently express how I'm feeling right now, and I'm at a loss."

I'm glad he can't find the words; that means, to him, I'm not "Beautiful," I'm not "Precious," I'm not any of the terms of endearment that any client has ever called me—this is refreshing. Finally catching a grip on Zephyr's blazing gaze, I sip on my drink to keep myself cool.

With no more words between us, he's got my heart twisted and my thighs moist.

Zephyr breaks our stare to glance around the space and releases a gust of air.

"C'mon. Let's get outta here," he whispers, eyes alight with mischief.

Zephyr stands, shoulders broad and strong, and extends his hand to me. Taking his hand, I follow him, my heart in his hand, hopeful for happiness—hopeful for life. However, this won't last long if Angel finds me first.

I have some decisions to make.

Gemini

Freedom.

Cruising down Ford Freeway, sitting in the front seat with Zephyr, I feel like I'm dreaming. His hands stay on the steering wheel, but I catch his gaze flickering between the road and me. In any other situation, other men would've been warming cold, clammy hands between my thighs.

"Is there anything you wanna talk about?" he asks, breaking the silence. I draw in a deep breath and smile.

"Okay. We can be quiet," he says with a chuckle.

"No, I just don't know what to talk about. That's all," I reply, shrugging.

"Is there anything about me you want to know?"

"I really don't know what I want to know about you," I admit. "I never imagined us spending this much time together, much less what questions I'd ask."

Small talk carries us the rest of the thirty-minute drive when Zephyr pulls onto an exit and a few turns later he drives into a park by a tree-lined river. The area is secluded with exception to the occasional lightening bug adding its own light to the scene.

Light from the crescent moon dances on water ripples as it slowly rolls downstream.

"This place," I say, my gaze following the sparkling river. "It's beautiful."

A smile cracks Zephyr's face as he slides out of the driver seat and pops the trunk before coming to the passenger side. Opening the door, he holds a basket filled with white roses and orange tiger lilies. Moonlight dances in his eyes as his gaze locks with mine, and my heart pounds with the desire to know what his lips feel like once more.

A warm breeze blows as Zephyr takes my hand to lead me to a bridge that spans the narrow river, stopping in the middle, and getting a view of the far stretching river.

"What's this place?"

"I found it back in my college days," Zephyr declares, staring down the river, and putting on a smile that doesn't reach his eyes. "When I'm home, I come here just to listen to the water to clear my mind. I brought you here because I thought maybe this would give you a picture of who I am outside of work and family. Besides, the way I see it, we both could use some place to make some good memories."

Delivering a kiss to my temple, he takes my hand, and leads me to a large tree by the riverside.

Zephyr digs his hand inside the top of the basket, handing me the flowers. The sweet fragrance of the bouquet makes its way to my nose before I receive the gorgeous bundle. Pulling a blanket from the basket, he spreads it on the ground, taking care to flip the corners flat on the king-sized covering. He pulls off his suit jacket, tosses it down, and takes one knee in front of me.

As he reaches into his pocket, my breath hitches.

He produces a box and opens the tiny red package to reveal a princess cut diamond set in a band of baguettes.

"Know that the perfect place to ask what I'm about to ask is wherever you are," Zephyr whispers as I tremble, my knees feeling like rubber. "This place is where I want to start good memories with you and don't want to wait another moment … Aisha, I don't want to ask you to marry me. I want to know if you feel I deserve you. I want to know if you'll let me love you for the rest of our lives."

"Yes," I whisper, my gaze fixed on him. A smile splits Zephyr's face, wider than I've ever seen. Taking my hand, he slips the ring on my finger.

Soft fingers gently glide down my leg to the strap of my shoe. He loosens the strap; bright eyes sweep from my feet up to meet my gaze, and he offers me a smile.

I shake my head and giggle.

Lifting my foot, he takes off one shoe, then the other.

Zephyr stands, his hypnotic gaze holds me hostage to his devotion.

The warm summer breeze whirls collecting the smells of the water, the trees, and Zephyr. Winding one hand in his velvety locs, the other bears witness to the thunder that rolls in his chest.

Drawing in a deep breath, he trails his nose along the curve of my neck.

Zephyr lowers me onto the neatly spread blanket keeping his lips pressed to mine.

Quickly I unknot his tie and unbutton his shirt.

His already strong heartbeat accelerates, pounding harder. Holding his sparkling gaze, I undress him, his fervent erection ready to be released. Heat spreads from my thigh up and under my dress as Zephyr's hot, robust touch travels, finding its way under my dress. One finger twists around the band of my panties and draws the material down, removing the skimpy barrier.

Zephyr reaches into the basket, pulls out a condom, and sheaths himself.

Unzipping my dress his hand quickly resumes traveling up to the small of my back, my dress inching and wrinkling until he pulls it over my head and tosses it to the ground. Removing my bra, his large hand cups one breast, his hot lips wrap around my nipple. Pleasure racks my body. I weave my fingers through his locs to stroke his head. He nips my flesh and every nerve cries out in surrender to my need to have him.

Zephyr spreads my knees and kneels before me, erect between my thighs. He descends and dusts my inner thighs with soft kisses. He places one last kiss on my forehead. With his magnetizing gaze set on mine, he fills me with every inch of his love.

I suck in a rushed, deep breath; my body lurches, surprised by the pleasure of him, my breath hitches. Closing my eyes, I relish the sensation of him thick and strong, inside me.

"I love you, Zephyr Gray," I whisper as I caress his cheek.

He stares down into my face with warm, piercing eyes.

"I love you, Aisha."

His stroke is slow, deliberate, and intoxicating—he reaches the depths of my core naturally. Welcoming each thrust, I clutch his luscious locs in my hands and pull; his moan is music to my ears.

His momentum intensifies, his rhythm harder and faster, his energy coursing through my body. Zephyr pulls away from me only long enough to change my position, bringing my foot to his shoulder. He remounts and continues his stride like he never broke it.

Heavenly vibrations take hold and my body takes on a mind of its own, bending and twisting at Zephyr's command. Deeper. Harder. Faster. Stronger. My breath catching with every push, tears of joy break way with each thrust.

Wildly he thrashes into me until we both groan in sweet release. Exhausted, Zephyr lowers his body to mine.

I nestle into the locs that drape over my neck and shoulders; his scent, the flowers, and musk fills my nostrils. Our heartbeats crash against each other's chests while our breathing rides on the breeze.

Zephyr has always been an impossible dream, as I never allowed myself to imagine him being a part of my life. However, in this moment, I can't see how I could live another day without him.

Chapter 33

Gemini

The morning brings the smells of sage, fried eggs, and fresh biscuits. The gentle tapping of the rain outside encourages me to curl deeper into the down comforter, my thoughts stirring about my night with Zephyr. I don't know how he's up to doing anything. We were all over each other until the break of dawn. Even on the car ride back to his parents' house, he held my hand and kissed it every chance he got.

"Good morning, Love."

A smile works its way across my face. My heart sings when he calls me "Love."

Zephyr's smooth timbre lures me to turn in his direction. As much as I want to spring up to see him, turning over is a process. The ache I feel is delicious—every tender move reminds me of one of the many adventurous positions played during last night's love making session.

"Good morning, Zephyr," I say, stretching out a few kinks. He stands at the foot of the bed, clad in black briefs, holding a bed tray with breakfast and flowers from the garden. I sit up in the bed as he puts the tray over my lap. He dashes from the room while I bite into the fluffiest biscuit I've ever eaten in my life.

Zephyr walks back to my moaning and eyes rolling up into my head. He pokes out his bottom lip and furrows his brows.

"What?" I ask around the buttery goodness in my mouth.

Zephyr places a wine goblet filled with apple juice on the tray and lays a kiss on my lips.

"I thought I was the only one that could make you moan like that," he pouts.

I chuckle as I take a sip of juice to wash down my food and clear my throat.

"Don't be jealous of the biscuit, honey," I say, offering him a smile. "It might make me moan, but I promise it won't make me scream your name."

Zephyr's eyes light up as the corners of his mouth turn up. He crushes a passionate kiss to my lips, the taste of his skin mixing with the flavor of my apple juice. He sits next to me and swipes a turkey sausage link from my plate.

"So," he begins, taking a bite, "What do you want to do today?" Leaning back on the mound of pillows pushed up against the stately headboard, he eyeballs me, waiting for an answer. Then picking up a fork, he takes a bite of scrambled eggs from my plate. I watch him work his way around the scrumptious plate of food, trying to decide if I should tell him what I really want to do.

"We can do some shopping in Canada," he suggests. "We can stay home and watch a movie or two, or we can—"

"I want to find my mother," I interrupt.

Zephyr looks at me, eyebrows popped, like my request is somehow surprising. "Okay," he drags the word out. "How do you propose to get that done today?"

"I don't know. We have to go back to Cincinnati for work soon, and I need to know why my life has been hell or why she never called for me."

Zephyr bolts up from his relaxed position. "You're not going back, Aisha," he says firmly. A crease forms between his eyebrows as he stares me down. "You'll stay here, and I'll arrange for you to work from here."

This should sound like good news, but it isn't. I straighten my posture and turn in Zephyr's direction. "Are you serious? Do you think I'm supposed to stay here and hide out forever?"

"That sounds a whole lot better than you ending up dead."

"What you fail to understand is that we might all end up dead if Angel finds me here and I'm not so sure that isn't possible. It's been a little over a week. If I show up he'll beat the hell out of me and I'll be fine, but I won't be dead."

Zephyr leaps out of the bed, his face twisted in disbelief. "Do you hear yourself?"

"I heard it. I said it," I say plainly.

Zephyr turns away from me and cradles his face with his thumbs while all other fingers send up a prayer in what seems to be an effort to calm himself.

"You said in the hospital that he was going to kill you," Zephyr says slowly.

"I was scared, I was being dramatic," I say. "I make way more money for him than his other girls. He won't kill me."

"You're not going back," he whispers.

"Listen, this has been a nice vacation and I appreciate everything you've done for me, but if I have any chance of living and not causing any collateral damage along the way, I have to go back."

He spins back around, lightning in his glare. You call what you were doing living?" he roars.

"No," I roar back. "I'm not trying to get you and your family killed. Okay? *You* said his reach could be this far. This has been more time than I've ever been away from him without money being involved. So, unless you have fifty thousand dollars handy for the last week of my life away from him, I have to go back."

Zephyr stands before me poised to settle this argument, unfazed by the imminent danger of having me around. I peer down at my bare, branded shoulder.

"Do you see this?" He glances at the finger pointing to my tattooed shoulder. "You've never even asked what it is. This. Means. I. Belong. To. Angel."

Zephyr squints and shakes his head, in what seems to be an effort to process what I just said. "A roman numeral for two?"

"My brand, the symbol for my name, Gemini. Angel gave me that name, and he had me tatted the day I looked at a man too loosely. That was also the day he held a gun to my head. He said he would kill anyone who thought they could have me without his say so. Right now, you're living your fantasy, but this is my reality."

Zephyr stands rigid, breathing heavy, and silent.

"Where did you go the day I told you about Angel? You left me at the hospital and didn't come back. Where did you go?"

As Zephyr looks at me, every bit of anger melts into the floor. He plops back on the bed as if he's exhausted from his own short stint of anger and wipes both of his hands over his face.

"I went to a waiting room in another part of the hospital to think," he admits.

"To think about what?" I ask as he peers at the ceiling, quiet. "What did you need to think about? What your mother would think of you bringing home a hoe for a girlfriend?"

Zephyr twists his head to look at me and my gaze locks on his glare. "Were you thinking about what everyone at work would say? What was so pressing that you needed to leave the room and not come back?" My heartbeat keeps rhythm with the pouring rain outside while I wait for his answer.

He rolls over and props himself up on his elbow. Concern covers his face, the fire in his eyes dull to a dim sparkle; his normally happy aura disturbed. His gaze wanders my face, his silence creating more questions than answers.

"First, never refer to yourself as a 'hoe', that's not who you are. In my presence or otherwise, don't do it. Second, I have enough money to pay Angel for a year of your time, but I want more than a year and you're far more precious to me than paid sex. Paying him would only reinforce his thought that you belong to him … I left because I was angry, I couldn't think straight, and I felt stupid."

"You shouldn't have felt stupid … I didn't want you to know. I didn't want anyone to know."

"I understand that. But with one statement, with one name, I had to think if I could deal with that. I have to be honest—I almost didn't come back." The idea that Zephyr Gray might not be in my life is an unbearable thought. "I had to ask myself if my love for you was real or was I just trying to play out some fantasy that I could walk away from."

My tears have their way and falling without apology.

"But then, I couldn't stop thinking about your smile or about our first kiss or the sound of your voice when you say my first and last name as one name…" A smile slides across his face. "I love the way you feel in my arms when I hold you."

I put my breakfast tray on the nightstand and inch in close to him. He pulls me in tight and folds me into his body. He places one kiss on my forehead and then another. He draws in a deep breath as I nuzzle in closer.

"It was like I didn't know what my life was like before you. Every time I tried to imagine it, I saw what my life could be with you. I couldn't walk away."

I don't know who I'm trying to fool—I can't walk away either. The time I've spent with him seems like a lifetime. All I want to think about is a future with Zephyr: having his kids, holidays with his family, traveling the world … this is all I want, but the only way for any of this to become reality is to get away from Angel and the business, and that starts with finding my mother.

I pull away from his warmth and look into his eyes.

"I have to find my mother," I plead. "She might be the only one with any answers to getting out of this business."

"How do you propose to do this?"

"You know the lady I was talking with at the event last night?"

"Yes …"

"That was Nina, my childhood friend. We were playing in the front yard on the day I was taken. Last night while we were talking she mentioned that my mother is still in my old house."

Zephyr stares at me, pity in his eyes. "If I help you get your answers, will you

stay here where you're safe?"

I stare back into his eyes and see forever, my forever.

"I can't stay, Zephyr. At least not now," I explain. "None of us are safe while I'm here."

"Do you think I asked you to marry me for you to go back to that monster? That life?" Zephyr asks, frustration darkening his tone. He pulls the hand with the ring on it to my face. "This means I love you and will do everything to keep you safe."

"What if he finds me? Finds us?" I ask, loosening my hand from his. "He already killed Mr. Bashir. If I return of my own will, he'll make me work more to pay off my debt. I'll negotiate my release or something. Finding my mother has to happen first. She'll have the answers I need."

Zephyr stares at me, saying nothing, and his eyebrows drawn in as if he doesn't understand the language I'm speaking.

The rhythm of the raindrops becomes lighter and the sun shines through the large-picture window.

I snuggle into his hold, placing my ear on his chest. He buries a hand in my hair and rubs my scalp.

"Okay," he relents, his soft reply booming against my ear. "When do you want to start your search?"

I pop up and look into his eyes; Wonderland's Cheshire cat has nothing on my grin.

"Today."

Chapter 34

Gemini

It shouldn't be this easy.

For as long as I have been gone, I hadn't forgotten my old address— I dreamed about getting back home often. Thoughts of home stayed on my mind, but remembering how to navigate the way back from a place that was once familiar to me is challenging. The Gray's home is only blocks away from the yacht club that my family and I used to visit. It's crazy to me how close we lived to each other in another space in time.

"Are you ready?" Zephyr asks, disrupting a string of questions in my head.

My heartbeat hammers as I clasp my hands to keep them from shaking. Zephyr caresses my hand, parts the knot they're in, and laces his fingers with my left hand.

"Are you sure you want to do this? I mean we can go back and … you know," he says wriggling his eyebrows.

"I'm ready," I whisper.

Zephyr kisses my hand, offering me a slight smile, and inputs the address into his GPS.

The usually comfortable silence between us seems strange, even strained. His gaze flickers from the road to me while he drives as an internal monologue overpowers any potential banter we might have.

Has she missed me? Will she recognize me? Have her looks changed? Her hair is probably gray from worry. I can't wait to see her. I wonder if my room is still the same...

The ride was shorter than I expected, only twenty-two minutes. Turning the corner onto the street where my childhood ended, the houses seem familiar, but don't quite look the same.

Trees stretch higher, shrubs and lawn figurines decorate some of the yards, and window boxes make even the smaller homes appear to be grand. The street appears much shorter than I remember but seems to grow longer the further we ride down.

The painfully slow creep ends as the car stops in front of the house neighboring my childhood home. Aside from the tan brick façade, the house doesn't seem familiar, like it's not my home, like it may have never been my home.

My eyes sting, I rub them before any tears can fall.

Zephyr takes my hand and places a kiss on the back of it.

"You've got this, Aisha," he encourages, locking his gaze on me. "This is what you want, right?"

This is what I want, what I need.

The sun, which had been darting in and out of the clouds for the duration of our short drive, found its place behind the clouds as rain started to fall. Peering into the front yard, I imagine the last day Nina and I played there with our dolls, every moment as clear as it happened yesterday.

"Aisha!" My mother's voice booms in my ears. I quickly cover my ears and crouch down. I put my head on the dashboard. A gentle touch glides back and forth between my shoulders.

"Hey, Love? Are you okay?" Rising from my bent position, I draw in a deep breath. "Aisha, are you sure you want to do this?"

His beautiful onyx eyes, full of concern, hold me in their grip.

"I'm okay. I'm going in now."

Zephyr leans over and places a kiss to my forehead. I muster some semblance of a grin.

Leaving the car, Zephyr follows me on the walk to the brightly painted red door of my old home. The distance feels football fields long.

"I need to do this … alone," I say, halting his steps.

Sounds of laughter and music play as I stand on the patio, listening to the hustle and bustle of what doesn't sound like the home of a solitary woman.

After ringing the doorbell, I fold my arms under my breasts, holding myself as tight as I can.

The voice of someone who isn't quite an adult, but older than a small child, grows louder as the person comes closer to the door.

The door rattles, then swings open. My breath catches as a milky-skinned, sandy-blonde girl with bright hazel eyes stands in the doorway. Her thick hair looks like it was forced into the braided rope that lays over the front of her shoulder. Studying the girl's face, I'd guess she might be ten or eleven. Her eyes have a mossy brown quality of green like mine. I don't know anybody else with hazel eyes, not like mine anyway.

"I-I'm sorry," I stammer. "I must be at the wrong house." Stepping away from the door, I turn to walk toward the street.

"Nadira, who's at the door?"

I whip back around at the sound of my mother's voice coming from the house.

"I don't know, Mama," the girl says looking over her shoulder. "It's a lady. I don't know her."

My throat dries out as my stomach ties itself into knots.

Mama?

Watching the door, I look to confirm what I thought was my imagination.

A bright smile from the short, olive-skinned woman who stands behind the little girl she called Nadira. She looks just like I remember—no gray hair, not one wrinkle. My heart pounds as I run back to the door.

Blowing past the girl, I wrap my arms around my mother's diminutive frame as hot tears pour. She smells like olive oil and roses, just like I remember.

"Mama, I've missed you so much," I cry into her neck.

She stands stiff and silent, but I don't care. I hug her even tighter.

"Fatma, is everything alright?"

My celebration is halted with the resounding bass of a man's voice. Loosening my grip, I wipe my eyes. A thick-bodied, light-skinned man stands in the living room, his eyebrows furrowed as a steely gaze demands answers.

A more sober view of the room uncovers a crowd of people with children running and laughing in the area of the house I remember being the den. A further scan shows balloons, streamers, and super hero decorations.

My mother pushes her way out of my hold, stepping away from me, her eyes unreadable.

"Yes, Jaffe. I'm fine," she assures the man, her cold gaze still locked on me. "Is Kareem ready to cut his cake?" A little boy with bouncy light-brown curls and dark, twinkling eyes cowers behind the man. Malik was shy, but not like this little boy.

"Who is she, Mama?" The boy asks peeking around the man's leg. A sharp pain hits my head as the second of two children calls my mother, 'Mama'.

My mother glowers, and my energy pools on the floor as my soul slowly bleeds at one biting glare from her icy, green eyes. Her chest rises and falls like an ocean tide, and she places one hand over her stomach. "You … you're supposed to be dead," she whispers. "You … you're dead." She repeats shaking her head.

This isn't how I thought this meeting would go.

Each aching heartbeat takes more and more of my breath away. "But … Mama, I'm not dead. I'm here."

She twists her face like she's biting into something sour, giving me and my meager smile a once over.

Once more I reach out to fold her in my arms and she recoils as if offended by the gesture.

"He … he said that he'd handle you, that I wouldn't have to worry, he'd handle you," she cries balling her hand into a fist on her stomach, her breathing becoming more erratic.

The room that once hummed with chatting and laughter is now quiet enough that a pin drop can be heard.

My glance bounces around the room; from the crowd, to the man, to the boy, to my mother, and finally lands on Nadira as she moves to the little boy and grabs his hand.

"Daddy, I think it's still too early to cut the cake. Kareem still needs to play his games." Nadira says, looking to her father. She glances over her shoulder at me, a measure of concern in her eyes. "C'mon, Kareem. We still need to pin the tail on the donkey." Yanking on the boy's hand, she pulls him along, and he follows without any fanfare. "C'mon everybody. We still have games to play," Nadira demands as all the guests follow her out of the living room.

"Are you sure you're okay, Fatma," Jaffe asks echoing his distress.

"Go with the children, dear," she replies without even turning in his direction. "Don't wait for me. Go and be with our guests. I won't be long."

His cold eyes rifle with confusion, Jaffe takes his turn to stare me down, lingering far too long before finally leaving my mother and I to ourselves. Jaffe, whoever he is, isn't at all threatening. My mother is the one running things around here. I'm pretty sure that even Nadira's balls are bigger than his.

My mother stands before me, indignant. Not as a joyful mother whose lost child has returned, but livid with the anger of a woman who just met her husband's mistress.

"Why are you here?" my mother questions. Her tight lips demand an answer to her question.

My answer sticks in my throat as tears build in my eyes. The petite woman, who had the arrogance to walk like a six-foot-tall runway model for the snooty members of the yacht club, quivers, her squinted green eyes glowing like a snake. "Why are you here?" she spits. "Why?"

My mother draws long, deep breaths; her chest rises high and falls, like mine does when I need to calm myself.

I measure my words, trying not to make an apparently bad situation worse.

"Mama …"

"Stop calling me that," she roars as her body shakes.

Nadira runs into the living room, but backs up behind a wall. "Why are you here?"

Tiny black rivers run from her eyes down her cheeks as she chastises me for being alive. A sharp pain shoots between my shoulders as tension builds with my mother's theatrics. My heart aches as every word that Angel and even Ryan spoke reverberate in my mind.

"Stop calling me that!"

"Your mother doesn't want you. It might be a good idea for you to leave her wherever she is." The voices mock my effort to reunite with my mother. Heat creeps up my neck as my mother stares me down, begging for an answer to her question.

I fold my arms under my breast once more, tilt my head to one side, and return her glare. "Tell me … Mama," my voice cracks, breathing becoming uneven, "Who exactly was supposed to *handle* me?"

My mother's eyes widen then narrow, her nostrils flare, but she doesn't reply.

"Mama?" I ask hardening my glare on her. "*Who* was supposed to handle me?"

Still, she offers no answer. I close the distance between us in one stride as she stretches her neck to look up into my eyes.

Nadira peeks around the wall behind my mother.

My mother looks up at me, draws in a deep breath, and shoves me in the chest.

Taken by surprise, I stumble and fall to the floor.

Nadira's eyes pop wide as her mouth drops.

As I lay on the floor, heat rises up my back, and sweat droplets form along my hairline. I suck in a deep breath and glance in Nadira's direction. My mother steps in close and peers down at me. Sweat beads across her twisted lips.

"Every day that I looked at you, you reminded me. You reminded me of that day," she seethes, wagging her finger in my face. "You were the reason my family disowned me. You were the reason I could never go back home to see my mother before she died. I sent you to the man who wanted you. You are supposed to be dead. It would've been better for you to die the day your cheating father and Malik died—which was what I planned, but your father wanted his *princess* to stay home. You should be dead."

She could've ripped my heart out of my chest with her bare hands and it wouldn't have been as painful as the words that spewed out of her mouth.

Nadira's hand flies to her mouth as I tremble violently on the floor.

"How was I the reason, Mama?" I inquire just above a whisper, despite my rage. My heart is racing like it does when Angel says he needs me for anything. My arms tremble under my weight; I want to beat the hell out of her.

"Get out… now," she barks.

Nadira quickly disappears behind the wall as if my mother was talking to her.

I back away from my mother, her intense glare following me. "I said get out," she growls. "You are ruining my son's birthday."

"Fuck your son," I scream. "I'm your daughter. I've spent my last twelve birthdays in hell while you went on with your life apparently thinking that I was dead! I want to know why."

"You … are … dead to me," she jeers.

Her unremorseful eyes demanding my exit, watch me as I rise from the floor, swing back, and slap her across her face.

Blood trickles from her nose down onto her lip. Narrowing her gaze on me, she doesn't move, doesn't even seem surprised. Her lips curl into a weak, yet delighted smile. I draw back once more and slap her, causing her to fall into a wall.

"Does Gillespie know you're here, Aisha?" she teases, pulling herself away from the wall.

I don't even satisfy her question with a blink. She didn't have to touch me to knock the wind out of my chest, but I won't let her see me sweat about this.

"Of course, he does," I lie. Realizing that she knows Angel and her willingness to have me dead gives me all the reason I need to deny her the satisfaction of my shock.

"I'm sure he has no idea you're here to see me," she says, her smirk striking the same chord in me that sends chills down my spine when I'm around Angel—they're twisted with the same yarns of evil like kindred spirits.

"He knows I've wanted to see you since the day he met me," I sneer. "My trouble always came because I wanted to know just where you were. And so, it seems that every beating I ever got for asking where you were was well worth getting."

My story is reasonable even if most of what I said is a lie. I beam as I watch my mother's face drop and twist into a frown.

"Get out," she growls through clenched teeth.

I walk backward toward the door, staring my mother down, barely holding onto every emotion that begs to be released. Zephyr throws the car door open and Nadira peaks again around the wall. I don't give away her position. Who knows what her mother would do if she knew all Nadira had witnessed. I feel sorry for her and the boy.

Nadira stands in the living room window while my mother looks on from the front door as Zephyr and I leave.

She made me pay for her transgression and then had my father and brother killed. I think it's time I return the favor.

Chapter 35

Gemini

My mother doesn't want me.

She replaced us all … The fact the she mentioned Angel by his given name makes me wonder if he was the one that killed them. Ryan told me to leave her wherever she was, so he has to know something about this. I have more questions now than before I came to Michigan.

Being loved by Zephyr has been all I could've asked for in life; hell, he damn near worships me. Head-to-toe massages, flowers from the garden, extravagant meals, and surprise trysts to out of the way places for mind-blowing, love-making sessions. His imagination is endless when it comes to the many ways he demonstrates his love for me. But, all of that hasn't fixed anything I thought it would fix: I have no family—my father and brother are dead, and my mother wishes I had joined them.

Zephyr's family is great, but they aren't mine. I thought I'd at least have my mother. All I've wanted since I was taken from home is my mother and to be loved—

Angel and Dane were no replacement for that.

I'm over two hundred and fifty miles away from Angel, but wake up from nightmares of him taking a blade and carving his name into different parts of my body to pay for my disobedience. If he doesn't already think I'm dead, he'll surely want me dead when or if he finds out that I'm not.

Zephyr and I spent one last night making love before he went back to Cincinnati for work three weeks ago, making me promise to stay in the house where he thought I'd be safe. We set up a bank account for my financial needs and bought a cell so that we could keep in touch. He aimed for an airtight plan, but this miscalculation in his judgment gave me time to make a plan of my own.

Every day after the family leaves in their various directions I go to the gun range for target practice. It's been said that it takes upwards of ten thousand hours to become an expert in almost anything. I suppose that could be true, but I've always been a fast learner. Firing a gun is no exception.

Pulling in my target, a smile works across my face as I see that I missed center by a hair and every other hole was where I intended them to go—the head and groin areas. Not bad for three weeks of four-hour practice sessions a day.

I've practiced with a few different guns, but I've found the same .357 magnum that Angel once held to my face is the one I prefer. There's a powerful energy that flows through my body when I hold that beauty, imagining myself returning him the kind favor, looking him dead in his eyes. Not just holding the gun to his face, but to his temple every time I hold my weapon up to shoot. It's a thought that's all too appetizing.

I don't have to think twice about it—I'm buying a gun. However, I need something smaller than a magnum. Something that fits close to my body.

* * *

There's something to be said for feminine wiles; I'm pretty sure that buying a gun and ammo based on a wink, smile, and a hundred dollars is illegal, but the sense of having protection and the plans I have for the gun make it worth the risk.

The ride from the gun range is long as the Uber driver drones on about events happening in the city. All I think about is how long Zephyr has been gone. If the time moved any slower, I'd swear it was going backward.

Lonely days and long nights steal my appreciation for the safety that Zephyr has afforded me. If I were back home, I wouldn't have time to think about what he's doing. I'd be looking forward to seeing Caren at the Millennia and drinking a bomb ass Rum and coke that she'd have the bartender make for me. I wouldn't have time to think about my mother wanting me dead. I wouldn't be ruminating about Mr. Bashir's death. I wouldn't miss Zephyr's scent of sandalwood—it's very faint in the room we shared before he went back to work. I wouldn't miss his touch. I still can't believe Caren and Angel … the thought sends chills up my spine, but even so, she was my friend before all of that madness took place. She's now on that list of every other person that's broken my trust.

Maybe this can work in my favor. A phone call will tell me all I need to know.

"Hello?" The familiar Angie Stone type voice rings in my ear.

"Is this Caren," I ask, just to make sure I didn't dial a wrong number.

"Aisha?" she asks, hesitating as if trying to recognize my voice.

"Yes," I reply. "How's everything? I've missed you so much."

Caren is quiet on the other end, but she doesn't hang up. Considering how we left things the last time we spoke this conversation should be interesting.

"Listen," I say. "I'm sorry about how I left things. I've really missed you."

"I've missed you too, honey," she says, her tone more relaxed than when she answered. "Where have you been? You know I need to see your face in the audience when I'm on set."

"I'm keeping a low profile these days. Are things going well with your music career?" People talking in the background sound familiar.

"Not as good as I had planned," she says with a chuckle. "I brought my happy ass back to McFadden & Tate because I've got rent to pay. I've only performed a few times in the last couple of months."

"Oh, wow. I'm sorry to hear that."

"It's all good. I was hoping to see you here. What's up with you not coming to work? Sasha told everybody you quit suddenly and that there's possibly a thing going on between you and Zephyr Gray?"

Interesting bit of gossip since I haven't quit.

"I had some business to handle in Detroit and it's taking me a little longer than I thought to get it done. I haven't quit. And as far as Zephyr Gray and I, rumors are what Sasha does."

"Yeah, I guess you're right," she says with a laugh. "Detroit, huh?" she asks. "Nice … I can't wait to see you. How soon do you think you'll be back?"

The cell rings and it's Zephyr returning my earlier call. "I'm not sure when I'll be back, but I gotta take this call. I'll call you later."

"Is this a good number to reach you if I want to just talk, you know girl talk?"

"Sure. I'll talk to you later." I hurry and swap calls.

"Hello, Zephyr Gray," I sing. His smooth 'Good afternoon, Love' makes my heart flutter.

"I'm sorry I couldn't call before now. My schedule has been really hectic since seven this morning. How's your day been?"

"I've been keeping busy … missing you."

"I've been missing you too," he replies, sounding like his smile is broad. "I'm coming home this weekend. You've been out of my arms for way too long."

"I agree. I can't wait to see you." We chat about plans for the weekend, which for me is to be wrapped up with him and only come up for air when I need a drink of water. The most enjoyable ten minutes of my day ends all too soon when he has to answer another call.

"I love you. I'll call you later."

"Love you, too."

The Uber driver pulls up to the Gray residence and the sunshine brings thoughts of gratitude—thankful for the day, thankful for a place where I'm safe but wishing, hoping, and dreaming these days aren't numbered. I can't see myself ever going back to the life I had before.

Even having a relationship with my mother is not on my mind the way it was before, though I do think about Nadira and Kareem. My mother's admission of guilt and the rift between her and her family—a story I've never heard from my father is a hard pill to swallow. Angel only alluded to knowing my mother, never saying he was contracted to kill anyone.

Picking up the cell, about to send a text to Zephyr, I see missed call notifications from Caren and a voicemail light up the screen. Climbing into the bed, I get comfortable, and hunker down into the comforter.

"Hey, Baby Girl," says Angel's gruff voice as the voicemail plays. "I've missed you … you know, your girl here doesn't get me off like you do."

Angel spares no change on his words or his sentiment. "At any rate, expect a call from Ryan for further arrangements. I look forward to seeing you. We have a lot of catching up to do," he warns, ending the call laughing.

That was easier than I thought. Clearly, I can trust Caren to side with whoever is making her moan at night since I can't trust her for anything else.

A meeting definitely has to happen, but it's not going to be what he thinks it's for. Still holding the cell, the call I was told to wait for comes through.

"Yes, Ryan," I say, finding no sense in carrying on with niceties.

"Listen," There's a sense of urgency in Ryan's voice that I wasn't expecting. "You shouldn't have left the city. Pops tells me he hasn't slept since you've been gone."

"I haven't been gone that long and I couldn't care less."

"You've been gone almost two months. Pops is different, like he's lost his mind or something."

"Really now? Let's talk about how he's always been crazy."

"Listen, there's stuff about my Pops that you don't understand."

"What is there to understand about a lunatic, Ryan?"

"Pops went through some foul shit as a kid. He used to tell me how he was so glad to have a son because he wanted to give me what he never got. I know it doesn't mean anything to you, but I tried to make life easy for him when I was around."

"And?" I ask. "Since you're being so open with your father's business, give me some insight. Why did he give me my name?"

Ryan sits silent, again, like he's mulling over what information he wants to share.

"His mother was a Gemini. She was killed in front of him on her birthday. It was a debt killing. I don't know why he would've given you that name. She was a junkie who wasn't very good at turning in her money from her tricks."

"How does Angel know my parents?" I continue questioning, impatient for more answers.

"Well," Ryan begins. "They all went to school together—"

"College?"

"No. They met each other like sophomore or junior year in high school. After everything that happened with his mom, Pops was kind of on his own. He made friends with some of the smart kids at school, so he could get tutoring for free. Your dad was at the top of their class. Your mom was the popular girl. Fatma was Pops side chick until just before they graduated."

This certainly isn't the story I recall.

"So, what does this have to do with me?"

"Pops and Mom had me when Mom was in middle school, so they were always a thing. Pops met Fatma at the beginning of sophomore year and they coupled up."

"So? It just sounds like he knew how to get what he wanted from them. Sounds like he's always been greedy."

"I guess. Somewhere in their senior year of school Pops told Fatma that they were exclusive, but he …"

"Lied?" I say, completing Ryan's sentence with my own words.

"Changed his mind. Your dad and Pops were pretty tight. So, as payback, your mom laid it on your dad in the band room during lunch. Fatma liked your dad as friend, but she was trying to make Pops jealous. Her parents thought she was a good girl," Ryan says, finishing his statement with a snicker.

My face contorts as if he can see me.

"Is there a joke?"

"No, there isn't. It's just that your mom was popular with all of the guys and she had, let's say, a forbidden preference in dudes. Her parents thought she was a virgin until they found out she was pregnant. And she was pregnant by a black guy? They kicked her out of the house the night they found out and they never looked back. She tried to go back home, and her younger brother beat the hell out of her in broad daylight while her parents watched and told her she was dead to them."

Unbelievable. This story only vaguely matches what my father used to tell me about him and my mother. My father never mentioned Angel, but this is clearly what my mother was talking about when she blamed me for her exile.

"Why should I believe anything you're saying, Ryan?"

"Listen, you don't even have to believe that the sky is blue on a clear day, but I'm giving you the answers to your questions. And with all of that aside, we need to negotiate bringing you back home."

"Home?" I scoff, "I'm not going anywhere."

"Wrong answer," he says, sounding dejected, "I'll be there tomorrow. I know how to find you."

Ryan disconnects the call.

The threat is concerning—maybe asking about my mother gave him clues, but he wouldn't know to find me in Zephyr's home.

I know this—he's not the only one who has plans for this meeting.

Chapter 36

Gemini

Light from the sunrise wakes me from a good night's rest. Between an open window, unusually cool, early summer Michigan temperatures, and a fan on high speed, the room is uncomfortably cold for an early morning rise. Pulling the comforter over my shoulder, I keep warm a little longer.

Sounds of food sizzling and the aroma of sage and waffles make me quickly sit up in the bed. Grabbing the cell, I look at the time. *7:34 a.m.... Who's in the house?* Glasses clink. Tapping that sounds like the glass is being set on the countertop. The refrigerator opens and closes.

My scalp tingles as my curiosity turns into fear. *Ryan did say he knew where to find me, but how would he know to come here?* Checking both wrists for scars from an implant of a lo-jack or something that I don't remember getting doesn't ease my angst. Peeling back the covers, I put my feet on the floor.

A splash and gurgle of something being poured.

I sneak over to my purse and pull out the .9-millimeter Kahr I bought yesterday. Turning toward the door, gun in hand, I'm stopped dead in my tracks. Butterflies take flight in my stomach at the sight of Zephyr standing in the doorway holding a tray of food and flowers. His raised eyebrows ask a question without words.

A smile zips across my face as I fumble to put the gun back in my purse.

"When did you get here? It's so early."

Zephyr smiles, puts the tray on the bed, and wraps me in his arms placing a kiss on my forehead. He pulls back and sets his warm gaze on mine.

"I got done with my work and postponed all appointments because I needed to get back to you," he says in a soft, smooth tone. Tightening his embrace, he kisses the curve of my neck. "I came in late last night and you were already asleep, so I watched you until I got tired. I didn't want to disturb you, so I slept in the living room."

"I'm so glad you're home." I reach up to nibble his ear, but he pulls back.

"What's with the gun, Aisha?" he inquires, holding me captive in his arms and his gaze while I figure out what to say.

Stepping back from Zephyr, I lower my gaze. My face gets warm as I get ready to give him an explanation for a gun he didn't give to me and wasn't in my possession before he left.

"Um, I just wasn't feeling safe by myself," I explain as he listens intently, the story lacking the complete honesty I have with him. "Your family is always busy and—"

Zephyr's lips slide to one side of his face. "Come better," he retorts, shaking his head, "If you're gonna lie, make me feel it."

"What do you mean, make you feel it?"

"Aisha, you don't have to lie to me … about anything."

He rebukes me with one kind, but disapproving look. "Why wouldn't you have told me that you weren't feeling safe?"

A knot balls in my throat. I can't think of a good excuse fast enough. "I feel like you don't trust me."

The hurt in his eyes is more than I can bear, so I turn from him to gather my thoughts. "I've never had the occasion to trust anyone," I confess. "Depending on myself is all I know how to do."

"I want to be able to trust you, so you have to be honest with me even if you think I don't want to hear it."

I marinate on this thought for a moment and turn back around. "I've been practicing at the gun range since you left."

Reproach turns into confusion as a wrinkle forms between his eyebrows. "Why would you do that?"

Swallowing past my pride and the lump in my throat, I stare out the window. "I need to protect myself in case Angel shows up," I say.

Zephyr searches my flushed face, squinting as if he has to focus at this close range.

"Tell me, what makes you think he's around here?"

Reasoning within myself if I should tell him about the one phone call that let Angel know I was actually still alive, I drop my head.

"Well? Why are you so paranoid?" he asks.

"I'm not paranoid." I sigh. "Angel knows I'm not dead. He's looking for me. I must have some sort of protection when you're not around."

Zephyr's face hardens at the admission.

"Why are you looking at me like that?"

"You haven't answered my question."

The debate in my head continues. *To tell him or not?*

"Aisha, this is why I didn't take you back to Cincinnati with me. As big as the city is, I knew he'd find you there. I just need you to be safe."

"So, your idea is to keep me imprisoned here?" The words whip out of my mouth without thought or regret. Zephyr's normally brown cheeks turn crimson, a single vein on his forehead confirming his level of distress. "How is it any different than Angel keeping me?"

"Well, for one thing, I'm not selling your ungrateful ass to the highest bidder," he snaps.

My heart stops as his bitter tone cuts me to my core.

"But I'm still not free," I plead, meeting with his pained gaze. "And, I'm grateful. I know it doesn't seem like it, but I am. You love me. I never knew what is was to be loved before you came into my life and for that I'll be eternally thankful, but I won't stay under lock and key forever … not one more minute."

Zephyr's chest rises and falls with calculated measure. He looks away as a single tear traces his cheek. The smell of roses and sage waft about the room as silence threatens to choke the life out of me.

A glance at the ornately arranged tray shows sumptuous servings of food and flowers. I quickly turn back to Zephyr as he slumps against the doorjamb and rubs his forehead.

"I just need you to be safe … how can you think I'm keeping you a prisoner?"

"I appreciate your protection, but I have to put an end to this with Angel. He'll never stop looking for me as long as he knows I'm alive. I have to get away from him … permanently."

Zephyr's horrified eyes zip to mine as if he put meaning to my words.

In a pleading tone, I add, "I need to end this."

"You need to stay here."

"He knows I'm here."

"How? How do you know that he knows where you are?" I plop down on the bed, exhausted from the conversation.

"I called Caren. I know you said the phone was just to call you or your family, but I wanted to see if I told her where I was how fast it would get back to Angel. In less than an hour Angel called."

I drop my eyes to floor, and Zephyr sighs.

"They slept together once. Things were tense between us after that. Angel called me from her phone and left a message."

"You told him you were here?"

"I told Caren I was in Detroit," I explain. "His son Ryan called me, and I started asking questions about my mother. That may have given him a clue because before he disconnected the call, he said he knew where he could find me. Now that I'm thinking about it, I'm not too sure my mother didn't call him."

"Your mother knows this guy?"

"Intimately."

Staring out the window at the sunlight cascading over the yard helps me avoid looking at Zephyr. I never wanted him to know about my life, particularly this part. "I tried to tell you that you didn't need to know this about me."

He wipes his hands over his face. "You're not going back. Especially if you're planning to kill this dude."

"What do you propose that I do then?"

I already know what he'd like me to do, which to me is no different than what Angel was doing—keeping me to himself whether or not it was something I wanted. "I refuse to spend my life looking over my shoulders."

"You don't have to. I hired a private investigator," Zephyr admits, leaning his head on the doorjamb. "Now that we know where Angel is, it'll be easy for the police to capture him, keeping you out of harm's way."

As much as I love Zephyr, I don't need his approval to do what I need to do, especially if it's to keep us safe.

Zephyr pulls himself together, picks up the breakfast tray from the bed, and goes back into the kitchen. The ache in my chest travels through my body until every nerve tingles. I need him to touch me.

Water runs from the faucet. On then off again. Every clink draws a tear; I wonder why he can't understand that what I want to do is for everyone's best interest.

Walking into the kitchen, I watch Zephyr as he puts away the last of the dishes, he cuts his eyes at me over his shoulder.

Stealing to his side, I slide my hands around his waist and splay my fingers near the family jewels, but his body goes rigid.

"Zephyr Gray?" I whisper, my cheek against his back like a kid hugging her favorite teddy bear. I need him to hear my heart.

He braces himself against the countertop; his body betrays his pride as his shoulders shift down. He exhales and places a hand over mine. I snake around his side and face him.

He diverts his gaze from me.

"Look at me," I beg, searching for the connection we have. Reaching for his face, I trace his taut jawline down to the curve in his neck, placing my hand on his chest.

Zephyr lowers his eyes to meet mine. "I want to make love to you … please," I whisper. "I love you."

"Aisha, I love you, but we're not doing that," he says, removing my hands from his body. "One of the qualities I admire most about you is your determination to see things through to the end, but this, My Love, has me fearful. Your safety comes first."

His words sear my ears like he's rebuking me for needing the affection he's been so generous in giving me up to now.

As I reach to kiss him, he sidesteps out of the space we share.

"I need some air," he says turning toward the door.

With his simple request, Zephyr walks through the front door toward the main house.

The cell rings from the bedroom and I glance at the clock on the microwave- *8:57.*

My knees quake, my jaw stings, saliva seeps into my mouth—I need to eat.

I put together a plate of food, but the first bite proves to be disappointing as Zephyr isn't dining with me, but it's something to kill my hunger pangs and keep a headache away.

The cell starts ringing again—back to back.

Finishing off breakfast with a cup of almond milk, I flip the cell over from the nightstand and it reveals four missed calls and four voicemail messages from Angel's number. Curiosity over takes any fear and I call Angel directly instead of listening to my messages.

"Baby Girl," Angel exclaims with more enthusiasm than I expected, "I see you got my messages."

"Actually, I didn't," I say, reciprocating his eagerness with boredom. "I figure all of the back-to-back calls means you wanted to talk to me personally."

A gunshot rings out over the phone.

"Daddy!" A small child screams from the background.

"Alright, Baby Girl," Angel's tone is even between heavy breaths,

"You need to come and visit your mother … maybe for the last time," he warns as he ends the call.

My skin crawls just thinking about what I heard over the phone.

Did he shoot Fatma? No, the child's voice said 'Daddy'… Did he make Kareem watch him kill his father?

Swiping the screen, I open the voicemail.

Message- 9:01: "Hey Baby Girl, I'm here for a little family reunion. It's time for you to come back home." He sounds sickeningly sweet. Not like Angel at all.

Message- 9:03: "I'm not gonna wait all day. We have unfinished business to take care of."

Message- 9:03: *click*

Message- 9:04: "Hurry up and get your ass here!" Angel's voice growls from the phone.

That's the Angel I know.

An unfamiliar, but welcome confidence eases over me as I look at my phone and call for an Uber. For the first time in as long as I've lived with Angel, I'm not afraid of what my consequences might be.

Alive or dead, I'll be free from him.

Digging through the closet, I fish out the perfect outfit for our meeting and get dressed. I can't stop replaying everything that happened this morning in my head.

Zephyr really shouldn't be upset about this. I just want us, safe and living in peace, and Angel won't let that happen.

The Uber arrives. I lock up and leave the house not moving fast enough to avoid Zephyr before he tries to stop me.

"Aisha, what are you doing?" He huffs, as he tries to block my path to the car.

"I'm going to see my mother." I try to side step him, but he follows my step as if we're dancing. He wraps his massive arms around me—he feels so good; I want to melt.

"Listen, I'm sorry. I'm just trying to keep—"

"Me safe. Yes, I know," I interrupt his less-than-profound apology as I push myself out of his grasp, my gaze now laser aimed into his. "I'm going to make us all safe."

Chapter 37

Gemini

No cars pass as tree leaves gently rustle with the ebb and flow of the wind on the street I used to call home. Not a single black squirrel hanging out when they usually cavort and play between yards and trees anywhere in the city on a sunny day.

The familiar Mercedes and the Escalade sit parked in the driveway and Angel seems to have made himself at home.

The Uber driver is patient while he allows me to wait for a few minutes before leaving the car, hoping to see if Angel would come out to his truck.

Ryan, not Angel comes outside. He readily blends into the environment with his preppy polo shirt and khaki pants. Strolling around the Escalade and scanning the street, it doesn't take him long to notice the Uber idling.

"Is there a problem, Miss?" the Uber driver asks.

I guess I'm taking too long getting out of the car. "No … there isn't a problem."

I wait until Ryan returns to the house to move. As I inhale deeply, my heart pounds against the gun nestled in my bra holster. I'm as ready as I'll ever be to see Angel face to face again.

Scanning behind the Escalade toward the house, I watch the open front door so as not to be taken by surprise.

A glance up to the second story picture window that used to be in my room reveals Nadira holding her knees to her chest, heaving. Slinking against the side of the house, I reach the back corner before a strong hand yanks me back.

"What do you think you're doing, Gemini?" Ryan whispers, pulling me in so close that spit showers my face with his question.

"Angel has a reunion planned," I inform him as if he doesn't know the reason I'm here. "That's why you're here, right?" I ask giving Ryan a sly smile.

Looking over his shoulder, he curls his lips in and tightens his grip on my arm.

"This isn't a game," he warns through clenched teeth.

"I'm well aware of what this is," I whisper, leveling a hard gaze on him, making my indignation clear, "And in case you weren't aware, I'm. Not. Going. Anywhere."

Ryan glances over his shoulder once more then back at me.

"Believe it or not, I'm actually here because I'm trying to help you. I just need you not to fuck this up."

Ryan and I stand off, neither of us blinking.

"And how, exactly, are you trying to help me?" I say, locking my gaze on his.

"Let's go," he demands, yanking me forward to follow him, though he really doesn't have to.

"Where's the girl, Fatma?" Angel roars from inside the house. "I can break her in and send you back the proceeds, like I did with Gemini."

The proceeds?

Ryan pushes me into the house where Fatma lays on the floor sobbing, pants torn from the waist down, her dark Rapunzel like hair strewn over her face. Her man, Jaffe, sits against a wall shaking, bald-head dripping sweat, his pants covered with blood. Kareem is squeezed as close to his father as he can be without sitting on him and it occurs to me that Angel doesn't know Nadira's in the house.

I look at Ryan before my gaze travels to Angel standing across the room. Angel's face lights up, though it doesn't improve his sickening appearance. He looks as if he's aged ten years since I last saw him, his face gaunt like he hasn't eaten in the time I've been gone.

"Hey, Baby Girl," he purrs, his smile wide. "It's really good to see you."

His bloodshot eyes glide over my body, studying me—from my body that has gained a few pounds in all of the right places, to my straightened hair that reaches the middle of my back, to my off-the-shoulder tunic dress that displays his tattoo, to my knee length gladiator sandals—from across the room I can tell by his disturbing smile he's excited to see me. Oddly, he doesn't seem to be angry like I expected him to be. Fatma's disheveled appearance says Angel has already has his way with her, but the bulge in his pants says his appetite wasn't satisfied. My heart pounds as I scan the room thinking of how I'm supposed to do what I came to do.

"So, do you want me to put her in the car and we can get outta here, Pops?" Ryan asks.

I whip my head in Ryan's direction, but movement outside the front door, that's still open, catches my eye. My gaze zips to Angel.

Zephyr pulls up in front of the house.

Before anyone can say anything, I flash a smile and pretend I'm happy to see my Angel. "Wait, Ryan. I'm not ready to leave just yet."

Ryan glares at me, appearing confused by my friendly response. "It wasn't until now that I realize how much I've missed Angel."

That lie is as far from the truth as east is from the west—it's hard not showing how disgusted I am to even let the words come from my mouth.

The energy that I have to use to look at Angel with adoration and sincerity is making my head throb, but I pull it together. Leaving Ryan's side, I maneuver my way around the bodies in the room to Angel's side.

"I'm sorry, Angel," I say, reaching up to caress his face. Angel locks his dark, dead gaze on mine.

I place a soft, lingering kiss on his lips. The bitter taste of stale beer and cigarettes almost cause the plan to derail. The nausea will wait this out.

"I've missed you, Baby Girl," he whispers as he combs his fingers through my straight, silky locs.

"I know, Sir," I say. Taking Angel by his hand, I kiss it. "I've had time to think about how wrong I was for leaving and I'm sorry. I hope you can forgive me. I want to make it up to you, if you'll allow me."

Angel takes his time placing his hands on my body. His fingers glide down my arm and reaches around to the small of my back. He lifts the hem of my dress and strokes my round derriere, lovingly rediscovering what once belonged to him. Gently pulling his hand away, I deliver another kiss to his hand, and lace my fingers with his before this journey gets too close to where I'm keeping my weapon.

Fatma still lies in the floor, her sobbing all but halted.

I kneel down next to her, while Ryan's disbelieving eyes follow me like he's watching a movie.

"Listen, Fatma," I whisper loudly enough for the monster next to me to hear it, "Angel and I have some catching up to do and he deserves to be serviced now. Do you mind if we have the use of your bedroom?" Peering back at Angel, I give him a wink.

"You're a little bitch," Fatma manages to breathe out.

"So, then you don't mind. Thanks … Mom."

Angel and I step over Fatma as if we're jumping the broom for our nuptials. A quick look out the door again shows Zephyr moving fast toward the house, the lines on his forehead telling a story. Hoping to distract Ryan long enough that he doesn't see him, I step into Ryan and sweep my gaze up and down his firm body neatly packaged in college preppy garb.

"Wanna join us," I ask, the corners of my lips turn up into a foxy grin,

"It would be just like the first time, only this time you'll be crying … with pleasure."

Ryan's cinnamon complexion quickly turns scarlet. I sidestep Ryan and watch Zephyr stalk toward the door, his face anguished as I shut the front door.

Putting one foot onto the first stair releases the shadows of Malik and I racing each other up the stairs like a dream before my eyes. Grief and regret weigh heavy in my chest— I never had the chance to mourn the loss of my brother and father; I was busy comforting Fatma, who only wanted me dead.

Angel is going to die, for everything he's ever done to me, for everything that's ever happened to me. Taking me from home. Losing my baby. Putting a gun to my head. He can't live. I won't live another day looking over my shoulder.

Reaching the top of the stairs, I thank God the door to Nadira's room is closed. I wish she were any place else, so she wouldn't have to be subjected to any of this.

Time stands still as I open the master bedroom door. The walls are the same creamy yellow and every piece of cherry wood, Queen Anne style furniture is in the same place that it was on the day I was taken. A sumptuous emerald-green comforter with golden threads adorns the four-poster bed that sits high off the floor. The less-than-spacious room doesn't offer much in the way of a variety of places to get this party started.

Turning, I stare into Angel's eyes. I didn't think his eyes could be anymore empty than I remember. It's like he's the walking dead. Killing him will be doing him and the world a favor.

A smile splits Angel's darkened face as I pull down his pants and do what I've never done before—prepare to give myself to him willingly.

I can't do this…

Angel sucks in a deep breath and runs his hand over my sleek hair with one hand and offers me his hearty erection with the other. A crash rings out from downstairs halting the session.

As Angel twists toward the door, I bite his thigh so hard that it bleeds.

"Shhhit," he growls, grabbing a fistful of my hair.

Pain zips through my head and the room spins as he throws me to the floor. Angel rocks back and forth squeezing the spot I attacked. He holds his thigh as he examines the fresh bite mark I left.

"Where is she?" Zephyr's voice booms from downstairs.

"I see you've forgotten your place, Baby Girl," Angel snarls. "And you brought in outsiders?" His twisted lips don't hide his disgust for what he thinks is a lapse in my judgment. "No good, Baby Girl … no good."

Angel yanks me up off the floor and my gun tumbles from its once secure place. He scowls, his gaze flickering from me to the weapon.

My heart races like an out of control freight train as I try to pull away from Angel's grip as hard as my dizziness will let me.

Angel reaches for the gun.

I kick it out of his reach.

The back of Angel's hand comes across my face with a force that causes my ears to ring. My knees are already weak. I have to hold myself up on the side of the bed; I refuse to collapse.

Angel reaches for my gun again and Zephyr bursts through the door and kicks Angel, forcing him to land in the narrow space between the dresser and the bed.

"Let's go," Zephyr roars pushing my hair away from my face as he tries for a quick exit despite my slumped body.

"You have no idea who you're fuckin' with," Angel growls as he gets up from the floor. "This one belongs to me and I'll kill anybody who thinks they'll change that." Zephyr's ordinarily chiseled features seem sharper, his silence ominous.

Moving across the top of the bed to the other side of the room, I watch Angel size up Zephyr, his fist balled into a hammer. Angel draws back, and Ryan dashes into the room, police sirens from outside trumpeting his entrance.

"Pops!"

The blow that's intended for Zephyr, meets Ryan's face, knocking him backward. Nadira rushes in and jumps on Angel's back as he charges Zephyr, glass shattering as he pushes him into the mirror over the dresser.

"Leave my sister alone," Nadira yells.

Angel yanks Nadira's arms, but her grip is firm.

"I see you need to be trained like your sister," Angel says reaching over his head and pulling her braid.

"Nadira," I say, stumbling, still dizzy from the blow to my head. "You're going to get hurt."

Nadira growls as she punches Angel in the head.

He catches her arm, throws her to the floor, and prepares to land a kick to her stomach. Before he can hurt Nadira, Zephyr kicks him to where Ryan is lying.

Swiping my gun from the floor, Nadira pulls the trigger.

"No," Zephyr yells.

Blood spatters across the floor as Angel falls to the floor gripping the back of his thigh, trying to cover the freshly made bullet hole.

My gaze flickers between Angel who's writhing and moaning, and Nadira. Her milky cheeks are red, and she's poised to pull the trigger again.

"Don't do it, Li'l Mama," Ryan begs Nadira as he steadies himself on the doorjamb.

Nadira doesn't flinch as she aims the gun at Angel.

"He hurt my mom and dad and scared Kareem," she says, narrowing her eyes on Angel.

"Look at me, Angel." I demand through clenched teeth. He angles his head, looking me dead in my eyes. "How does it feel?"

"Shut up," he mutters.

Zephyr slowly extends his hands to me as I reach for Nadira and take the gun from her hand.

"Babe, don't do it," he whispers. Worry draws his eyebrows to the middle of his face.

I rear my foot back and kick Angel in his jaw and stomp on his head. Blood spills from his crusted mouth as he groans.

Perspiration trails down my temple, my body trembling like a leaf. Crouching into his face, I take my finger off the trigger, wrap my fist around the gun, draw back, and slam the butt of the gun into his face. I draw back once more and come down again. Tears blur my vision, but not so much that I can't see my target. Each blow to Angel's already bloody, swelling face comes harder and faster. Every hit sends me into a high that only a mind-blowing orgasm can bring. I continue to pound into him until I'm weak.

Nadira stands next to me, her gaze locked on Angel.

Zephyr pulls me into his chest, holding me as if he's trying to bind my broken pieces.

Twisting and squirming, I try to loose myself from his tight embrace.

He holds me tighter until I'm too tired to fight anymore and drop the gun to the floor.

Angel moans, holding his injured leg with one hand, and the other moving toward me.

In a move that I didn't anticipate, Angel charges for the weapon.

Nadira kicks him, grabs the gun, and pulls the trigger.

Angel's bloodshot eyes widen as blood pours from his neck.

Chapter 38

Gemini

The police crashed into the room. One stony faced officer took in the bloody scene and pulled out a pocket-sized notebook.

Questions flew while his partner checked the doors on the second floor.

Nadira's heart-wrenching sobs echoed down the stairs while the officer called for medical assistance. Burying my head into the curve of Zephyr's neck, I used his shirt to catch my tears as his splayed hand rubs the back of my neck as he gives one assurance:

"It's over now," he whispered.

The forty-five-minute interrogation ended with me in a pair of handcuffs and a ride to the precinct for the attempted murder of Angel and carrying a concealed weapon without a permit.

This can't be how I'm going to spend the rest of my life.

* * *

Between praying to a God I'm not sure I believe in and a migraine, sleep didn't come until morning. Every crack and dusty corner of the cold, gray cell has been inspected from top to bottom from the flat padded bottom bunk where I tried to get some rest.

I've never seen the inside of a jail cell. Angel always made sure my clients were wealthy people, not notable people who would have the eyes of any kind of press on them all the time—a gag order of sorts was always part of the arrangement.

This reduced the risk of ever being caught or, at least, that was what Angel thought anyway. One investigation was opened against Angel, but one witness was reported missing and the other was found in a park with a gunshot to the back of her head.

Some of his newer additions had been to jail, some several times, but that was before Angel "saved" them. Once Angel got them cleaned up, they thought they were living a good life. I don't see how; they got what I got—only they had to share the three-bedroom apartment Angel paid for out of their intake. I'd never choose this life no matter what expenses were covered.

Ryan and Zephyr round the corner with a guard and the scent of sandalwood makes the stale air easier to breathe. Zephyr flashes a smile, like he's found a treasure.

Ryan's lips curl into a smile, though his eyes appear sad. He reaches for his back pocket and flips open a wallet with an identification card and gold badge.

The guard opens the gate and the two of them step into the cramped space. Ryan hands me his wallet and I read the contents.

"Wai … Officer?" A light breeze could knock me down right now. "What is this, Ryan?"

"Undercover," he says, his eyes appearing brighter. "When I ran away from home, I went to live with my girlfriend's family," he explains, starting to answer the question I asked him when he first came back into my life. "I only told them I needed safety from my dad. They were gracious and let me stay there until my girl and I moved to Dayton for school. I was sure Pops wouldn't look for me outside of Cincinnati. I got my GED and went to the Police Academy."

I tilt my head, searching his eyes for any truth to his statement.

"Let's just say a lot of stories weren't told during the application and interview process."

That's what I was waiting for. Nothing he's saying is making any sense to me, but it could be that I'm tired as hell.

"Get to the point," I snap, wasting no patience with what sounds like a drawn-out explanation for his absence.

"Listen, I'm trying to answer the questions you had when we met at The Millennia. Every day I wanted to come back for you. I just couldn't figure out how to do that without one or both of us getting killed." Ryan says, averting his gaze to a corner of the cell. "I'll never forgive my pops for doing what he did to you … " He pauses, his Adam's apple shifts, emotion consuming his words, "I don't know that I'll forgive myself for what I did."

Murmuring and shuffling from other inmates in their cells are all that keep the momentary silence at bay.

"With every girl I had to lock up for prostitution, I knew that I had to find some way to repay you for how I hurt you. And after my daughter was born, I knew Pops had to be stopped."

I don't say anything so that it doesn't sound like I don't appreciate what he's saying or what he's doing for me.

"You have a daughter? That's great." I glance over at Zephyr's tired face—he looks like he hasn't seen any sleep either.

"Yeah. I named her Aisha, after the only little sister I ever had. 'She who lives," he says, stating the meaning of my name.

Staring into Ryan's proud papa face, I can't help but smile a little.

"So why are you two here?" I ask. Changing the subject abruptly seems like a good idea. The trip down Ryan's memory lane doesn't need to be long.

"Pops—Angel is dead. X-rays showed that you cracked his skull pretty good. You put a hurting on him."

"Frankly, I didn't hurt him enough," I retort, setting my chin on my drawn-up knees.

"He didn't survive the gunshot to the neck," Ryan explains after another long pause. A chill runs down my spine as I snap my head off my knees. "He bled out before he arrived at the hospital. The hollow point bullet tore him up."

"Is Nadira okay?"

"She's a tough cookie like her sister," Ryan assures me. "But she'll need some counseling."

"What about Fatma? What's she saying about what he did? Why was Angel here in Detroit?"

The sparkle in Ryan's light-brown eyes dulled instantly.

"She said he was a long-time family friend that she invited into her home … she said you lured him to her bedroom to have sex with him. She heard a commotion that sounded like an altercation but didn't know what happened once you got him upstairs."

Ryan couldn't dispute that since he was a witness to that much himself.

"What about Angel raping her?"

"She won't report it as a rape."

"Her husband? Angel shot him in front of their son!"

"Fatma and her husband have a nice, short list of issues. After searching the place for anyone else who might've been in the house, we found enough crack cocaine to put them away for a few years. They're being charged with possession of a controlled substance."

I wipe my hands over my face. "She told me that she had my father and brother killed."

"I'll be working on getting murder charges filed."

"Where are the kids?"

"The kids have been placed in foster care." Ryan offers a crooked smile.

"This isn't looking good, is it?"

"I started an investigation against Pops for drug running and operating a prostitution ring in Cincinnati, but I'm not sure how that's gonna play out since I needed you back in the city to make sure we caught him in all of his operations. You're the only one who has an extended history with him."

I'm embarrassed—Angel could've been shut down before now if I'd answered Ryan's calls or cooperated.

"That's why I was trying to get back in touch with you. I needed you to make this case happen and put Pops away … I needed you to get justice."

"I don't know what to say," I admit, ashamed for giving Ryan a hard time when he returned. "I'm really sorry I messed things up."

"We'll figure it out," Ryan assures me, checking the time on his cell. "We actually collected enough evidence against him to put him away for a while. But as it stands, we'll have to use this evidence in a connected case."

My gaze locked on his, I ask Ryan a question that didn't come up in our meeting at The Millennia.

"What about Dane? Where is she?"

The sparkle in his eyes dims as he tells me of his mother and Caren's incarceration.

"Wait … How did Caren get involved?" I ask. My jaw hangs open—there's no hiding my shock that the woman I've called a friend for almost the last year got wrapped up with the likes of Dane and Angel. I feel bad that I didn't tell her who Angel was.

"Pops was using her to keep the books while Mom took in the girls and the money from the streets," he accounts. "I've been tracking you all for over a year. Unfortunately, Caren got wrapped up in the money. She said Angel promised her a bonus if she could get you to come back home."

Every bit of my life has been spent as someone's tool or fantasy. The happy beginnings that I dreamt of in my life after Angel didn't look anything like life in prison and without family.

This is not how my life is supposed to end.

"Mr. Gray has set up counsel and is prepared to post bail after your arraignment," Ryan declares, shaking Zephyr's hand. A smile creeps across my face and tears well in my eyes, as I look to Zephyr. "I don't think there will be any problems at trial either because we'll be claiming self-defense for your actions."

Zephyr extends his hand and pulls me from the cot into his embrace.

"I love you so much," I whisper into his shoulder.

"We're getting you out of here," Zephyr says, as I steady myself.

Ryan calls for the guard, and Zephyr and I say our goodbyes.

I have no regrets, no matter how this ends. I feel safe knowing Zephyr will be waiting for me.

Chapter 39

Zephyr

Smiles and handshakes go around the conference room as Peter Wines is named the newest company partner. I can't be mad, Peter is a good dude, though word has it the only reason he was named partner is because he's a 'yes' man. I was never going to be that kind of partner.

One good thing for the company—Charles and his special "offers" were terminated. It's never a good idea to approach a woman who has eyes on all of your accounts, especially when she's paying attention to the company's bottom line. I guess nepotism didn't cover his ass this time.

Opening the doors to Gray and Associates Investment Solutions in Detroit has been the greatest accomplishment so far in my life.

After having Adelaide do a little research, she found a good number of staff members and executives were looking for other opportunities with a company with more advancement possibilities and diversity. With capital from the investors, the company had enough money to offer relocation incentives. My seven-figure client even came through with an apology bonus in addition to becoming one of my first clients. I'm pleased to say when my clients were informed of my newly established business, they were all more than happy to move with me. Along with four other executives and all of their clients taking almost fifty percent of their bottom line, I'm not sure how McFadden & Tate is going to stay in business.

The gag order and hiring bonus I put in the contracts has been handy—not even Sasha has been able to get any information to share.

Adelaide and Winfree report that the renovation of the riverfront office property is coming along beautifully, and all of the new hires look like they'll be great for building the foundation of the company.

Vanessa finally had the test done. I feel sorry for the boy, as I was number three in a line of potential fathers.

The days following Aisha's arrest, news reporters camped outside my parents' home, questioning us all about our connection to the case. Once investigators were satisfied that my family wasn't involved, I sent them all on a vacation to France—an early birthday gift to my mother.

In all of this, I'm on pins and needles waiting for the call from the lawyer I hired for Aisha's case. I'm confident in her ability, but Aisha's premeditation didn't make her case slam-dunk that Ryan had predicted. I don't think I've lived a week this long in my life.

Getting away from all the fanfare, I sneak out to answer the vibrating cell in my pocket.

"Zephyr Gray speaking."

"Hey, Zephyr Gray."

My heart skips a beat as Aisha's voice chimes from the other end. "Not guilty."

"Yes," I shout, turning the heads of a few staff members as I have a personal celebration of my own. "When are you being released?"

"In a few hours."

"I'm on my way now," I say, rushing to lock up my office.

"I need you to do a favor before you get on the road," Aisha appeals, as I'm ready to speed back to Detroit.

"Anything," I reply.

"Can you find Nadira and Kareem? I won't let them grow up like I did, not knowing any family, raised by strangers or worse."

"You know what?" I say as a smile splits my face. "I knew you'd want them, so I arranged with their caseworker for them to live with us after we take all of the necessary classes. Right now, they're safe. I've been checking on them."

"Thank you," she says, and I can hear how wide her smile is. "Words don't express how much I love you."

"I know, right?" I say with a chuckle. "I love you more."

As soon as the call ends, another call rings in.

"Zephyr Gray speaking."

"Mr. Gray," begins the real estate agent hired to sell the condo, "After having multiple offers on the table for your condo, if you're willing to sell it completely furnished, we have an offer for one-point-four million."

"Sold. Just let me know when they're ready to move. My offer on a home in Detroit has already been accepted."

"I'll let you know later today."

I end the call and look at the screen, waiting for it to ring again.

There's nothing wrong with wanting to hear more good news.

Chapter 40

Gemini

Nadira brushes my hair into a ponytail while Kareem slips rhinestone-sparkled sandals on my slightly swollen feet in preparation for the intimate backyard ceremony that was planned for our nuptials at our new riverfront mansion.

"There," Nadira exclaims. "Your hair's perfect. Where are your earrings and necklace?"

Reaching over my round belly, I pick up the string of pearls that laid on the vanity in the bathroom we use as a makeshift beauty salon. Pulling up the ponytail, Nadira clasps the necklace as I put on the diamond and pearl drop earring that Zephyr's mother gave me as a gift.

"Thank you," I say, peering at my little sister and trying to think of a word for her that isn't 'beautiful'— she's so much more than that.

"C'mon, Aisha," Kareem pleads with excitement, pulling my hand to get me out of the chair.

"Are you ready, daughter?" Zephyr's father asks, peaking around the bedroom door. Nadira fluffs her sandy-blonde curls and Kareem straightens his bow tie as I take my time standing.

"Yes, I'm ready, Dad ... well, we're ready," I say, rubbing my belly, happily anticipating the next two members of our family.

Diamond dotted layers of cream chiffon drapes my motherly figure, I hold a bouquet of blush roses, the stems wrapped with the green silk scarf Zephyr gave me so long ago. A tear falls as I think that this life is more than I had ever dreamed.

Nadira rushes out the door and down the stairs wearing the floral V-neck gown Zephyr let her choose for this occasion.

Mr. Gray holds his elbow out for me to grasp. Although I'm not due for another three months, the twins are not letting me see my feet down the stairs.

The orchestra plays as Mr. Gray and I arrive at the sliding glass wall that's already open, letting in a magnificent breeze off the river.

Kareem takes Mr. Gray's place, walking me down an aisle decorated with tiger lilies in tall crystal vases.

The guests are few with his family, Adelaide, and Derek Winfree in attendance.

A smile cracks Zephyr's face as he wipes his eyes.

Kareem takes me to Zephyr's side and jumps to a front-row chair.

Turning to Zephyr, I'm spellbound by the sparkling gaze of the man who loves me, beyond what I was, beyond the damage another man caused.

"Zephyr Gray," I say, being first to declare my vows "I didn't trust you. I'd never had the occasion to trust anyone, as doing so was not to my benefit. But you came into my life, asking to be a part of my story. And every day that I couldn't run you off, I fell more in love with you. You made me understand what love is with no judgment and no strings attached. No words will ever express how eternally grateful I am for you. You asked me if you deserve me. You more than deserve me and I vow to love you the way you deserve to be, the way you've loved me."

Never having seen Zephyr cry, I kiss his tears before we're supposed to salute and before he speaks his vows.

"I don't know how I'm supposed to beat that," Zephyr says, laughing as the guests chuckle. "Aisha, I told you I was going to marry you and I knew that on the first day I saw you. There's a power in you that shows, you are much more than your words and how does a man not love that? You say I taught you what love was, but you're the master. You protected me from what I didn't know and what I couldn't see and it almost cost you your life. You made me understand what love is and then you gave me life and are giving me life again. I want to be the best husband and friend to you and the best father to our son and daughter. I make no promises because they are meant to be broken. I vow to commit my love to you every moment of the day of the remainder of our lives."

"Aww," the guests sigh.

I place Zephyr's ring on his hand and with a little effort; he manages to get the ring he has for me on mine.

Zephyr cups my face in his hands and delivers the most tender kiss he's ever given me.

"I love you," he whispers.

"I love you more," I reply.

Teary-eyed guests descend on us as the clergy announces Zephyr and I as husband and wife.

Stealing away from the crowd, we take a stroll to the back of the yard. Zephyr kisses my belly.

"Thank you for making my life better than I could've ever imagined," he says as he holds my gaze while caressing our babies.

More than I'm grateful, I'm astonished. For all of my hopes and dreams, there was always a thought that I might not make it out alive. Not only did I rise from the ashes of my life, I'm living a life beyond every thought I ever imagined and with the most beautiful love ever created.

And *beautiful* is what *this* life is.

MarZé Scott is a lifelong resident of Ypsilanti, Michigan and graduate of the University of Michigan. A lover of all things creative, MarZé loves to read, write, draw and do makeup artistry when she's not taking care of her family.

MarZé has been writing short stories and poems since elementary school and developed a taste for writing about provocative topics like the consequences of casual sex in high school.

You can find MarZé on social media sites:
Facebook- facebook.com/marzescott
Twitter- @marzefab
Instagram- @marze_fab
marzescott.com

Next Lifetime

Brown Sugar

MarZe Scott

Elijah Hargove's body laid on the beige shag carpet, apparent of one thing— a gunshot to his temple and a .9-millimeter handgun right next to him. However, those two things weren't enough for Daylin to believe he had taken his own life.

God should pay Daylin in cash for every prayer she ever whispered for Elijah. At least, then her relationship with him wouldn't have been in vain.

Tears streamed from her eyes as red and blue lights flashed onto the blood-spattered walls. Police and EMTs swarmed around the tiny apartment trying to find the beginning of answers to her boyfriend's untimely death.

"Baby, why?" she cried, wrapping her arms tight around her knees. Her gaze followed the blue uniforms and neatly dressed investigators around the place she had lived a tumultuous life with a man she once believed was her Prince Charming but showed himself to be a monster instead.

"I'm sorry for your loss, Miss—?" one raven-haired detective said, narrowing her blue-eyed gaze on Daylin.

"Montgomery," Daylin supplied to the woman who she thought was too beautiful for this dangerous line of work.

Daylin and Elijah lived in an area of Deering Park, Michigan that was known for its bourgeois residents with mini mansions and manicured lawns. The small off-street apartment complex where she lived hidden behind a concrete wall, full evergreen trees, and brush was anything but elite. The sound of gunshots was as common to the drug-ridden community as city buses passing from the east side to downtown.

"Miss Montgomery, I'm Detective Voorhees. I need to ask you a few questions." The detective took Daylin's silence as consent to begin the interrogation. "Do you know if there was anyone who wanted the deceased dead?"

"No," Daylin barked, failing to tamp down her anger at such a dismissive term. "And his name is Elijah Hargrove." She maintained her spot in the corner, only shifting position to glance into the detective's somber face.

"Do you know if Mr. Hargrove used drugs?" Detective Voorhees inquired searching Daylin's face, her pen in hand ready to record any and all information that was shared.

"I don't think so," Daylin murmured, putting her head on her knees, the sudden weight had become too much for her to bear.

"Miss Montgomery, can you tell me where you were at the time of Mr. Hargrove's death?"

Daylin's head snapped up at the accusatory question and tone. Her heart raced; her gaze bounced between the EMTs and Detective Voorhees as the technicians lifted Elijah's body and placed it in a black body bag.

"I went shopping," she replied. "We had an argument, so I thought some retail therapy was in order."

Detective Voorhees lowered a cool gaze on Daylin as a tall man, with a tawny complexion, dressed in career blue shirt and slacks came over and whispered in Detective Voorhees ear. The new comer's face remained neutral as he glanced in Daylin's direction. The detective's eyes flickered from Daylin back to the officer's gloved hand that held a slip of paper. She recognized that it had been on the carpet near Elijah.

Voorhees shook a pair of gloves from her pocket and slipped them on before she took a letter-sized envelope from the officer.

"Miss Montgomery, are you aware if Mr. Hargrove was depressed? What was his behavior before you left the apartment?"

Daylin didn't want to discuss anything about her strained and often violent relationship with Elijah. Before she left the apartment this morning he had punched her in the thigh for wearing one of his t-shirts.

"I don't know if he was depressed," she admitted. "He didn't get any type of diagnosis from a doctor. He was upset that his job let him go. He said the manager didn't like him," she murmured, her anger diminishing as she thought about how this explanation was a typical response for an involuntary loss of employment.

Detective Voorhees flipped the paper open, examined the contents, and turned it to face Daylin who scanned the handwritten letter that delivered a gut punch to her soul.

"Oh my God," she groaned, nearly gasping in an effort to get enough air.

"Is there anyone else that you can think of that we can talk to about his state of mind?" Detective Voorhees inquired.

"Just his family."

Daylin offered the names and phone numbers to any of Elijah's closest family members, ones who had turned a blind eye to the bruises, broken nose, and bald patches, all signs of when Elijah had taken out his frustration on her.

"Thank you for your cooperation, Miss Montgomery," Detective Voorhees said as she handed Daylin a business card, "Please be advised that you shouldn't leave town until this investigation is over."

Daylin nodded as she moved to take the small card from the detective. She leaned on the door and closed her eyes, remembering the content of the letter.

Daylin my Love,

How could you do this to me? I thought you loved me, but you had me fooled. I went out and bought a ring. I was finally ready to propose and make you my wife. I'm sorry that I wasn't good enough. I trusted you, but I shouldn't have. I found the texts about your pregnancy. I thought we would be a family, but you had to go and mess everything up. I hope you're happy now. Congratulations, Daylin! This is all your fault.
Good bye,
Elijah

Heat built up around Daylin's face as Elijah's last words bounced around in her mind. Not only had he chosen to end their relationship this way, but also blamed her for why he decided to end his life and he had ended it on a lie.

Daylin and Elijah had a chaotic relationship, but could never be said that the high school sweethearts ever experienced the sweet part of what love was supposed to be. Desires of leaving their hometown died as Elijah's childish tantrums and pleas grew into full on abusive episodes every time Daylin talked about moving on. Only God knew what she was going through and felt betrayed that her prayers didn't make Elijah a better person. If there was a wish that had been granted, it was one that only her heart uttered— to be loved by a man she could call a friend.

Daylin took in the mess Elijah had left for her to clean and a pitiful groan escaped her lips.

"Selfish bastard," she said through her teeth to the chilled space as she went to retrieve her cell phone from her purse. "I've never cheated on you as much as you've given me reason to."

All Elijah had to do was love her instead trying to make her as crazy as he was. His melodramatic existence took precedence in something as simple as ordering pizza.

Daylin read through the texts that Elijah used as the reasoning for his dramatic life exit.

She tapped the screen and waited for the call to be answered.

"Hello, Maurice," she said when he picked up. "Can I meet you somewhere? We need to talk."

She never wanted to return to the place where heaven and hell met her each day.

Chapter 3

A broad, flirtatious smile and runway model swagger made Maurice the breath of fresh air that Daylin needed, giving her the friend that she never had in Elijah. Common interests in travel, music, and the occasional debate about Daylin's Wolverines being better than Maurice's Buckeyes made for frequent and sometimes raucous lunchtime breaks at Atwater Bank and Trust.

More than a few women in the building were envious of how well the two worked together even knowing that he was spoken for with a baby on the way. Maurice was confident, supportive, and creative—everything that Elijah was not.

Sitting in the dimly lit corner booth of Shane's Bar and Grill, the restaurant was packed like it was Valentine's Day. Daylin didn't know if she would pass out from fear or happiness when the six-foot tall ebony superman made his way to the booth.

"Hey handsome," her voice trembled as she stood to hug her friend, ignoring the ogling eyes from women whose gaze wandered from the companionship of the men at surrounding tables to the appearance of what could be considered perfection.

"How are you, Beautiful?" the bass voice sang from a wide smile from a handsomely chiseled face.

The words to explain her situation became caught in her throat.

"Did he hurt you again?"

"He's dead."

Maurice's gray eyes widened to size of half dollars as he shifted to wrap his arms around her trembling body.

"Are you okay?" Maurice tilted his head as if he was hit with a sudden thought. "Did you?" He slowly released Daylin and lowered his gaze so their eyes met.

"Did I what?" she snapped.

"You know…"

"I would never," she replied, twisting her face in horror that her best friend would think that she could harm Elijah, even if he deserved it. "We got into a stupid argument. I didn't do anything to him even after all he's done to me. He killed himself and left a letter blaming me for it."

Maurice closed his eyes and exhaled.

Embarrassed, Daylin looked away from the man who'd been her rock when life became overwhelming.

"He found our texts about the baby."

"But it was *his* baby."

One wayward tear set the path for more to fall and Daylin couldn't stop the flow if she tried. A server ambled toward the couple and took one look causing Maurice to wave him away.

"It … It was," she stammered and then took a deep breath. "I didn't get the chance to tell him because I miscarried. At some point he went through my phone and found the texts. I guess that sent him over the edge and he …"

Scooting into a padded bench seat on either side of the booth table, Daylin fixed her gaze on Maurice. His eyebrows creased the middle of his forehead, something that always happened when he was thinking of how to solve a problem. The type of man that kept a cool head he was always the voice of reason. The only advice that Daylin hadn't followed was to report the abuse and leave Elijah.

"I'm here for you," he whispered. "What do you need? A lawyer? Money?"

"Can I crash at your place for a while," she asked. "Or at least until the investigation is over. I mean, I can't stay at the scene of a crime, right?" She braced herself as the smile that didn't reach Maurice's gentle eyes held little hope of assistance.

He reached across the table and took Daylin's hands in his strong hands, his thumb caressing hers.

"That can't happen," he said shaking his head.

Daylin's breath quickened as if a sharp pain hit her chest. She wiped the pool of moisture from her cheeks.

"We've been friends for how long? Three or four years?" she admitted. "You've let me hang out with you before until the smoke cleared. What's so different now?"

"You know that my fiancée is expecting," Maurice explained as he leaned back in his seat.

Daylin felt a twinge in her stomach as she considered the loss of her own baby. "I remember. Are Faye and the baby okay?"

"She's really close to her due date," Maurice informed. "The doctors are trying to regulate her blood pressure. She's been ordered to go on bed rest. So, I'm making sure she's comfortable and the house is quiet. I need to focus on her."

Daylin withdrew her hands from Maurice's hold and crossed her arms across her chest. Despite her tumultuous relationship she hoped for a future with Elijah. She wanted her baby. She wanted Elijah to care for her the way that Maurice cared for his family.

"Daylin, I want to help," he declared reaching into his jeans pocket, pulling out his wallet, and placing a credit card on the table in front of Daylin.

"This card is clean and has a five-thousand-dollar limit. You can stay in a hotel for the duration of the investigation. Maybe get a massage to help you relax. Just please don't max it out," he said with a chuckle trying to make Daylin smile; his friend's watery gaze wasn't lost on him.

A stocky blonde man dressed in dark slacks and a crisp white shirt advanced through the dimly lit restaurant toward the couple, his expression wary given the emotional scene he walked upon a few minutes earlier.

"Hi, I'm Justin your server," he said avoiding eye contact with Daylin. "Can I start you out with something to drink?" Daylin lowered her gaze to the table and shook her head.

"I'm sorry, Justin," Maurice said sliding the menus in. "We're leaving. We apologize for any inconvenience."

The server inched back as Maurice stood and handed him a ten-dollar bill. Daylin sighed, feeling overwhelmed by the day's events.

He reached for Daylin, took her hand, and led her out of the restaurant to the less noisy area of the off-street parking lot.

"Listen," he said, placing the card firmly in her hand. "Get a room. Get you some room service and take it easy."

Daylin slid the plastic inside one cup of her bra; her mind was in other places. *Body bag. Don't leave town.*

"What am I supposed to do, Maurice," she cried as she tucked a loose lock behind her ear. "Elijah's gone."

"You're better off," he said with a harshness she had never heard from him before. "Black eyes, busted lips, and bruises. Stressed out. He's shown up at the job and caused a scene after scene. Need I go on?" Maurice's eyebrows shot up as if to let Daylin know he had mentally recorded every offense made against his friend. "Now you can be with someone who deserves to have you, the way that you gave your heart to Elijah."

Daylin's bottom lip quivered as shame washed over her for agreeing with the facts he presented. Even though she was valedictorian of her graduating class, matters of the heart overrode commons sense and logic when it came to Elijah.

Maurice wrapped Daylin's curvy frame in his massive arms while she fell apart. Squeezing her as if by his strength he could put the pieces of her broken world together, he splayed and wove his fingers through her dark tresses and cradled her head.

Dailyn's tears fell relentlessly, wetting the white t-shirt that covered his chest. She looked up at the only person who helped whenever she needed to find some type of peace.

"I'll call you in a few days to see how you're doing," Maurice said placing a heated kiss to Daylin's forehead. Feeling safe in his hold, she couldn't remember the last time she'd felt so good in a man's arms. Releasing her, she missed the heat that holding her so close had created. A cool breeze blew between them, sending a chill racing up her back while directing heat to other places.

Maurice walked Daylin the distance down the crumbled blacktop to her car that was parked in a dark area of the lot.

"Thank you for everything, Maurice," she whispered, her words working past the lump in her throat.

"What are friends for," he asked his smile not reaching his eyes.

Daylin slid behind the steering wheel of her Malibu as Maurice closed the door and stepped back. Turning the key in the ignition, she avoided his gaze as he waited for her to leave. As she drove away, Daylin glanced in the rearview, her stomach in knots. Thoughts about the investigation, life without Elijah, wishes of trading places with Faye swirled around in her mind.

How has fate been so cruel?

Some amount of serenity should've been a part of Daylin's world now that her abuser was dead. However, peace was elusive as she could only find it in stolen moments at a nearby park while writing in a hot pink leather-bound journal, a birthday gift that she had received from Maurice.

The days following Elijah's death proved to be even more troubled than when he was alive. Police questioning her at the hotel made for a less than relaxing stay and prank calls from blocked callers kept Daylin awake at night.

Cars whizzed up and down busy Harbor Avenue during lunchtime traffic as Daylin returned from a break away from her job and friend.

"So you mean to tell me that you're fine having a murderer work for this establishment," a petite and portly woman with a dark complexion yelled in the lobby of the bank that was jammed with customers.

The balding middle-aged manager had seen this woman on a few occasions under more friendly circumstances, but now stood with his face so red it looked as though the woman may have slapped him on both cheeks.

Daylin rushed to the woman, brushing past customers to try and calm her down. The sweet floral scent that wafted from the well-dressed woman didn't match the unpleasant twist of her lips as Daylin reached out to touch her.

"Ms. Hargrove? Why are you here," Daylin whispered observing all of the onlookers in the area.

Elijah's mother snatched her arm away from Daylin's contact as anxious observers moved away from the trio. Two customers held up their phones to record the drama.

"Listen, Joan," Mr. Shelton said, defending his star employee, "Daylin is a great worker and I have no problem with her. And as I understand it, your son's injury was self-inflicted."

"And you believe the lies she told you?" she screamed. "She killed my son. What you need to know is you'll have more than a problem if I come back tomorrow and she's still employed here," Ms. Hargrove warned, her large protruding eyes narrowing on Daylin's face. "She's still under investigation for my son's death. She shouldn't be walking around free while I have to bury my only child."

Daylin's mouth dropped as sweat beaded on her forehead— how could such an accusation come from the only woman she felt close enough to consider a mother since her own mother was killed in a car accident before high school graduation.

"Let me come back and see her here, Mr. Shelton." Ms. Hargrove's angry gaze flashed over to the bank manager's weary expression, "Channel 7 will be here to film your regret for the evening news."

Ms. Hargrove turned on the heels of her black church mother pumps and stormed out the door. Silence hung in the air as though the bank were devoid of customers.

"I apologize for the commotion ladies and gentlemen," Mr. Shelton declared. "We'll get you taken care of as quickly as possible. Thanks again for banking with Atwater Bank and Trust."

Business resumed, customers shooting accusatory glances and murmuring amongst themselves.

Heat blew up Daylin's neck, blood rushing to her golden cheeks. Her clinched fist shook as her chest ebbed and flowed like the waves of the ocean.

"Come with me, Miss Montgomery," Mr. Shelton directed as he walked toward a corner cubicle at the back of the bank.

Daylin trailed the manager fighting back her tears. Neither sat down as they reached the desk, instead huddling in a corner that was obscured from the customers' view.

"I was clear when you said that your boyfriend killed himself. What is Ms. Hargrove talking about?"

Mr. Shelton wipes his hands over his face as Daylin explained at length life with Elijah, his family, and the unnaturally close relationship he had to his mother.

"He was her only child and she had him late in life. He was twenty-eight years old and it was like he couldn't breathe if she wasn't a phone call away. And believe me that's all she needed to be at my door."

Exhausted, Mr. Shelton leaned on a wall near him and crossed his arms over his chest.

"Listen Daylin, you're a great worker and the customers love you, but this kind of disruption is bad for business. I'm not inclined to suspend you, but clearly you need to keep a low profile. I'm transferring you immediately to the Centerline branch. There's an opening for a loan officer that'll be good for you."

Daylin loved where she worked, however she knew that Ms. Hargrove's words were not a threat, but a promise. She didn't want to make any more bad press for the company.

"Take the rest of the day off while I figure out what to do."

Daylin scrambled to gather her jacket and golf umbrella from her desk and was exited out of the front door before co-workers stop her for their own personal interviews.

She hoped that things wouldn't get any worse, but she soon found that was too much to ask.

Want more? Pick up your copy of . . .

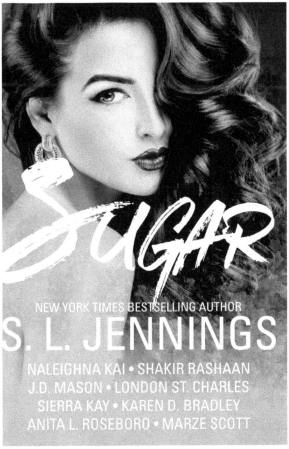

Nine authors, featuring *New York Times* bestseller, S. L. Jennings, bring the unexpected with unique short stories that are sure to leave a sweet taste on the tip of your tongue. Among the delicacies penned by national bestsellers Naleighna Kai, J. D. Mason, Shakir Rashaan, London St. Charles, and also **MarZé Scott,** Sierra Kay, Karen D. Bradley, and Anita L. Roseboro, are contemporary fiction, suspense, women's fiction, erotica, and even romance that will warm the heart. This anthology is a perfect blend of authors at the top of their game who have crafted stories that will leave you wanting more.

WWW.NKTRIBECALLEDSUCCESS.COM

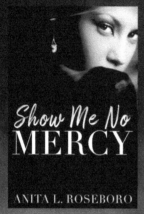
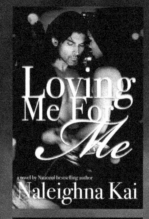
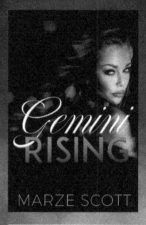

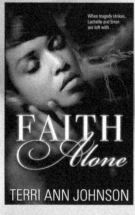
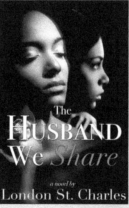
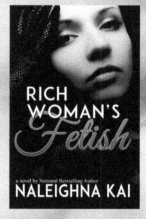

CPSIA information can be obtained
at www.ICGtesting.com
Printed in the USA
FFHW02n0256211018
48849451-53072FF